HOT AS HELLER

LUCY LENNOX

Cover Art: Natasha Snow Designs

Cover Photo: Wander Aguiar

Editing: One Love Editing

Proofreading: Victoria Rothenberg

Beta Reading: Leslie Copeland, May Archer, and Shay Haude.

KEEP IN TOUCH WITH LUCY!

Join Lucy's Lair
Get Lucy's New Release Alerts
Like Lucy on Facebook
Follow Lucy on BookBub
Follow Lucy on Amazon
Follow Lucy on Instagram
Follow Lucy on Pinterest

Other books by Lucy:
Hostile Takeover
Made Marian Series
Forever Wilde Series
Aster Valley Series
Twist of Fate Series with Sloane Kennedy
After Oscar Series with Molly Maddox
Licking Thicket Series with May Archer
Virgin Flyer
Say You'll Be Nine

Visit Lucy's website at www.LucyLennox.com for a comprehensive list of titles, audio samples, freebies, suggested reading order, and more!

1

DECLAN

"But, Sheriff—"

"But nothing, Penny," I told my dispatcher over my earpiece as I strode down the sidewalk in the center of Aster Valley one bright June morning. "I don't care how nicely the *Gold Rats* production team asks, we are not closing down Cade Road on short notice for them to film a high-speed chase. The movie people have disrupted things enough around here."

They'd disrupted *me* enough.

I'd left Los Angeles for this tiny Colorado town six months ago for a reason, and that was to get as far away from Hollywood and its players as I could. But now, here they were. Like a fungus I couldn't get rid of.

Especially the one exceptionally entitled actor I'd had a run-in with the night before.

Finn Heller.

The man had a face that belonged on the big screen, alright—a face that had been awfully hard to get out of my mind when I tossed and turned in bed last night—but his ego had been bigger than Rockley Mountain, leading me to believe that all the rumors I'd read about him were true.

He was a spoiled brat. A troublemaker. A party boy. A child-star-turned-adult-wannabe. The personification of everything I'd hoped to escape when I'd fled LA.

I'd been minding my own business at a friend's party when the kid had asked me to *valet his car*, for god's sake.

So, no, that movie crew wasn't getting another damn concession out of me.

"Penny, I've gotta go. Meeting the new deputy."

"Tell him I say hi," she said before clicking off. "And if he's cute, maybe ask him out. I could stand an office romance to spice things up around here."

"That's not happening. Ever," I assured her.

"Morning, Sheriff Stone!" Chaya called out from behind the counter as I stepped inside the coffee shop. "How's it going?"

It was such a sweet, simple thing, being greeted by name. I still hadn't quite gotten used to it in the months I'd lived in Aster Valley, Colorado, but I liked to think I was getting there.

"I'm doing just fine. Ravenous, though."

"Well, we can take care of that." She nodded toward a table near the window and lowered her voice just a fraction. "New deputy's waiting on you. Punctual, which is great, but straight and single, which isn't great for you. Great for me, though..."

What was with these people? I didn't need a man. And... she'd learned all that in five minutes? His dating status and that he was straight, too?

I blinked, opened my mouth to—Jesus, I didn't even know what. Offer Chaya a job getting hardened criminals to confess?—then closed it again. No, I *definitely* wasn't getting used to small-town living anytime soon.

"I'll be over in just a second to take your order," she added brightly.

"Great. Cup of coffee, black, if you don't mind?" I suddenly wondered what my beverage order said about *my* integrity, but I reminded myself that I'd already proven that.

In fact, I'd proven it more than once.

"Deputy Graham? I'm Declan Stone." I offered him a welcoming smile and reached out a hand to shake. He stood up to take it, and his grip was warm and firm. "Nice to meet you in person finally. Hope you didn't mind meeting me here. I was thinking an informal breakfast meeting would be a great way to welcome you to town. How was the move?"

Shawn Graham had come strongly recommended by a friend in the FBI, who'd worked with the officer on a missing persons case down in Durango. From everything I'd seen in his application and on his resume, we were lucky to get him.

He gave me an affable smile. "A pain in the ass the way you'd expect, but please call me Shawn, Sheriff. Everyone else does."

I pulled out the chair across from him and sat down. "And I'm Declan. The sheriff thing's still fairly new."

"Yeah, I heard about the trouble with your predecessor." Shawn took his seat.

"You *heard*, huh?" I gave him a sharp look, and the man looked a little embarrassed. "Didn't know the news had traveled as far as Durango."

"Well, my brother is chief of police over in Meeker. Jay Graham. Maybe you know him? Anyway," he hurried on when I shook my head, "when I told him I was looking at a job here, he gave me a rundown on the whole extortion plot Sheriff Stanner cooked up, and how a couple of the deputies were involved. Small department like Aster Valley's, losing part of the force like that had to be a blow."

He said this so sympathetically, it was impossible to take offense. And besides, it wasn't like he wouldn't have gotten the rundown from Chaya or a dozen other Aster Vallians within the next twenty-four hours.

"It was hard on the whole town," I admitted. "Building back trust in the department is our primary goal these days."

"Must've been tough on you personally, too, after you dealt with almost the same thing back in LA."

I gave him another sharp look. "More information from your brother?"

"Nah." He shrugged sheepishly and wiggled his fingers in the air like he was typing on an imaginary keyboard. "Google. I wanted to find out more about my new boss."

I chuckled. I'd have done the exact same.

In fact, I had, back when I'd first accepted the job. Too bad Google didn't tell you when your boss was a biased asshole. Good riddance to that one, but now I had to fill the shoes.

"Didn't expect to find court transcripts, though," he continued, sipping his coffee calmly. "Is it true your partner—?"

"If you read the transcripts," I interrupted, "you know all there is to know. I'd rather not talk about it, if it's all the same to you." The movie crew in town had dredged up enough LA memories.

Shawn nodded. "Sure thing."

Chaya bustled over to our table with a mug of coffee for me and took out her notepad with a flourish and a smile. "What'll it be?"

"Croissant sandwich," I said without hesitation. To Shawn, I added, "Aster Valley insider secret: you have *got* to try these things. They make the croissants from scratch, the bacon is perfectly crispy, and they're the best breakfast food in town. I have one at least a couple times a week. I always know it's gonna be a good day when I do." I was practically drooling.

Chaya's smile faltered. "Well, hell, Sheriff. We're out of croissants this morning."

"Out," I repeated. I looked around the nearly empty cafe. "Out?"

"Out." She rubbed her lips together. "*Gold Rats* got them all."

I sucked in a sharp breath through my nose.

Of course they fucking did.

"*Gold Rats* went and cleaned out all the fairy lights at the hardware store," Curtis Twomey piped up from the line at the counter. "Not sure what they're doing with 'em, but I sold out all my stock from last Christmas." He sounded positively gleeful.

"And *Gold Rats* took every single one of Connie Mac's begonias!" Florence Wimple interjected happily from the table behind us. "Even the half-dead ones."

Wilber Wimple scowled at his wife. "Well, I've had just about enough of *Gold Rats*. They're a menace. Clogging our streets like they own the damn place. Do you know, I was fifteen minutes late for *Judge Judy* the other day, because the *Gold Rats* had blocked off half the road out by Rockley Lodge?"

"I could offer you gentlemen a sandwich on a brioche bun." Chaya's flirty grin tried to make up for the terrible croissant news. "Or... toast?"

"A brioche bun would be terrific," I lied with a smile. "Nearly the same thing, right?"

It was not even remotely the same thing. One more thing to hate about Gold freakin' Rats invading Aster Valley.

"Uh." Shawn frowned as Chaya hurried away. "I'm gonna guess they're not talking about actual rodents?"

"Huh?" I was still busy backing up my salt truck over this latest outrage. "What rodents?"

"The Gold Rats. Help me out here. Are they a motorcycle club? A gang that... traffics fairy lights and begonias?"

I snorted, unwillingly amused. "Worse," I informed him. "They're a movie crew. A big blockbuster action-adventure film with the worst, weirdest name ever, and some big-name director and a bunch of party-hungry actors."

"I don't know about that," Mrs. Winple said. "Crystobell Edmund signed an autograph for me the other day, and she was lovely. Beautiful, poised, and gracious."

I drank my coffee and acknowledged this with a grunt. Too bad Crystobell's male counterpart had been an absolute pain in my ass the night before.

"Sheriff." The sound of Penny's voice in my earpiece almost made me jump. "10-91. Report of a wild animal attack over on Thistledown. System says you're up."

"Yeah, alright. Send us the address," I told her. "Shawn, you mind taking breakfast to go?"

When we got out to my vehicle a minute later with our sandwiches, I asked Penny, "Any idea what kind of animal?"

"Man was freaking out. Sounds like maybe a bear? If so, we can call Charlene Candycorn. There's no better trapper in Rockley County."

There was quaint small town, and then there was Candycorn.

"Did you say Charlene Candycorn?"

"No, sir. Well, yes, but not like you think. Charlene Candy married Clara Corn."

I sighed. This was the price I paid for leaving LA. There'd been pros and cons, and sometimes the cons were doozies. "And they became Charlene and Clara Candy-Corn."

"Not really. They kept their own last names, but after the divorce, Charlene fell in love with Clara's brother."

Welp, that's what I got for asking. "Listen, Penny. I'm going to stop you right there. Shawn and I have about three minutes to choke our breakfast sandwiches down before dealing with a potentially rabid bear, okay? You can tell us about Charlene later." Or not.

"Yes, sir. Good luck. And hi, Shawn! Welcome to Aster Valley! Oh, and also?"

"Yeah?" I said around a mouthful of sandwich.

"Bears can get rabies, of course, since they're warm-blooded. But it's rare, and there's no recorded case of a human catching it from one. You should be good. Well... except for the mauling, of course."

Yes, thank you. Except for the mauling.

The GPS directed me to a very out-of-the-way mountain road I wasn't familiar with yet. Even though I'd been living and working in Aster Valley for over six months already, there were still plenty of areas I hadn't had a chance to explore yet.

Thistledown Cove was one of them.

The old mountain cabin homes along the street became fewer and farther between until I got to the end. The road simply stopped in a pile of dusty pine needles and a tangle of downed branches. The gravel driveway to my right sported an old brown truck that looked about as tidy and clean as the pile of debris on the road.

I parked and reached into my glove box.

"Bear spray," I told the deputy. My utility belt held pepper spray, but bear spray was both stronger and able to deploy over greater distances. I had no intention of getting closer to the bear than I had to.

Shawn nodded, like wild animal calls were just a part of life, and it occurred to me that growing up in Meeker, which wasn't much bigger than Aster Valley, it probably had been.

It turned out we didn't need to bother with the bear spray. After following high-pitched yelps and calls for help, we found our way into the cabin's small, cluttered kitchen where a big, burly man sporting a thick, ragged beard and wide, bugged-out eyes stood on the table clutching one hand to his chest with the other.

"It bit me!" He pointed in the direction of the violent perp.

A fluffy squirrel looked at me and, swear to god, rolled its eyes as if to say, "Yeah, no shit. Drama much?"

I looked back and forth between the squirrel and the mountain man. "The squirrel bit you?"

He nodded rapidly. "Get it out! Get it out!"

"If it bit you, we need to trap it to test it for—"

"Get it out of here oh my god get it out!"

I blinked up at the big guy and wondered if there was substance abuse involved. "Sir, if we don't have the animal tested, you'll have to be presumed exposed to rabies. That means—"

He roared, leapt off the table, hopped over a pile of newspapers and empty cardboard boxes, and yanked open the back door before running out of it. The squirrel looked at me for a beat before bolting after him. Shawn and I exchanged a brief, incredulous glance before darting after the squirrel.

Outside, the man was now standing on a picnic table, whimpering and sniffling through tears. "Hurts like a son of a bitch."

I reached into my pocket and pulled out some gloves before asking to see his hand. Sure enough, there was a tiny bite mark on the meaty part under his thumb that was welling an impressive amount of blood.

"You're going to have to go in for treatment. I really wish you'd let us trap him." I peeled off the gloves and called dispatch to give them an update. "The first shot has to be given as soon as possible. Come on. I'll drive you. Save you the cost of an ambulance ride."

On the ride to the hospital, I asked the man—turns out his name was Coleman—what had happened.

"You see, it's like this," he began, hugging his now bandaged hand to his chest. "I love animals. I do. So, sometimes I like to feed them, you know? Just do a little something nice for my fellow creatures. And I have a raccoon that comes around. I call him Jolly. Well, Jolly is pretty particular about his breakfast foods."

Why did I ask? This was like the Candy-Corn story all over again.

But in the passenger's seat, Shawn was nodding along, like picky raccoons named Jolly were all in a day's work.

"He likes berries, but only if I serve them with something else, like chicken or mice or frogs."

Welp, that escalated quickly.

"And this morning, I sprinkled some nuts over the top. So, really, it's my own damned fault. Squirrels like nuts, you know?"

I nodded solemnly. "So it seems."

He shrugged. "I left the door open because I like to watch and see if Jolly likes his breakfast. We have kind of a... camaraderie, you could say."

I bit my tongue against pointing out Jolly represented the largest rabies risk to him among his menagerie. No raccoon friendship was worth a fatal rabies infection.

"But then, easy as you please, in comes this jackass squirrel. As if I'd prepared him a meal or something."

As if. The gall of that wild animal pursuing nourishment. Quelle surprise.

Once again, I wanted to say many, many things. But I figured none of them would help. I kept my mouth shut and let him get his story out.

"So then I tried to grab him to take him outside, and that's when he bit me."

I glanced over at him to see if I was being played. "You... tried to grab a wild squirrel. With your bare hand?"

He set his jaw and nodded. "Little punk-ass needed to be taught a lesson."

Oh, now he was Mister Big Scary Mountain Man. Mm-hm.

I asked him a few more questions, gently suggested he change his wildlife feeding habits, and wished him well in his intense two weeks of treatment. When we finally handed him off to the friendly intake personnel at the hospital, I sat in my vehicle and typed up the incident before laughing to myself.

Potentially rabid wild animal attacks weren't common in Los Angeles, but it was nice to know both human hubris and fear were universal.

"You handled that well," I told Shawn as we headed back to town. He'd grabbed us some fresh coffee from the cafeteria while I'd written the report. "I'm guessing you'll be right at home here. Did you miss exciting stuff like this in a bigger town? Is that why you moved away from Durango?"

He smiled. "Partly. I wanted to move closer to my family," he admitted. "But I have no desire to work for Jay, so I couldn't move back to Meeker. This was the next best thing. As you can imagine, my mother is thrilled I'm a little closer. I'll be able to go on the father/son annual fishing trip again. And don't be surprised if the entire Graham clan turns up in the department one day to meet everyone, and if she tries matchmaking everyone in sight distance, I apologize in advance."

"You're a bigger man than I," I admitted. "My parents live in LA, and I'm enjoying the distance. They're wonderful but very opinionated."

Shawn's laughter was warm and easy. "Well, to be honest, Jay being chief of police isn't the only reason I didn't want to go back to Meeker. My mom truly is hell-bent on getting grandkids. And dating any of the women in Meeker would be like dating one of my sisters. No, thanks. Being an hour away is just about perfect as far as I'm concerned. I only hope it won't take too long to make some friends here. I don't care about the dating scene so much as having folks I can kick back and enjoy a beer with. It never really happened for me in Durango, even after five years of trying."

"Then I'd guess you'd better come with me to Pie Hole tonight. I'll introduce you around." I closed my laptop and made sure I had my phone and keys. "You like football?"

His grin widened. "Hell yeah. Cowboys all the way, baby."

I shook my head. "Tonight you're a Houston Riggers fan, I'm afraid. Tonight's a going-away thing for Tiller Raine. He's headed to Texas for the preseason tomorrow."

The look on Shawn's face was priceless. "Tiller Raine? *The* Tiller Raine? Heisman winner and Super Bowl MVP?"

Maybe being friends with celebrities wasn't quite so bad.

As long as they weren't Hollywood actors.

"Yeah. He and his boyfriend got engaged last night, so I guess we're celebrating that, too."

"No shit? That's awesome. I read an article about them buying a place in Colorado, but I didn't put two and two together it was Aster Valley."

I spent the short drive explaining that Mikey and Tiller had purchased Rockley Lodge and the old, defunct ski mountain in hopes of reviving it and reopening it in the future.

"It's part of why they agreed to let this film crew come in and film on location here," I said, stifling a sigh. "They're hoping to start getting some positive media coverage about the place. The ski mountain was closed down twenty years ago after an unfortunate accident, and they want to replace those old stories with some new, feel-good ones."

"Oh man, I'd love to live in a ski town. I'm not great at it, but I'd love to learn."

I pulled up outside the new bakery in town. "Gonna grab some donuts and bring 'em over to the fire department," I told Shawn. "I want to thank Russ Grant and his crew for their amazing response to a false alarm over at the high school last weekend. Half the firefighters were playing a softball game in Valley Park, and they dropped everything to race over there in case any summer school kids were in the building. Thankfully, the building was empty, and the alarm had somehow been tripped accidentally. But they went above and beyond."

"Best part of living in a small town," Shawn said happily.

And he was so right. *That* was the kind of thing I should be focusing on. Not hot, entitled troublemakers. I was determined to put the movie people out of my mind entirely, and I did...

For about four minutes.

"I don't understand," I told Darius behind the counter. "What do you mean no bear claws?"

"I mean... we delivered them all down to the *Gold Rats* set. For craft services, you know? That movie has been amazing for business," he enthused. But whatever expression he saw on my face had him licking his lips nervously. "Sorry about the bear claws, though, Sheriff."

"Not at all. Don't give it another thought." It wasn't Darius's fault that the movie people were on a mission to destroy my breakfast and my peace of mind.

But the strikes against *Gold Rats*—and seriously, *what was that name even about?*—were adding up.

After dropping off the donuts and chatting up the firefighters for a while, Penny radioed to tell me they needed Shawn to fill out some paperwork. He and I spent the rest of the afternoon going over department protocol and housekeeping. He was easygoing but alert and attentive, and I decided I liked him.

When we joined the rest of the guys at Pie Hole, I introduced Shawn around. He played it cool with Tiller and gave his same easy smile to everyone at the large table.

"Any more trouble with the film folks since last night?" Tiller asked me once we'd ordered a couple of pitchers of beer and some pizzas.

"Not exactly." I did not mention the breakfast food debacle.

"Wait," Truman asked. "What happened last night?" The smaller man was tucked against his boyfriend's side. Sam looked exhausted, and I was sure he'd been working his ass off getting the lodge and the chalets ready for the cast and crew who would be staying there for the next few weeks. As the general contractor on the lodge and ski resort project, he was undoubtedly burning the candle at both ends.

I opened my mouth to explain it was no big deal, but Chaya, who'd tagged along with Truman, leaned in and took over the story.

"That kid from *Cast in Clover* thought the good sheriff here was some kind of parking attendant," she said. "Asked him to take care of his McLaren."

A tableful of gasps surrounded me. "Oh no he did not," Mikey said with a mischievous grin. "Finn Heller thought you were the valet?"

I shot Chaya a look. "How do you even know what happened?"

Her dark eyes danced almost as wildly as her big curly hair. "Because I heard him and his little groupie pal talking about it after you left. I was going to tell you about it this morning, but we were slammed."

Tiller chuckled. "I hope you took that bad boy for a joyride."

For a split second—seriously, just a sliver of a hot moment—I pictured a naked Finn Heller mounted on top of me. But then I realized Tiller had meant the *car*.

"No kidding," Shawn said with eyes twinkling. "When in your life would you ever even get a chance to *see* a McLaren, much less drive one?"

I didn't point out that I'd come here from the land of the douchemobiles. Expensive sports cars did absolutely nothing for me, and I'd also witnessed my fair share of them being repossessed from people who couldn't actually afford them.

I swallowed a sip of beer. "Suffice to say, dealing with that prima donna was confirmation I did the right thing moving here," I said lightly. "I wanted a slower pace of life, more natural beauty around me, and a town full of nice, genuine people. So far, so good on all three. Hopefully they'll shoot their film and get gone without causing trouble along the way."

Gentry Kane, who was a celebrity in his own right as a musician, leaned forward and clinked beer mugs with me. "Hear, hear. I found everything I ever wanted here in Aster Valley, and I don't want the paparazzi to come in here and mess it up."

After taking a sip of his beer, he leaned over and pressed a kiss onto his husband's cheek. Winter blushed and turned to meet him with another kiss on the lips.

My heart did a strange twisty thing I was beginning to recognize. It was a combination of happiness and envy. I loved having so many new queer friends in town, but they all seemed to be matched up with their perfect someone already. While it was great for them, it made me more painfully aware of my single status than I usually was.

Maybe I hadn't been completely truthful with Penny in my attitude about being single, but that still didn't mean I wanted an office romance. It was my job to make sure the sheriff's department was completely aboveboard. But maybe I could find someone else here in Aster Valley. Someone normal and nice.

LA had been too much of a hookup scene and not enough of a dating scene for my taste. I was almost forty. Hookups were fine, amazing even, but I wanted a partner. I wanted a family. Seeing these men and their partners made me want it even more.

"You okay, boss?" Shawn whispered from the seat next to me. "Don't feel like you need to stick around to make me more comfortable. Your friends seem awesome."

I opened my mouth to say they weren't really my friends yet, but I realized that wasn't exactly true. I'd been in Aster Valley for almost six months, and I'd known these guys for at least four of them. Even though we'd originally met through a case when I'd been a new deputy in town, these guys had gone out of their way to include me in social events ever since.

When was I going to think of myself as one of them?

I met Truman's eyes from across the table. He frowned and mouthed, "You okay?"

I nodded quickly and turned to Shawn. "No, sorry, just feeling ornery about the meeting I have with the show runner out at the *Gold Rats* set in the morning. I'll be fine. Besides, Crystobell Edmund and Logan Shaw were able to do a casual signing outside the cafe the other day without creating a crowd problem. Maybe this film situation won't be as bad as I keep expecting. Maybe last night's encounter was the worst of it."

But I knew that was wishful thinking. Thankfully, Gent's uncle Doran piped up to change the subject.

"Now, what's this I hear about your big emergency callout today?" the older man asked with a snicker. His thick, white mustache quivered with excitement. "If I recall correctly, you said something about wanting a slower pace of life, more natural beauty, and a town full of nice, genuine people. Tell us about rescuing Coleman Harrow from a rabid grizzly squirrel. Seems to me you got the trifecta all in that one case..."

The stress banding my shoulder muscles broke apart as I remembered the mountain man's high-pitched calls for help.

"Be careful what you wish for," I said through my laughter after giving them the basics of the story. "If the rest of my cases can be that straightforward, I'll be a happy sheriff."

Shawn clapped me on the shoulder. "Don't worry, boss. I'll take the dangerous ones off your shoulders. You handle the squirrels, and if that Jolly raccoon ever gets moody, just know I've got your back."

We spent a couple more hours in good company, laughing, eating, and drinking before promising Tiller we would guard his fiancé with our lives while Tiller was in Houston.

When Shawn and I left everyone and headed back to the SUV, he asked why Mikey just didn't go back to Houston with Tiller for the season.

"Someone needs to stay here and keep an eye on the cast and crew who are renting their lodge and the chalets on their property," I explained. "In case something happens."

Shawn shrugged. "They're all professionals and adults. What do they think would happen while they were gone?"

I remembered the raging house party my partner had been called out to one night in Santa Monica. "Finn Heller is known for throwing out-of-control house parties," I said. It was the understatement of the year. "And after all of the work Mikey, Tiller, and Sam have put into renovating the property, I'm sure they don't want to see it destroyed by drunken dilettantes who have no respect for other people's..." I realized my bias was showing. "Anyway. I get why they'd want to keep an eye out, but I know Sam has offered to watch over it for them, too."

Shawn looked over at me. "Your friends are good people. Thank you for including me tonight. You didn't have to do that, but I really appreciate it."

I nodded and mumbled something to acknowledge his gratitude. They were good people, and I felt as fortunate as he did to know them.

"I remember how I felt when I first moved to town," I told him. "It's not easy to make the leap from deputy to friend with the locals, but once you do, you learn how great the people of Aster Valley are. Genuine, kind, and helpful. One of the few places I've ever found where you can be accepted as your true self without putting on an act."

Which was a concept the Finn Hellers of the world would never understand.

2

FINN

"This fucking cabin is like being on set at a remake of Little House on the Fucking Prairie," Kix said, flicking the corner of a patchwork quilt that lay over the back of the small love seat.

He was right. The "chalet" they'd put me up in was pretty rustic, but I could tell it had been recently renovated. Most of the fittings were brand-new and fairly high-end, but the decor was homey and welcoming. Not exactly what Kix was used to back in his luxury apartment on Sunset Boulevard, but I kind of liked it. It wasn't the cold, ultra-modern style so many people had back home with hard angles, steel and concrete surfaces, and neutral grays.

The bedroom was my favorite, with its colorful rug that my bare feet had sunk into late last night when I'd been practically sleepwalking after a long day of driving. The crisp, cool sheets had been heavenly, and the fresh, mountain air flowing in gently from an open window had put me right to sleep. I'd come to this project after months... years... of churning, working as much as I could, as hard as I could to change my image from Chip Clover, the sitcom boy next door, to a dynamic adult actor who could take on nuanced, dramatic roles. But no matter how many degrees I'd earned, people wanted to keep me in a Chip-shaped pigeonhole.

I was so damned tired.

"I like it here," I said, kicking off my shoes and stretching out my legs on the small ottoman in front of my chair. The nearby stone fireplace made me almost wish it were wintertime. A night dozing in front of the fire in a cozy mountain chalet sounded just about right for my current mood.

"You would," he muttered under his breath.

I tried not to take his comment personally. First of all, he was right. I would and I did. Secondly, I knew how boring I was. It had been a problem for me my entire life so far. My mother had worked her ass off to make me more fun and engaging, and she'd be annoyed to see me chilling in front of a fire when I should be out socializing with the other cast and crew. *"Finn, you have to take advantage of every moment you have while on location. There's no better place to deepen those bonds than on the road."*

I glanced over at Kix. "Crys was pretty cool on set today, didn't you think?"

He rolled his eyes. "If by cool, you mean an ice queen, then yeah. Cool."

"Did you see her helping Yuki with the scene where her mother dies?"

Kix flipped the corner of the quilt again and bounced his leg in a way I recognized as pure, restless boredom. He wasn't going to stick around here shooting the shit for very long, which was fine by me. He was welcome to go back to his room in the lodge at any time. I was ready for the day to be over.

"Yuki is a suck-up. How hard is it to act bereft when your mother dies painfully from radiation exposure?"

I opened my mouth to argue. Yuki Makino was young and eager to please. She was terrified of letting down a big star like Crystobell Edmund. But Kix was jaded, and rightfully so. He'd worked his ass off for years in this business, just to get cast in supporting roles over and over again. I had my own opinions about why that was, but I wasn't about to say them out loud anymore, especially to Kix himself. Last time I'd tried, I'd gotten a snarky "Gee, thanks, Chip!" for my trouble. So I closed my mouth instead.

Kix resented Yuki for getting such a strong part in the film after only one decent credit to her name. As a result, he immediately put her in the "enemy" basket and treated her like dog shit.

It made me feel very uncomfortable.

"It's so fucking boring here, I can't imagine how we're going to survive four more weeks of this crap."

I shrugged and reached over to crank the nearest window open. The distant sound of an owl hooting made its way through the screen. "I think it's relaxing. A nice break from the city. Things are nuts in town this time of year, and, honestly, I don't love the heat."

He barked out a laugh. "How can you live in Los Angeles and not like the heat?"

That was easy. The answer was two words. *Lola Heller.*

"It's either LA or New York," I said instead. "At least LA has good climbing nearby."

"You and your climbing," he said. "If you lived in New York, you could still climb, you know. I'm sure there are a ton of climbing gyms there."

"Not the same as Point Dume and Echo Cliffs," I countered. "And while I don't love the heat in the summer, I do love being able to climb outside year-round."

Kix closed his eyes and groaned. "God, even this conversation is boring. Let's do something."

"Like what?"

"Anything, Jesus. I'm aging as we sit here." He lifted his fingers to his eyes and pulled at the edges to smooth out the nonexistent wrinkles. "Let's find some dick."

I thought of the sleepy mountain town we were in for the filming. "In this place? Pfft. I opened Grindr last night, and it literally showed me a photo of a cricket." It wasn't true. I'd actually opened my Discord Shakespeare chat group, but I was never going to tell him that.

He grinned. "Not true. But most of them seemed like either jailbait or jailbait's grandpa. No one just right. I'm like motherfucking Goldilocks up in here."

I stretched and leaned forward. "Maybe we should get some beauty sleep. Today was a long day, and tomorrow could be the same. I don't want to lose sleep before we've even gotten into primary filming."

It wasn't true. I wasn't on the schedule for much tomorrow, but I also didn't want to go skulking around a sleepy town looking for a hookup like some kind of pathetic loser. Besides, I was here to do a good job. I needed to impress the director. My mother, agent, PR manager, and I were all working hard to transition my reputation from child star to serious adult actor, and being seen in town trolling for a hookup wasn't the way to sell Nolan Trainor on my professionalism.

"Why do you care so much?" Kix asked.

I blinked at him. "Why do I care about doing a good job on the film?"

"It's an action movie. You look sexy and blow shit up. Hardly the stuff of legends."

He wasn't wrong, but the comment still grated. "I told you why this is important to me."

He flicked a hand in the air. "Nolan promised you something douchey if you do this. Yeah, I got it."

"Not something douchey. Lucentio in his big-budget production of *Taming of the Shrew*." I waited for a reaction even though he'd already heard me talk about this before.

"Yes, yes. Shakespeare. Guaranteed box office smasher. Oh, wait."

I sat up in the chair. "Do you have any idea what this kind of historical production could become with Nolan attached to the project?"

"What I know is that Nolan Trainor is crazy. Certifiable. Everyone says so." Kix shrugged.

"Not everyone. If it were *everyone*, he wouldn't be in charge of a big-budget project like this one," I argued. "Besides, people have said that about lots of great directors. Stanley Kubrick, Kurosawa, Orson Welles. Being unconventional is a good thing."

I wasn't sure why I was defending the man so hard. I hadn't been a fan of Nolan Trainor or his smash-'em-up blockbusters until the possibility of me playing Lucentio had been floated. But now that it had, I was looking at *Gold Rats* as a very long, involved audition for my bucket list role.

"I don't even understand why he would want to go from action films to historical dramas," Kix mused.

"It's a comedy," I muttered.

"Whatever. He's never made anything like a Shakespeare film. Why not make *Gold Rats Two* instead? I don't even care how good the acting is. With Crystobell's face on the ads and this mountain getting blown to bits, it's going to make truckloads of money. Might as well knock out the sequel right away."

The opportunity to act in a big-budget Shakespeare remake was a dream come true. It had been worth any amount of bullshit, including being treated like a joke by some of the cast and crew of *Gold Rats*. Nolan himself had pretty much admitted that he'd only cast me in *Gold Rats* because my rock climbing fans from years of *Cast in Clover* were now the target demographic for this film. I was a ticket sales draw, plain and simple.

Which was fine with me. Being an action movie star had never been my goal. But the better *Gold Rats* did in the box office, the more money we'd all make and the better chances the *Taming of the Shrew* project had of keeping its green light.

"They'd have to knock out the sequel without me if they moved it ahead of the Shakespeare project," I said, knowing it was hardly a threat. They'd simply find someone else to play the part of Ladd Masters, small-town police officer and avid rock climber with a heart of gold. Maybe it would be Kix's big break. But if they did… it would mean the Shakespeare project would be put on hold.

Again.

Kix groaned. "I'm tired of this whole conversation, and I don't really care. Let's go sign some tits."

Now I was annoyed and restless from letting doubts about Nolan's intentions on the project seep into my thoughts. I stood up and stretched. "You don't even like boobs."

"No, but I like seeing you blush when you have to touch 'em. Let's go fuck some shit up." He slid his feet into his shoes and pocketed his phone. "Logan tweeted they'd be at that little roadhouse place in fifteen. Let's go have a few drinks, sign a few cocktail napkins, and blow off a little steam. Once you get back here, you can get your beloved beauty sleep, okay?"

My mom's voice in my head had the deciding vote, as usual.

"No one ever made good connections from staying at home, Finn. The fans want to see you, and you never know who you might meet along the way."

I blew out a breath and grabbed my wallet. I wasn't in the mood to meet anyone tonight. Not only was I tired of the game, but I was tired full stop. But years of media training had prepared me to hide it under a million-dollar smile.

I pushed down my natural inclination to avoid the spotlight.

The way I always did.

3

DECLAN

The brash squawk of my radio woke me out of a dead sleep. If dispatch was trying to raise me on the radio, it meant they'd tried my phone already with no success.

"Sheriff Stone," I mumbled, getting up and grabbing my clothes out of habit.

"10-101 at Merry's Roadhouse," Janine said. "Sorry to bother you, Sheriff, but Matt Jancer asked for you specifically. Said he won't take no for an answer."

I sighed and told Janine to tell the bar owner I'd be there in less than ten minutes. After a quick visit to the bathroom and a shot of bottled iced coffee down my throat, I was off. The clock in the dash said it was almost three in the morning. Matt tried to close up the bar by half past one most nights, so if he was still having trouble with some drunk patrons, he'd most likely tried all his usual tricks.

When a few of my brain cells kicked into gear, I called back to Janine and asked which deputy was supposed to be on duty right now.

"Well, that's just it, you see." Our evening dispatcher was young and a bit too into local gossip for my taste, but since her mother was on the county council, I'd decided not to rock the boat by reassigning her to something a little less sensitive. "I sent Rolly over there, but you know how he is."

Yes. I knew how he was. Rollins Kepplow was a well-meaning doofus, a leftover hire from the old regime. Had we been in any other town than Aster Valley, I probably would have insisted on letting him go straightaway. But, like with Janine, I'd decided caution was the better part of valor in making big personnel changes in my first few months. Hearing the young deputy hadn't been able to manage helping Matt close out the bar made me rethink my stance.

Sure enough, when I pulled into the parking lot of the Roadhouse, the place was filled with vehicles including a sheriff's patrol vehicle. I strode through the front door of the bar in time to catch Deputy Kepplow taking a selfie with one of the actors from the movie.

"Fuck," I muttered under my breath. Of course this disturbance was caused by those assholes from California. Leave it to the film people to wake me from a dead sleep.

After a few friendly hellos from patrons leaving, I stood on a nearby chair and slipped my thumb and middle finger between my lips. My shrill whistle split the air, bringing the happy chitchat to a sudden stop. "Everybody, out. Last call was more than two hours ago. Unless you want to see poor Matt get shut down for serving violations, I recommend you save your thirst for another night."

The bar owner met my eye from across the crowd. His expression was full of exhaustion and gratitude. I wasn't fool enough to think he'd tried too hard to get everyone out as long as the money and fun were still flowing due to the notoriety the actors had brought to his place. Penny had mentioned the new social media hashtags popping up all over Instagram, and Matt had been the source for at least a few of them.

I caught a few teenaged girls begging the actors for body autographs, so I hopped down from the table and cut through the crowd to put a stop to it.

"Melanie and Samantha, right?" I lifted an imperious eyebrow at the girls. "Don't you have Mr. Reyes for summer school tomorrow?"

The girls both dropped their jaws in shock. "H-how did you know that, Sheriff?" one of them asked.

"It's my job to know where everyone is supposed to be at any given time," I lied. "And if I'm not mistaken, at no time are you two supposed to be at a bar after hours. Do your parents know where you are?"

The truth was, I'd helped Daniel Reyes track down his lost wallet a couple of weeks ago, and for the first hour, he'd insisted he'd most likely been pickpocketed by a couple of girls in his summer school class.

But I wasn't about to tell them that. Especially since the wallet was later found in Dan's own gym bag in the faculty lounge locker behind his own combination lock.

The girls panicked and bolted, leaving one of the actor twerps drooling in their wake. I didn't recognize the drooler or the two women sitting at the table, but I definitely recognized two of the other men as the brats who'd asked me to park their car at Rockley Lodge the night before.

"Let's go," I said, placing my hand on the shoulder of the man closest to me. The body under my hand stiffened. I looked down to see my hand on Finn Heller's shoulder. *The* Finn Heller. The famous actor who'd played Chip Clover in the long-running sitcom *Cast in Clover*. The kid America had watched grow up from their living rooms. The asshole who'd treated me like the help the night before.

When I'd seen him at Tiller and Mikey's house, I hadn't realized who he was at first. He looked nothing like the smart-mouthed boy next door who'd made millions flashing his dimples in front of American households on Thursday nights for all those years.

He was all man now. Even though he still had distinctive freckles scattered across his nose and cheeks, he also had tattoos I'd never noticed before inked on his muscular forearms and the rounded shadow of shoulders and pecs defined under his shirt.

I cleared my throat and pulled my hand away. "Time to go," I said again. "This isn't the Bayou on Santa Monica for god's sake."

The beach-blond man I'd pegged as Finn's sidekick the night

before raised one corner of his lips at me, and his eyes turned preda-
tory. "You know the Bayou?"

"Sure do. And I also know that Colorado has a mandatory
community service requirement for first-time DUIs. You look like the
kind of guy who might want to stick around after filming is done to
help beautify our little hamlet here. What do you say?"

Finn answered before his friend could mouth off at me. "He's not
driving. I am." He met my eyes, and his gaze held a potent combination of defiance and exhaustion that made me feel enraged and
shockingly protective all at the same time. My stomach pitched a
little like it might qualify for a DUI even without the alcohol
consumption. "And I'm sober."

I had no idea why I did it, but I grabbed Finn Heller by his biceps
and hauled him out of his chair and toward the door of the bar.
"We'll see about that."

What the hell was I doing? The kid was cherry-cheeked, sure, but
he didn't actually seem drunk. But once I'd started this ridiculous
charade, I was going to finish it.

"Could you... go easy on the optics, please?" His voice was soft as
if he only wanted me to hear him.

I glanced sideways and noticed a few people watching me haul
him out of the bar. I loosened my grip and instructed him over to the
side of my vehicle where I proceeded to ask him a few questions,
followed by holding out my finger and moving it side to side for the
first part of the field sobriety test. Normally, that would be followed
by the walk-and-turn test, but it was clear to me he wasn't drunk. Now
that we had an audience with a few cell phones out, I decided to
spare the town the additional drama.

"Wait in your car while I check with the bar owner. I'll escort you
back to your hotel."

Finn opened his mouth to argue with me, but I glared him into
changing his mind. After making sure Matt was able to close the bar
down peacefully, I returned to the McLaren. Several fangirls were
swarming the vehicle with their boobs and fluttering cocktail
napkins.

The sidekick was drinking it all up, but Finn himself just looked tired. He must have still been hungover from partying the night before after arriving in town.

"Alright, let's go," I said in a voice that meant business. I made significant eye contact with the fans, and they scattered like dandelion seeds.

The sidekick pulled his celebrity schtick on me again. "Do you have any idea who this is?" he asked with a laugh.

I tried to skewer him with my crusty, middle-of-the-night eyeballs. "Yes. I'm fairly sure it's the man who asked me to park his car last night."

Sidekick snorted. "Well, you should know he barely ever drinks. The man's a total bore."

Right. And I was Aristotle. "Be that as it may, I'm actually the sheriff of Aster Valley. And when I say it's time to go, that means it's time to go."

Finn actually blushed. What the hell? "Sorry, man. I didn't know," he murmured to his lap.

So now he was playing the innocent schoolboy. Not interested in that garbage.

"Now you do. And now the *sheriff* is going to escort you back to your hotel."

Finn looked up at me. "Yes, sir. We're staying at the Rockley Lodge property."

Normally, I didn't appreciate being "sir'd." But when that lush mouth did it? Jesus Christ on a motherfucking hot bed of coals did I have thoughts screaming through my head in response to it.

I cleared my throat to keep from squeaking like a hormonal teen. "Follow me."

As I turned to my vehicle, I heard the sidekick murmur, "Yes, Daddy."

I clenched my teeth against a smart retort. The McLaren's hungry engine followed me through the dark mountain roads until pulling safely into the drive of Rockley Lodge.

The drama was over.

Until the following night when the same damned thing happened all over again.

This time, I wasn't nearly as polite as I'd been the first night. I was exhausted and running on less than fumes. Janine had woken me up again with a loud radio squawk, and I was contemplating running over the damned thing with my vehicle.

"What is it?" I growled into the radio mic.

"Matt needs y—"

I didn't even let her finish. "On my way, and tell Rollins to bring his sidearm and badge to my office first thing in the morning." Aster Valley had no use for a deputy who couldn't help Matt close his damned bar in the middle of the night. Was I being an asshole? Maybe. But at least the command would scare him into compliance.

When I arrived at the bar, the entire vibe was different. It wasn't quite as late as it had been the night before, and people were still emptying their glasses from the recent last call. Music continued to pipe through the speakers, and a game of pool was in progress at the table in the corner.

I went directly to Matt before approaching Rolly.

"What the hell is going on?"

Matt pursed his lips in anger. "It's those Hollywood guys. They offered everyone free drinks and conveniently forgot to close out. Every time Dakota tries to present them with a bill, the crowd around them squeezes her out. So I went over there and demanded a credit card. The kid put a stack of cash in the folder instead. When I got it back over here, I saw it was singles. Nowhere near enough to cover what they bought."

Dakota leaned over the bar and whispered. "Honestly, he's too drunk to realize what he's doing. I say we just grab his wallet."

I held up a hand to stop her. "Let me handle it. What's he still owe you?"

When Matt handed me the new bill, my eyes nearly bugged out of my face. "Congrats," I muttered to Matt before walking over and disbursing the crowd around our erstwhile actors. On the way, I found Rolly and told him to get out to the lot and make sure no one drove drunk.

Sitting at the table was the same group of three men and two women from the night before. Finn, his blond groupie, another actor I recognized as Logan Shaw, whose roles in action films usually embodied every aspect of toxic masculinity, a petite woman with long ebony hair straight as a board down her back, and a woman with full cheeks and a big smile, who seemed to giggle drunkenly at every-thing around her. There were also a few fans interspersed between them, and I noticed Russ Grant had his arm around Finn.

"Closing time," I said, grinding my teeth. Some of us had actual work to do during the day and couldn't keep waking up at all hours to put the kids to bed. "And the bill is due. Which one of you has a credit card for Matt?"

Everyone's eyes went to Finn. He seemed to be swaying in his seat, and his eyes were unfocused. I flicked my eyes to his blond friend. "I thought you said he didn't drink?"

The friend snorted, and someone elbowed him.

"Kix, don't be an ass," one of the ladies said. "It's true. He doesn't usually drink. But he was... different tonight."

Kix snorted again. "Different like horny."

Russ squeezed closer to Finn in the large booth. "Shhh. Don't worry. I'm going to take care of you tonight."

Like hell he was. I knew Russ was an upstanding guy, and he probably meant well. I just didn't care. "Credit card," I said again.

One of the ladies leaned over to Finn. "Finn, they need your card to pay the bill."

He almost fell out of the chair trying to get his wallet out of his pocket, but when he did, he handed the entire thing to me. "I know you're not the valet, okay? I know. You're..." His face suddenly creased in confusion. "The waiter?"

Everyone at the table started laughing as if it was the best joke that had ever been told. They were all hammered.

I opened the worn leather wallet and saw Finn's driver's license.

Finnegan Joseph Heller with a familiar address in Santa Monica. He also had a condom that looked like it had been in there a while, a membership card to someplace called "Jack's Personal Fitness," a health insurance card, a bank card, and a black American Express card.

He was twenty-four years old. A newborn baby.

I slid out the Amex card and handed it to Dakota. "Add twenty percent," I told her under my breath.

"Make it thirty," Finn slurred. "She never once got mad at us."

I nodded to Dakota and turned back to Finn. "Come on, let me help you up. Deputy Kepplow can take some of you home, and I'll take the rest."

When Russ slid out of the booth and stood up, he gave me a firm nod. "No worries, Sheriff. I'll make sure Finn gets home okay. My place is just around the corner."

Finn's forehead crinkled in confusion. "But I'm not staying at your place."

"Tonight you are, babe," Russ said with a chuckle. "You're way too hammered to get home by yourself. You can sleep on my couch." He paused. "Or in my bed."

"I don't think so," I said as calmly as I could. Dakota brought back the bill, and I set it in front of Finn. If I hadn't known how wealthy he was, I might have felt more uncomfortable about having him sign it while he was this drunk. But Matt and Dakota deserved to get paid, and the bill was peanuts compared to a big night out at Nobu for guys like this.

Once he'd signed the tab and stood up, Finn wobbled a little. "Why am I tipping over?" he murmured under his breath.

I shot a look at his friend Kix. "So much for the sober bullshit from last night."

He waved me off. "Whatever, dude. I don't care if you believe me or not, but he doesn't usually drink much."

The woman with the cheeks leaned in to speak softly to me. "He's right. I know Finn got a call from home. He wouldn't say what it was, but maybe it was bad news."

Russ tried pulling Finn back under his big muscular arm. "Finn needs a friend. And I'm just the man for the—"

I gently guided Finn around to the other side of me until I was between the two of them. "Nah. I've got it from here. Thanks anyway, Russ."

The man opened his mouth to argue, but I shook my head firmly. *It's not happening, asshole.*

He gave me a narrow-eyed look, then stepped around me and took Finn's hand. "Tomorrow, then. Meet me back here, okay?"

Finn looked at the guy like he'd never seen him before in his life. "I don't even know where *here* is," he said under his breath.

Russ laughed like it was a joke and then pressed a kiss to Finn's hand. Just the sight of all that ink on Finn's forearms sent a shiver of need straight to my dick. I pushed it down. Ink had never done it for me before, and I sure as hell didn't need to get an ink fetish now.

I bit back a laugh when I saw Finn wipe the back of his hand on his jeans as soon as Russ turned to leave.

Finn's friend Kix called after him. "Rusty! Russ! Whatever your name is. I'm down if you are."

Russ turned back with a decidedly hungry gleam in his eyes, only this time it was aimed at the bleach-blond guy instead of Finn. "Yeah? Let's go, then."

Kix blew a smirky kiss to Finn and followed the firefighter out the door. As soon as they were gone, Finn seemed to sag against me.

"I'm sorry," he whispered.

I grabbed his elbow and led him out into the dark night. Rolly had stepped up for once, organizing rides home for everyone, because it seemed like the parking lot was mostly empty.

Before we got to my vehicle, Finn yanked himself out of my hold and bolted for some nearby bushes where he proceeded to hurl up his evening fun.

I stayed well away from his pukefest, but I gathered some wet wipes and a bottle of water from the back of the SUV for when he was done.

He finally stumbled back over to me looking like death. "Fucking hell," he said. "I forgot how bad it was. No wonder I stopped drinking. But my mom called and... you know? Sometimes it's like that. Like drink needs."

He wasn't making much sense. I handed him the water and wet wipes and looked anywhere but at him while he cleaned up his plump lips and sweaty face. The idea I found this puking *man child* attractive was untenable. It was a testament to how delirious I was from sleep deprivation.

After settling Finn in the passenger seat of the SUV and clipping his seat belt around him, I forced myself to pull away.

"No sniffing the drunk celebrity," I muttered to myself as I walked around the vehicle to the driver's side. *Even if he smells like the best combination of coffee and woodsmoke.*

It was a surprising combination, especially since it held no hints of vomit. I would have expected a man like him to wear something expensive like Tom Ford or Dior, but whatever scent he was wearing was completely different. Not floral or citrusy.

I wanted to press my nose into his neck just to see if I could figure it out.

Is that why? Survey says no.

I stretched my neck side to side. The lack of sleep was getting to me. This kid was the opposite of everything I'd ever wanted, and having to pull him out of a bar after closing time two nights in a row was proof of that.

When I got into the car and started the engine, I heard Finn singing softly to himself. It was a little endearing, and since I had no interest in having soft, positive feelings for this troublemaker, I decided to cut him off.

"Two nights in a row now. You know this isn't LA, right? Just because you and your friends want to stay out until all hours basking in the attention of your adoring fans doesn't mean people like Matt and Dakota should have to stay up and serve you."

He slow-panned over to face me. "What?"

"I'm just saying, this is a small town where we roll up the red carpet before midnight. How is Matt supposed to get up and be ready to receive his deliveries in the morning if you keep him up till three every night? And Dakota is a student at Rockley Tech. She probably has classes in the morning. That's why they close at one."

He glanced at the clock on the dash and squinted comically. "But it's two now."

"Exactly my point. Your people kept them open because you wouldn't pay the bill and leave when they asked you to."

"No, but..." He drifted off, seemingly distracted by something out the passenger side window. Just when I thought he'd forgotten he was in the middle of saying something, he continued. "I didn't pay attention to the time. I didn't want to come out, and then I didn't... I didn't want to drink. And I didn't pay attention to the time. My mother says punctuality can be the difference between a starring role and the gutter."

I glanced over at him and noticed the hank of brown hair that had fallen over one eye. My fingers itched to push it back.

"She's right, but I'm not sure how that's relevant to respecting closing time at the local pub."

"It's about respect," he said.

That was rich coming from someone who'd thrown a house party back in LA so large and destructive they were recreating it as a training exercise for new recruits at the police academy to learn crowd disbursement techniques. Finn Heller's reputation preceded him.

"Exactly. Think about your actions and the way you treat people. Actions have consequences."

Finn's head bobbled as I pulled down the driveway to Rockley Lodge. He'd mentioned staying at one of the chalets, so I took the turnoff to head farther up the mountain property.

"Yes, sir," he said, sounding both exhausted and annoyed now. "I appreciate you so much."

That was sarcasm. I made a grunt of surprise.

"In fact, I'm grateful someone like you is here to help me see the error of my ways. My mom wanted to come, but she was offered a chance to join Stavros Pagonis on his yacht instead. So now I have you here making sure I behave just right. So. Fucking. Grateful," he ground out.

I threw the SUV into park behind the chalet with the McLaren. He must have ridden to the bar with someone else.

"Seems you're sobering up," I said. "Or maybe you're still shit-faced if you can mouth off to a cop without blinking an eye."

He finally turned to me with steel in his eyes. "I'm not drunk enough to miss the fact you've found the one person in a group of, what? Five other cast and crew, who you're convinced is responsible for not leaving. Well, you know what? I wasn't driving. And also... also... I was trapped in that booth. I told them I didn't want to go out. And then I told them I didn't want to stay." As he spoke, Finn's voice got louder and more belligerent. "And then I told them I wanted to go home!"

He threw open the door to the SUV and lurched out, almost landing flat on his face. I hurried around to help him.

"Careful," I murmured, grabbing his elbow.

He sniffed. "I didn't want to go out."

It was on the tip of my tongue to ask him why he didn't want to go out. What had the phone call been about that had upset him to the point of becoming almost blackout drunk? But then I reminded myself he was a spoiled actor whose problems were most likely tied to not getting a role in a film rather than anything life changing.

"Well, you did. And actions have—"

He finished the sentence with me. "Consequences. Thanks, Sheriff Daddy. Now kindly fuck the fuck off."

Finn stumbled to the front stoop where he crawled up the two stairs and then lay down on the welcome mat. I stepped forward to help him into the cabin but then stopped myself.

If he was going to tell me to fuck the fuck off, then he could sleep on the damned welcome mat for all I cared.

I turned and got back in the vehicle wondering how long it would be before the first hints of sunrise would sneak over Rockley Mountain. I radioed in my status and told Janine I would be coming in late today.

When I pulled into my own driveway, all I could think about was returning to my bed for a few more hours of sleep, but when I walked up to the front porch, I realized that wasn't in the cards.

Tessa, my friend and next-door neighbor from LA, sat curled up on one of my rocking chairs. Her big belly was hidden by a hoodie sweatshirt, but I saw the evidence of the pregnancy in the fullness of her face.

She was beautiful.

"Oh honey," I said, reaching out to shake her awake. "What happened? Why'd you leave LA?"

As soon as she woke up and saw me, she burst into tears.

4

FINN

Being the lead actor on a fairly big-budget film came with many perks, and right now, the luxury trailer I was in was the one I was most grateful for.

I lay back on the sofa and groaned. The cold compress the makeup assistant had given me felt like heaven over my eyes.

Kix wasn't quiet as he rifled through my fridge for a drink. I bit back the desire to tell him to get the hell out of my trailer. He only had access to a shared trailer with a few of the other cast members who had smaller parts, and if I mentioned it, he got angry. I'd learned back in high school that Kix's tongue got even sharper when he was angry.

"That firefighter dude had a nice fuckin' dick," he said. "Except he kept asking me about you, so I told him I'd get you to agree to a three-way later."

I pulled off the cloth and glared at him. "Not happening."

The idea of sharing dick with Kix made my stomach crawl. He was a player and didn't seem to discriminate much when it came to taking it from strangers. Which was fine but not really my speed. My speed was more like glacial cornball "making love" speed. The kind that meant I pretty much never had sex. Ever. And I for damned sure had never had a three-way.

Kix wouldn't know that, though, because I did a very good job of making myself fit in.

"And anyway, I'm here to work. No more nights out," I grumbled. "That was a colossal mistake."

"Yeah, whatever," Kix said before throwing himself into a nearby chair and spilling some of his water on the floor. I put the cloth back over my eyes.

"This is going to be a big release, Kenny," I said, forgetting the stage name he'd picked when we were preteens. "I have to nail this part if I want Nolan to offer me the—"

"Save it," he snapped. "I don't want to hear another thing about that damned period drama. Besides, how the hell do you expect to nail your part if I hadn't kept you out late enough both nights to watch a real cop in action?" He snorted out a laugh.

I thought of the gorgeous but very frowny sheriff who'd driven me home.

Declan. I'd heard the bartender call him by name the other night. *Sheriff Declan Stone.*

"I can nail my part," I muttered. "It's not a problem."

"That's not what I heard." He sang the snide comment in an annoying way. I didn't want to take the bait, but I had too much riding on this project to ignore a comment like that.

I whipped the cloth off and sat up. "What did you hear?"

Kix was tossing a water bottle in the air and catching it. "Lina overheard Nolan complaining to Shelly something like, 'I asked for the Rock and you gave me a pebble.' And then he supposedly said, 'Chip Clover himself would make a tougher cop at this point.'"

My skin prickled with embarrassment. "That doesn't even make any sense. I *am* Chip Clover. Chip Clover was me. If Chip would make a..." I let the complaint trail off since it was stupid. "What do they expect me to do?"

The idea they would have cast me without thinking I had enough talent to pull this off didn't make any sense. If I couldn't pull off this role, then why hire me for it?

"Don't worry about it," Kix said, tossing the water bottle up again. "I'm sure he was talking out of his ass. And why do you even care? You'll get paid your millions regardless of how well it does."

That was patently false. But it wasn't about the money. If Nolan didn't think I had acting chops, he was never going to give me a shot at the Shakespeare.

I needed some advice. "Hey, I have a call with Iris in five minutes. Would you mind finding another place to hang out while I talk to her?"

He rolled his eyes but got up from the chair. Before opening the door, he turned back to me. "You're a good actor, Finn. Don't listen to that blowhard Nolan, okay? He's an asshole, desperately trying to stay relevant, and everyone knows it. You're going to be great. Just maybe... take some asshole lessons from someone. You're too nice to portray an angry cop. You need to find your spleen and then spray it at everyone."

I thanked him instead of explaining I didn't think that was how spleens worked. As soon as I was alone, I dialed my agent.

"I need your help," I said as soon as the call connected. I told her what Kix had heard.

"Honey, don't listen to *Kenny* Rowe. He's a wannabe who is using you for your connections. I've told you this a thousand times."

That was true. She had. But Kix and I had come up through the children's role audition ranks together, and at the age of eight, I'd given him the raging case of chicken pox that had prevented him from auditioning for the role of Chip Clover. He'd always joked I'd done it on purpose since I had to have known I'd have never gotten the part had he been able to audition.

While I knew it was just a joke, part of me still felt guilty. I'd spent years trying to make it up to him by introducing him to people in the industry and giving him tips on auditions when I heard of them. But, after missing the opportunity for *Cast in Clover*, things had never really happened for him the way he'd always dreamed.

So, yeah. I felt guilty. He'd gotten chicken pox, and I'd gotten cast in a career-making role.

"Does that mean you don't think Nolan doubts me?"

She hesitated. "I didn't say that. I only said take what Kix says with a grain of salt."

Great.

"I need to know if there's something else I can do to prepare for the role. That's why I'm calling. What should I do?"

"Have you talked to your mom? What does she say?"

I hated that after all this time she still thought of my mother as the person in charge of my career. "She's on a yacht right now. I didn't call her. I'm asking you. Do you think I can nail this role?"

This time, she didn't hesitate. "Absolutely. You're a good actor, Finn. I believe in you, and I always have. Even when you could have rested on your laurels with *Cast in Clover*, you took as many acting classes as you could. Hell, you worked hard enough at UC Irvine to get Franklin Burkhoff's attention, and that's no small feat. So yes, you can nail any role you set your mind to." She paused significantly. "But that's different than convincing the director you're better than your reputation."

I ignored the mention of my college mentor. If there was one person who would absolutely not be up for talking to me about how to nail a blockbuster action hero part, it was Barry.

"Explain what you mean," I said.

"You and I know you can nail this role, but the rest of the world still thinks you're Chip Clover, including Nolan. We talked about this. He needs to know you're serious about this role. He needs to see you doing the work to get it right, even if you already know what you're doing. It's about perception. Optics. You know how it is."

"So how do I make him think I'm taking this seriously?" I tried not to remember myself shutting down the local pub two nights in a row. That probably wasn't high on the list of how to win friends and influence directors.

"I have an idea," she said after a minute. "Hang tight and I'll call you back in a few."

After she hung up, I let out a breath. Other than giving my mother too much of a say, Iris had never steered me wrong. Thanks to her, I'd had a lucrative acting career, even through the years I'd spent pursuing my master's degree. And with her help, I'd kept the lion's share of the money well managed and away from my mother's clutches. With residuals constantly coming in from *Cast in Clover*, I could retire today and still live in luxury for the rest of my life.

Then why are you here?

I ignored the voice in my head. There was no mystery about why I was here. I wanted the Shakespeare opportunity. If there was going to be a big Hollywood remake, I wanted to be involved in it.

When Iris called back, she sounded excited. "You have your car there, right?"

"Yes."

"Okay, I'm texting you the address of the local police station. I pulled some strings and got you a ride-along with the sheriff himself. Apparently he used to work here in LA and—"

Her words were lost behind the slight roaring in my ears. The sheriff? As in, Officer Hotpants who hated my guts?

"I'm not sure that's such a good idea," I said feebly. "I've met the sheriff, and he's..." Gorgeous? Stern? Strong? Easily annoyed? "Unlikely to agree to such a scenario," I finished.

"Don't you worry about that. He owed someone a favor, and it's all set. You're to show up at the police station after your wardrobe fitting. He'll be expecting you."

"But..." I let out a breath, deliberately not correcting her that it was the Rockley County Sheriff's Department and not a police station. I may have done some googling while waiting for a fight training lesson yesterday. The photo of the sheriff on the department's website was damned fine. I also may have saved it into the photo folder on my phone. "Why do I need to do a ride-along when we both know I got rave reviews from that season of *SEAL Team Charlie*? That was super similar to this. I can do this. I can—"

"It's not about whether or not you can do this. It's about the optics, remember? Besides, getting in tight with local law enforcement is always a good idea on location. If you have any problems, it won't hurt to be on a first-name basis with the chief."

"Sheriff," I mumbled. "Fine. I get your point. I'll spend the day riding with him. Thank you."

"The week. It's for a whole week until primary filming starts. He knows to work around your work schedule."

My hands were sweating. "A week?" I cleared the panicked squeak out of my throat. "Why a week? Isn't a day plenty of time?"

"It's just a few hours a day around the other things on your schedule. I know you have choreographing for the fight and climbing scenes, fitness training sessions, wardrobe fittings, and blocking meetings. So, really, it won't be more than a few hours a day with the cop. Ask lots of questions. Seem interested in doing the best job representing his... industry, or whatever, you can. He'll eat it up."

After getting off the call and making my way over to the wardrobe trailer, I remembered my centering techniques. Just because I'd made a terrible first (and second... and third...) impression on the sheriff, didn't mean I couldn't turn things around.

I was Finn Heller. America's beloved boy next door. I was known for my charm and ease.

And if he didn't like it, well, too bad. My only goal was doing what I needed to do for this film so I could move on to what mattered the most.

And that wasn't Sheriff Declan Stone.

5

DECLAN

I was running on two hours of sleep, a giant cinnamon roll from the new bakery, and a vat of coffee. To say my mood was less than ideal would be an understatement.

So when one of my brothers called to ask me a favor, I was inclined to tell him where to shove that favor. The only thing that kept me from biting his head off was the knowledge I owed him one. A big one. He'd been the one to offer pro bono legal help to my partner when all the shit had gone down with the department's bribery scandal back in LA. And even when Nick had been clearly guilty of the charges against him, my brother Patrick had given him a strong defense and had negotiated an impressive plea deal for him.

I owed Patrick big-time, and seeing Tess, Nick's ex-girlfriend, on my stoop last night was a reminder of it.

"Can't I have one of my deputies do it?" I asked with a sigh. "You have no idea how high-maintenance Finn Heller is."

Patrick laughed. "No way. I promised her he'd get the best man on the force. One has to assume that's you, Peanut."

Leave it to one of my brothers to be loving and condescending in the same breath. "How do you even know this agent? Is she a client?"

"You know I can't tell you that. But I can tell you she's Olivia's tennis partner at the club. She and her husband are friends of ours. In fact, you've probably met them at the holiday party before. Iris is tiny, and her husband is a giant. Olivia always makes rude jokes behind their backs about the physics involved during sex."

That rang a bell. I remembered the husband more than the wife. Sexy as hell, but a pompous jackass who name-dropped in every sentence.

"Yeah, okay. Whatever. But this is a big ask, so now you're going to owe me one."

His warm, familiar laughter made me smile. Moving away from my family had been the only downside to my relocation to Colorado.

"That's not how this works," he said. "We'll be even if anything. Don't you remember when Nick wanted to bribe the judge on his case?"

Heat flooded my face. My partner had hidden his corruption incredibly well until he'd been caught. Then it had seemed like almost a game to him.

My hesitation must have betrayed my emotions because Patrick's voice dropped the teasing tone. "It's okay, Dec. You know I'm used to shit like that. He wasn't even close to the worst of my clients. And I was happy to do that for you. Okay?"

I was the youngest of five boys. They'd always been just as protective and loving toward me as my parents had been.

"Okay. Yeah. Ah... speaking of Nick, Tessa showed up here last night."

"Really? Is she okay? I saw her about six weeks ago when Nick signed away his parental rights. Since you're listed as her next of kin, she told me I could disclose it to you."

I hadn't known she'd listed me as next of kin, but she'd told me about the parental rights. Thank god. Nick Kimball had never been father material.

I thought of how Tess had been so exhausted she'd burst into tears before I'd taken her inside and put her to bed. "She's not okay. It's been rough on her back in LA, financially and emotionally. Her business dried up, and all her so-called friends have suddenly evaporated. I told her to stay here with me for a while. I have room, and she needs someone in her corner."

"She's lucky to have you. It's probably good for her to disappear until this crap dies down. As long as some of these bribery cases are still making their way through the courts, it's going to remain active in the tabloids."

At least Nick's plea deal had saved us all that long, drawn-out process. He'd begun serving his long sentence as soon as Patrick had made the arrangements.

"I'll have to find her a doctor or midwife, but I have a friend whose sister is a nurse. I'm sure she can help."

"Good. Listen, I have to go. Things might not be busy in a small-town sheriff's department, but they're bonkers here. I'm due in court in about twenty minutes. Call Mom. She got downright sniffly the other night because you weren't there for her special spaghetti and meatballs."

I ended the call laughing. Our mother made spaghetti from a jar with frozen meatballs and tried to pass it off as an old family recipe passed down through generations from some Italian ancestor who didn't actually exist. As soon as we were old enough to figure it out, we started calling it "Mom's special spaghetti and meatballs," and it cracked us up every time.

Leave it to Patrick to lift my spirits. My improved mood lasted all of ten minutes until Penny announced the arrival of "that adorable boy from that show."

"Send him in," I grumbled.

Somehow in the twelve or so hours since I'd seen him last, Finn Heller had become exponentially more attractive. Maybe my mind was playing tricks on me with an attempt to downplay his looks in my memory. But here he was in the flesh, about as sexy and compelling as a human being could possibly be.

What was it about him that made my breath come faster and shallower? He was too young, too... perky, too... *everything*.

"Hi, Sheriff," he said, holding out his hand. "I'd like to apologize for last night and thank you for your intervention."

He said this like he'd been rehearsing it on the way over. Still, I glanced down at his hand like it was going to bite.

"Just doing my job," I said. As soon as my hand clasped his, my lower belly tightened. His grip was warm and firm, but his hands were soft and tender. I didn't want to be attracted to him, but he was making it (and me) hard.

"Great. That's what I'm here to see. I appreciate you agreeing to let me shadow you this week. I hope it's no bother."

I bit back a complaint that of course it was a bother. I had a county to keep in order, new deputies to train, and a large film project causing all kinds of traffic, zoning, and crowd control problems.

"No bother at all," I said instead. "Have a seat." I led him into my office and gestured to the plastic guest chair in front of my desk before taking a seat in my own chair. "What exactly can I help you with?"

I figured the best course of action was to determine what he wanted to learn or observe and then dive right in. Maybe once he had the information he needed, we could finish early.

Finn blinked at me, sooty eyelashes dusting his cheeks just above the sprinkling of freckles that made him look so young. "I, um..."

"I was under the impression this was an action film," I said. "With shooting and explosions. Car chases and stuff."

He scraped a tooth over his bottom lip. "Well, yes."

"Which, as you probably know, isn't normal fare for a small-town sheriff's office in the Rocky Mountains," I added.

His forehead crinkled. "But you're not from here. You were a special operations detective in Los Angeles until recently. Weren't you?"

I nodded. "I was. But it was a rare day when I chased a suspect to the inevitable mountainside cave explosion," I said drily.

Pink suffused his face. "You know about the cave explosion scene."

I nodded again. "My first official day as sheriff was spent talking the county council down from allowing your people to literally blow up the side of Rockley Mountain. Yes, I'm familiar with the plans."

"They wouldn't have actually blown it up," he said. "Most of it is done with special effects."

He must have had more faith in his director than the guy warranted. Nolan Trainor had actually submitted a request to use blasting agents for a live explosion shot. Thankfully, Tiller Raine's attorneys had been better than Nolan's, and the landowner had prevailed.

"They actually attained approval for a live detonation of a temporary structure. So, they're still blasting, just not making a permanent dent in our mountain."

Finn's eyes widened. "They... they wanted to blow up part of the mountain?"

He was very good at acting naive.

"The movie apparently ends in an explosion that creates an avalanche."

He nodded. "Well, sure, but that... I thought that was the kind of thing that would be done with CGI."

"The show runner told me this director prefers shooting things as real as possible. Just be glad there's such a thing as a stunt double."

Finn's forehead creased in a frown. "I'm not using a stunt double. It's one of the reasons Nolan cast me in this role. You're right about him being a stickler for authenticity. There are several rock climbing scenes, and I'm... I'm good at climbing. I just didn't think it meant he'd want to blast into a real mountain."

He looked down at his hands which were clasped in his lap. Gone was the flashy celebrity who'd handed me his keys with a dismissive wave the other night in front of Mikey and Tiller's place. In his place was someone I couldn't figure out.

Finn Heller wasn't just good at climbing. He was famous for it. The show he'd been on was about a family known for their unusual luck. Everything went right for them, regardless of how dangerous or ill-advised. As a result, the youngest Clover kid had been a danger-seeker until finally finding his passion: rock climbing. Finn had spent the next several seasons playing a serious rock climber.

Finally, I understood why this particular actor had been cast in a big-budget action film. He was known for climbing, and the hero in the movie they were here filming was a rock climber. I only knew about it since they'd had to schedule extra security and crowd control perimeters the days they were shooting climbing scenes on the other side of the mountain.

No matter how skilled I knew him to be, when I pictured Finn hanging from Slye Peak, my palms started to sweat. Just one more piece of the Finn Heller puzzle that was driving me crazy.

I blinked away the image and got back to the point. "I certainly can't help you with the rock climbing portion of the film, not that you'd need my help for that anyway, so what other scenes are there I might be able to help you prep for?"

He looked back up at me. His eyes sparkled a little. "You know about my climbing?"

I didn't want to give him the satisfaction of knowing I knew who he was. "You mentioned you were good at climbing. I've never been climbing. Ergo, I can't help you with climbing."

Ergo? Jesus.

I cleared my throat. "But car chases I could help with." Finn's eyes widened with excitement, so I threw up a palm to deflect it. "Not by participating in one, mind you, but by discussing techniques and tactics."

Finn's expression still held excitement as he nodded. "I would appreciate that. Thank you."

His professionalism and gratitude made me uncomfortable.

Thankfully, we were interrupted by my new deputy.

Shawn ducked his head into my office with a quick knock on the doorframe. "Sheriff, sorry to interrupt, but there's a 10-59 at the Barking Lot, and Penny said..." He glanced at Finn and chose his words more carefully. "You'd want to handle it."

I stood up and gathered my things, halfway hoping this wasn't what I thought it was. "Deputy Graham, this is Finn Heller. He's shadowing me this week. Finn, Shawn Graham."

They shared a quick greeting before I led Finn out the back to my vehicle.

"What's a 10-59? Please tell me it's a robbery in progress. That would be amazing."

I turned to Finn. "It wouldn't be amazing for poor Louisa, who runs the shop."

He looked appropriately cowed. "No. Obviously. Sorry, I..."

"Get in the car."

When we got underway, Finn scrolled through his phone until he found a site with radio codes. "What's malicious mischief?"

I sighed. He was going to find out anyway as soon as we got there. "It means Mrs. Brainthwaite has decided Prancer needs a new sparkly collar, but she doesn't want to pay for it because she's still mad at Louisa for cutting Prancer's toe fluff too short."

I was quickly discovering Finn was the master of the slow-pan. "Say what now?"

"You heard me," I muttered, turning on my indicator before pulling into the open spot in front of the shop. "This is what I meant when I told you I might not be the best person to shadow for your role. This is hardly Los Angeles, and you're not going to see any exciting action here."

Finn followed me into the pet store where I spotted an angry septuagenarian being blocked from exiting the store by a harried dog groomer.

I nodded a greeting at both of them. "Louisa. Mrs. Brainthwaite. What seems to be the problem?"

Louisa remained calm despite being obviously peeved. "She has three Nylabones and a squeaky squirrel in her purse."

Mrs. Brainthwaite wouldn't meet my eyes. She crossed her arms in front of her full chest. "Don't be ridiculous. As if I'd deign to purchase any items from the likes of you."

Louisa finally snapped. "Who said anything about purchasing?"

"Marla," I said, softening my voice in the way I'd learned worked on the older lady. "We've been over this before. Either pay her for them or get them on Amazon. Which will it be?"

Now she met my eyes with fury. "I will not give my money to that corporate monstrosity! I support local or nothing at all, do you hear me?"

Louisa threw her hands up and huffed, but Finn was the one who spoke next. His voice was kind and gentle.

"But you're not supporting local. You're contributing to a locally owned business suffering. Is that what you want? For Aster Valley to go back to the way it was ten years ago when half the shops were shuttered and some of the store owners were forced to move away?"

I glanced at him in surprise. How did he know about Aster Valley's history?

"Of course not," Mrs. Brainthwaite said indignantly. "My own sister... my own..." She stopped and clamped her lips together, chin trembling a little. Her eyes darted to Louisa before she finally exhaled. "My sister used to own a T-shirt stand inside the main ski lodge. She... she was forced out of business when the resort closed."

Louisa looked taken aback. "I never knew Alicia owned her own business. I'll bet she was great at it. She's such a people person. She comes in here with Pickles all the time and makes everyone laugh."

Mrs. Brainthwaite's entire face softened. "She does?"

Louisa nodded and gestured toward a little rotating stand with doggie bow ties on it. "She was looking at that green-and-white-striped tie for Pickles but decided to wait for Christmas."

Mrs. Brainthwaite reached out to run a finger over the fabric of the bow tie. "But Pickles' birthday is next month..."

Once everyone's hackles had been lowered and Louisa had made a particularly large sale to Mrs. Brainthwaite, including the bones, toys, bow tie for Pickles, and a bag of organic, homemade treats—also made by a local Aster Vallian—Finn and I bid the ladies a nice day and made our way back to the SUV.

"You didn't arrest her for shoplifting," he said once we got strapped in.

"She didn't shoplift," I said with a smile. "Louisa didn't let her leave."

"But..." He looked back at the shop and then at me. "Small towns are different."

"That they are," I agreed. "It takes a little getting used to."

"I like it," Finn said softly.

We made our way back to the station, but before we arrived, Penny radioed in a 10-16.

"Negative. Have Graham do it," I said in response. Finn began scrolling on his list of radio codes again.

"A prisoner pickup?" Finn said, with a thread of excitement in his voice. "Why did you say no? That would be great."

"She needs to be taken down to Silverthorne. I assumed you couldn't be that far away from the set." It was a lie. I didn't want to be alone in the car with him for the long drive back after dropping the woman off at the lockup in Summit County.

"It's fine. All I have left today is a blocking meeting for a climbing scene. My trainer and I are doing it over dinner."

My mind interpreted that last sentence in an inappropriate way that left me feeling testy. "Fine." I called Penny back and told her I'd take the 10-16.

We swung by the department and processed the prisoner out. Finn listened to my safety instructions diligently and kept plenty of distance between himself and the woman. She'd been picked up on a routine traffic stop where the deputy had learned about an outstanding warrant on her in another county. All we had to do was transfer her, and since the deputy who usually did runs like this was on vacation, Penny had figured I'd appreciate the time away from all the chaos of the increasing tourist crowd in town.

She'd been right. Even the woman in the back of the SUV commented on it.

"What the fuck is all that for?" she asked as we drove down Main Street past a large crowd gathered outside the diner. She craned her neck to see if she could spot the cause of the gathering.

Finn sunk down in his seat and kept his head turned away from her.

"There's a movie being filmed in town," I said. "It's brought in a bunch of lookie-loos. Some of the actors are probably having lunch at the diner."

Finn turned to me. "Lookie-loos?"

I shot him a glare. "Fine. Idiot groupies with nothing better to do than stalk random people. Is that better?"

"I'm not sure anyone would call Crystobell Edmund a 'random' person," he said with a smirk. "Tell me you wouldn't sleep with her if she crooked her finger."

I turned to him at a stoplight and said it straight up. "I would not sleep with her if she crooked her finger."

The prisoner piped up. "Well, shit. You broken? Even I would sleep with the woman, and I don't swing that way. Did you even see *Party of Two*? The hot tub scene? Jesus on a jump rope, that woman can steam the pants off anyone."

I glanced at her in the rearview mirror. "I don't swing that way either."

Even though I didn't want it to be so, I had all of my antennae focused on Finn's reaction to my declaration.

He turned to look out the passenger-side window as if it was no big deal, but I noticed his grip on his phone turned white-knuckled. "Same," he said casually.

I didn't admit to already knowing about his sexuality. It was still my plan to not give him the satisfaction of thinking I knew anything about him.

"Great," the woman said from the back. "I can't even make up a sexual assault complaint with a couple of gays up in here."

I couldn't hold back a laugh. "That and there's two cameras in here."

She grinned wide at me in the mirror. "I'm just teasing. You seem nice. Too bad I didn't get the bust-up in Rockley instead of Summit. I woulda liked seeing you again in court."

Finn chuckled at that and began asking her what she'd been busted for. His questions were so casual, the prisoner had no idea she was confessing to crimes after she'd not only been read her rights but also after it had been clearly disclosed to her she was on camera.

I glanced over at him and caught his eye.

He winked at me.

I bit back another laugh and looked in the rearview mirror again. "Ma'am, you might be seeing me in court after all."

This time, it was Finn who had to bite back the laugh. I tried hard not to feel like the two of us were in on a secret together, but it was hard.

I didn't want to like Finn Heller. But that was hard, too.

Step one, I needed to stop palling around with this guy.

6

FINN

Riding along with Sheriff Stone was easier than I'd anticipated. I'd expected him to be harsh, annoyed, and stuck-up. He'd seemed to make a flash first impression of me that put me squarely in the "spoiled brat" category.

But today was different. He'd been kinder than I'd expected, and more patient in general. At least, *at first*.

After dropping the woman off in Silverthorne, Declan pulled into a sandwich shop so we could grab a late lunch. I asked him lots of questions about police procedure, but the minute I threw in a personal question about why he'd gone into law enforcement, his easygoing manner shut down.

"We should probably get back," he said, balling up the wax paper from his sandwich and shoving back his chair to stand up. "You have your dinner thing."

I looked down at my half-eaten salad. It wasn't very good anyway, so I went ahead and threw it out before following Declan to the SUV. When we were back on the road, I tried again.

"Are you from here?"

He glanced at me out of the corner of his eye before answering. "No."

"Oh." That wasn't a question people usually answered with only one word. "Where did you—"

He interrupted me to point out an elk off the side of the highway. "Quick, look over there. See the antlers?"

I stared in awe at the big animal, who stood frozen in a stand of trees. After spending my entire life in the city, it was almost unbelievable to think the elk was real and wild, not part of a zoo exhibit or something.

"Wow," I whispered as I craned my neck to look at it as long as I could before we were too far past it. "That's amazing."

"I often wonder if I'll ever get used to it," he said, almost to himself.

I kept eagle eyes on the edges of the highway after that, trying as hard as I could to spot more wildlife. The closest I came was seeing some kind of hawk fly over the trees.

"I can see the appeal of living here," I said after a while. "The people are friendly, and the area of Aster Valley is stunning. It's just as sunny here as in LA, but it's fresh and clean."

"So, you do your own stunts, you said?" Declan asked, turning the conversation away from himself again.

I opened my mouth to give my usual PR response about taking pride in doing my own stunts, but for some reason, I didn't feel like lying to him. "Technically? I mean, that's what we say. Most of the time, I do my own climbing stunts which is the bulk of what my career has consisted of so far. But when you mentioned Nolan's plan to use actual explosives in the avalanche scene..." I looked out the window at the rolling hills to my right. "Well, let's just say I hope he has some specialists who can show me what to do safely."

He turned to me with narrowed eyes and a frown. The intense look on his face made the hairs on my arms stand up a little. "How could you not know? Isn't it spelled out in the contract? Don't you have an agent looking out for you?"

"I have an agent who looks over everything. If she agreed to it, I'm sure it will be fine." Now I was definitely lying. As much as I appreciated Iris, I knew she was desperate to change my image from the clean-cut boy-next-door Chip Clover character to something edgier, more mature. I could see her accepting dicey stunt terms in an effort to make my image a little more badass.

But I wasn't a tough, brave guy who relished putting myself in danger. I was an awkward, too-small-to-be-an-action-hero guy who'd accidentally fallen in love with rock climbing after taking private lessons with all the best safety equipment available. There'd been one other action movie, but I'd played the weakest link on the team, and I'd been well prepared with plenty of action choreography ahead of time. I assumed the same thing would happen on this film, but I was a little nervous the show runner hadn't given me more information about it yet. Maybe I needed to take the initiative and ask. Regardless, I didn't want to talk about it.

I wanted to know more about the sexy but stern sheriff with the tiny rainbow flag icon on his watch face. Did that mean he'd be open to a little flirting?

"When did you move to Colorado?"

"Six months ago."

Talking to this man was like pulling teeth out of a rabid dinosaur. "Why did you leave California?"

"How'd you get into acting?" he asked instead of answering my question. The brush-off was rude as shit. He was behaving like an automaton.

"My mother took me to an open casting call as a newborn. She was a young single mom with delusions of grandeur, according to my grandparents. But her plan worked. I was offered a commercial. That led to modeling jobs for kids clothes and stuff. She used some of the money to enroll me in acting classes at a local theater program when I was very young."

He scoffed. "Typical stage mom."

That set my teeth on edge, not because he was wrong. He wasn't. My mom was the worst kind of stage mom. She was the reason stage moms had the reputation they did. But she'd done it out of a violent desperation to get enough money to get out from under the thumb of my conservative grandparents and out of the horrible neighborhood we'd escaped to when they'd become too much.

"You don't know me or my mom," I said as calmly as I could manage.

"Bet I do," he muttered, rubbing his hand over his face as if he was suddenly exhausted. "I've met a million people just like you."

"What's that supposed to mean?" So much for the flirting. The man was an ass.

He shook his head. "Never mind. Forget I said it."

"Not possible. But I appreciate knowing you've prejudged me and my mother. That's always nice. I'll go ahead and put you in the bucket of people who think they know me without ever fucking trying."

"I'm not trying? What do you think I'm doing right now? I've asked you a ton of questions about your work, for Christ's sake."

"You've used those questions to get out of answering questions about yourself. Don't pretend you want to get to know me. I know people just like you." I emphasized the last few words the same way he had.

We sat side by side in fuming silence. For the first time in a very long time, I wanted to punch someone.

"You tried to get me to park your damned car."

I threw up my hands. "I apologized for that! For fuck's sake, can you not let it go? So I got it wrong. I assumed Tiller Fucking Raine would have a valet service at his engagement party. Was that such a stretch to imagine?"

"I was wearing a sidearm."

"You had on a white button-down and black pants!" And he'd looked like sex incarnate. I'd wanted to fuck the sexy valet over the hood of my car, but I didn't dare tell him that.

"After I told you I wasn't the valet, you still asked me to park your car."

"I made a fucking mistake! I'm a nice guy. I swear I'm not the asshole prima donna you seem to think I am. I'm a nice, normal guy." At least, I tried to be.

"Okay, *Chip*," he said with a slight sneer.

"Are you fucking kidding me right now?" I shouted.

He smirked at me as if satisfied he'd gotten a rise out of me. "Whatever you say, *Chip*."

"That's mature," I muttered, crossing my arms and sitting back in my seat. "Real mature, *Sheriff*."

We sat in stupid silence as the miles passed under the vehicle. The tension was thick and hot. I rolled my window down to let the sweet mountain air blow in against my warm face.

He opened his mouth to say something, but I didn't want to hear another snide remark. Instead, I pushed a button on the dash. "What's this do?"

The bark and whoop of a siren split the air. Declan jerked in surprise. Before he could reach to turn it off, I pressed another one. "And this?"

A red light swirled on the dash, and the car in front of us began to pull over.

"Cut that shit out or I'll put you in the back," Declan growled, turning off the lights and siren.

I pushed another button. "And this?"

A phone rang over the car's speakers until a woman's voice answered. "Dec, sweetie? Would you pretty please bring some ice pops home tonight? I'm positively craving them. This baby has a strange way of telling me he has a sweet tooth."

We both stared at the button I'd pushed, and suddenly my stomach dropped from a great height.

The man was married to a woman with a baby on the way. So much for him *swinging* in a certain direction.

And I was a total fucking idiot.

7

DECLAN

After literally arguing my way out of sharing anything personal with this man, he accidentally called Tessa on the phone.

"Of course," I gritted out to Tess. "Anything else?"

"Yeah. Ham."

"H-ham?"

"And bacon. But something fancy like... like applewood smoked. Is there such a thing as boutique bacon? If so, get that. I stayed in a hotel once in San Diego that had the best—"

"Tess, honey, I can't talk right now."

"Okay. But don't forget the ice pops, too."

As soon as the call ended, the silence fell around us like wet sandbags.

"Sorry I pressed your buttons," Finn mumbled before turning to look out the window.

I bit back a laugh at the pun. For some reason I didn't think Finn would appreciate me laughing at him right now. We continued driving in silence before I finally joined him in the apology-making.

"I'm sorry for being an asshole," I said. "You were right. I don't know you, and I certainly don't know your mother. I apologize. I didn't get much sleep last night." *Or the night before, thanks to you.*

After a little while, Finn cleared his throat. "Is that your wife?"

"No."

"Girlfriend?"

"No."

"Oh."

More silence.

I hated how awkward things were between us, especially because I knew it was completely my fault. My attraction to him was inappropriate (and had scared the piss out of me), and I'd been determined to keep him at arm's length. Apparently, I thought keeping someone at arm's length was the same thing as shitting all over them.

Just as I was gathering up my courage to apologize again and maybe even tell him about my move from LA to Aster Valley, the radio squawked. Penny's voice sounded tense as she reported a 10-51 at a familiar address.

"You'd better get there quick, Sheriff. Deputy Graham is headed there now, but he doesn't know the history."

I responded before flipping on both lights and sirens and picking up the pace. I tried getting Shawn on the radio, but there was no response.

"What's going on?" Finn asked quietly.

"I'm dropping you off at the lodge on the way."

"I want to come with you," he said defiantly.

"I can't have you at a scene that could potentially turn violent."

The radio squawked again. "Deputy Graham called in a code eight. Possible firearm involved."

"Shit." I sped up. "Okay, but you have to do exactly as I say. Do you understand?"

"What's the situation?" Finn asked again.

"The suspect's two sons were recently incarcerated on assault charges, and his brother, Erland—the man who was sheriff of Aster Valley before me—was arrested for financial crimes. To say this guy's not taking it well is an understatement. We've had a few instances this summer of him getting drunk and belligerent. His threats seem to be escalating, but his wife refuses to provide a witness statement to help us charge him."

"Can you blame her? It's her husband," Finn said, gripping the dash as I took the mountain turns quickly.

"No, I don't blame her. She's already had to see her boys and her brother-in-law go to jail. I'm sure she doesn't want Gene there, too. Both boys are married and had recently started a family. Kimber is trying to take care of everyone by the skin of her teeth."

We sped up the mountain to the Stanners' property and pulled down the drive in time to see Gene waving a gun around while he had one of his daughters-in-law in front of him with an arm locked around her throat.

She was pregnant.

I thought of Tessa and quickly packed away the image to focus on the challenge at hand.

"Get down," I hissed. "I don't want him to know you're in here. Stay in the vehicle and do not move, do you understand? Lie down and stay down."

"Maybe I can help."

"No. Dammit, *no*," I snapped. "You aren't armed. You're not trained. You are an actor. Jesus. Let the professionals handle this. If I have to worry about—"

Finn held up his hands. "Sorry. Of course. Go."

"Stay here," I said again.

He met my eyes. "I promise."

I let out a breath and stepped out of the vehicle. Gene and the young lady were on the front porch with my SUV between us. Shawn was approaching the pair slowly from behind a pickup truck in the driveway. Gene's eyes were trying to take it all in, and the minute he saw me, he swung his weapon to point at the woman's head.

"Easy, easy," I called. "Gene, that's your grandchild in there. Your *family*. I know you don't want to hurt them."

"I don't, but I don't want you fuckers out here neither! Get away. Leave us be. We were fine before all you showed up."

Kimber stood behind him, shaking her head and wringing her

hands. "Gene, this isn't fine. Let her go. This isn't you. You don't want to do this."

Gene swung the weapon toward his wife. Shawn took the opportunity to move to the side of the house and edged a little closer. The movement caught Gene's eye, and he swung the gun back around toward Shawn and then me. I unholstered my weapon and moved away from my vehicle to get Finn's location out of the line of fire.

"Let's talk about this," I urged. "Put the gun down and we can talk."

"Like hell! You took everything from us. You and those other bastards," Gene slurred. "I want my boys back. I want my brother back." His voice cracked on the words. "And you can't do that. I want my baby boys back home. They did what they did because of me."

The arm holding the weapon waved around wildly as he spoke. The one around his daughter-in-law's throat tightened until she was standing on her toes to keep from choking. Her face was pink and blotchy, and tears streaked down her cheeks. I pressed the call button on the radio and calmly requested an ambulance to the address.

"Gene, I'm going to have the EMTs take a look at your daughter-in-law." If only I could have remembered her name. "Just to make sure the baby's okay, alright? When the ambulance gets here, we'll have them check her out."

He looked confused by my words, as if he couldn't figure out how they were going to do that while he still had a hold of her.

"I don't think so, *Deputy* Stone," he said when he finally decided it was a trick. "You took my boys away. You stole Erland's job. You stole *everything*."

He swung the weapon back to me, but his vision was most likely impaired by drink. I decided to take the chance. I met Shawn's eyes and said very calmly while pointing to my chest with my free hand, "10-53." *Person down.*

The rest happened in a blink.

As soon as Shawn nodded, I dropped to the ground, and Shawn rushed the pair of them, shoving the woman back into the house and grabbing for Gene's weapon. The gun discharged, and I heard the pop of a bullet striking the passenger-side door of my SUV.

Finn.

Shawn shouted, "Clear! Suspect in custody," as I radioed for Penny to give me an update on the bus.

My heart jackhammered in my chest as I scrambled to my vehicle. I'd told Finn not to move from the passenger seat, and then the bullet had gone right into it. Fuck, fuck, what if he'd been hit?

I wrenched open the door and saw an empty seat.

"Over here," a small voice said from the other side of the vehicle. I raced around to see Finn crouched on the ground outside my driver's door. His arms were over his head, and his eyes were wide enough to see the whites all around.

"Fuck," I croaked, grabbing him and searching his body for any sign of injury. "Fuck." It was all I could say. My brain was completely logjammed with fear.

His voice shook. "I'm okay. I'm sorry."

I stopped manhandling him and stared. "You're sorry? Why the hell are you sorry?"

"You told me not to move. I didn't listen. When I heard how mad he was, I got as far away from that gun as I could."

I grabbed his hand and squeezed it hard. "N-no, you did good. So good. You did the exact right thing. I'm the one who's sorry."

I wanted to say more, to kiss his face off and hug him until my heart stopped thundering, but I couldn't. The shrill peal of the ambulance siren cut through the clearing as the bus came storming down the driveway.

"You're okay?" I asked, just to make sure. He nodded. "Okay. Stay here." I took one more good look at his face and gently brushed the messy hank of hair out of his face before forcing myself to walk away to help Shawn and make sure everyone else was okay.

After the EMTs checked the young woman and declared her shaken but unharmed, they left. Shawn took Gene to be processed into custody while I began gathering evidence at the scene and taking down witness statements. Finn refused to let me arrange him a ride home, stating he wanted to watch the process. I thought it was more likely he didn't want to be alone. The poor guy looked scared and somber, a look that made me want to comfort him the same way I'd comforted Tessa the night before. Well, maybe not the *exact* same way.

I let him stay close to me as I explained what I was doing. Taking photos of the bullet hole in the door, measuring the distance from where Gene had stood, and emptying and bagging the firearm. One of my other deputies showed up to take the evidence into custody and type up the witness statements for me, and Shawn returned to offer me a ride since department policy stated my vehicle would have to be towed in.

When he pulled up outside of Finn's chalet, I murmured for Shawn to wait a minute while I walked Finn to the door.

Finn had been quiet all night since the shooting, and I was starting to get worried.

"Do you want to call your friend to come stay with you?" I asked quietly.

He reached the door to the small cabin and turned around to face me. "Kix? No. It's okay. I think I'd... I'd rather be alone than have to tell him what happened and have him ask a million questions."

I wanted to touch him, reach out and caress his lightly freckled cheek before skimming my thumb across his full lower lip, but I kept my hands fisted in my pockets instead.

"Call... shit, hang on." I pulled out a business card from my wallet and handed it to him. "My cell is on there. Call me if you need anything. If you can't get me, call the department and tell them to raise me on the radio. Tell them it's a 10-36."

His eyebrows furrowed in confusion, but I knew I'd piqued his curiosity enough to distract him from my leaving.

"Good night, Finn."

"G'night, Sheriff."

I turned and didn't look back. Once I was in the car, I asked Shawn to stop off at the 24-hour supermarket before dropping me home. They didn't have "boutique bacon," but I got the best they had of everything Tessa had asked for. When I got back in Shawn's patrol vehicle, he raised an eyebrow at me. "You hungry? I could have found a drive-thru."

I noticed a bleeding scratch on the side of his face. "Not for me. You catch a fingernail or something when you took Gene down?"

He glanced in the rearview mirror before backing out of the parking space. "He had on a ring that got me. Big stone one like the kind some Freemasons wear."

"I've got some stuff at the house we can clean it with," I said, pointing him in the direction of my house. When he pulled back up the same mountain road that led to Rockley Lodge and the Stanner place, Shawn shot me a look.

"You made me drive you all the way into town when you live near the suspect and the place Finn Heller is staying?" he asked with a laugh.

I shrugged. "You don't show up empty-handed to a pregnant lady, Shawn." His jaw dropped, and I almost laughed. "Come in the house and let me fix you up. Stay for a beer."

He followed me to the house and came up short as soon as he saw Tessa uncurl from the shadows of the rocking chair on the front porch.

As soon as her big belly came into view, the image of Gene Stanner threatening his pregnant daughter-in-law flashed into my memory. I grabbed Tess in a fierce hug and held her for a long minute. "So glad you're okay," I whispered into the side of her hair.

She held me just as tightly. She'd been with Nick long enough to know something bad had probably happened on the job, so she simply let me hold her until the moment passed.

I pulled back and held up the shopping bag with a forced smile. "Truckload of pork products and sugar syrup, just for you," I said proudly.

She clapped her hand over her mouth and bolted for the house.

"Are you crazy?" Shawn hissed at me. "You don't use the phrase 'pork products' around a pregnant lady. For god's sake, Sheriff. Don't you know anything by now? She looks at least seven months along. Where you been for the last seven months?"

I led him into the house and to the kitchen where I had him take a seat at the table. "I've only had her in my house since Tuesday night. She was in LA until then. So, no. I'm not all that familiar with cravings and sickness yet."

After putting the groceries away, I opened a beer and set it in front of him before getting one for myself. He took a sip while I went down the hall to my bedroom to find the first aid kit. When I got back, Tessa was sitting on a seat next to him with a tall glass of ice water in front of her, and Shawn was fussing around her like a granny.

"You cold? Want me to fetch that quilt? When my sister Madison is pregnant, she can never get warm enough," Shawn babbled. I noticed his cheeks were a little pinker than normal.

I cleared my throat, and he jumped. "Sorry, Sheriff. I was only trying to make Mrs. Stone comfortable."

Tess made a choking sound, and I snorted out a laugh. "This is not Mrs. Stone. And what happened to you calling me Declan at least outside of work? Tessa, this is Deputy Shawn Graham. Shawn, this is my *friend* Tessa."

She reached out her hand to shake Shawn's. "Nice to meet you. Sorry for the less than ideal welcome."

Shawn blushed some more. "It's understandable. He shouldn't have... said what he did." He blinked at me and realized he'd called me out in my own home. "Sorry, Sher... Declan."

I nodded.

Tessa said, "I'm just here visiting for a little while. I used to be with Dec's former partner on the force back in LA before... some stuff happened. Now I'm single, and I wanted to get out of LA for a while." She rubbed her belly absently.

"You're staying," I said gruffly before taking a gulp of the beer. "I think you should stay."

Shawn nodded. "Aster Valley's a nice place, ma'am. Much better place to raise that little one than LA if you don't mind a nosy opinion."

She gave him a small smile. "It's beautiful here. Are you from Colorado?"

The two of them made small talk while I thought back through the events of the evening. I couldn't get over the look of fear on Finn's face. I would have expected to feel smug, to think *I told you so* because police work was dangerous and unpredictable like I'd tried to tell him, but then I remembered his eager questions earlier in the day when he'd tried his hardest to get to know me, to make a personal connection. And I'd shut him down.

After a while I realized Shawn and Tessa had been talking for a while. I looked over and saw Tessa taping a clean bandage on Shawn's eyebrow. Debris from her little first aid session littered the place mat in front of them.

"Sorry," I muttered. "My mind was wandering. She get you sorted out?"

"Yes, and I'm grateful. But it's late, and Tessa here probably needs to get some sleep. I didn't mean to keep you up like this."

She grinned at him. "It's no bother. Now I at least know someone else besides Declan here in Aster Valley, so it was worth staying up."

Shawn fingered the uniform hat in his hands. "If you want... I mean..." His eyes flicked at me and back at Tessa. "I could show you around. I have the afternoon free tomorrow. Not that I know my way around all that well either since I just moved here myself. But there's a beautiful park in town. And we could kinda find our way around together?" He blushed furiously.

Tess stood up a little taller, her slender hand going automatically to her belly. "I'd like that. I mean... if you don't mind?"

He looked to me again as if for permission. Even though it was none of my business, I gave him the barest of nods. He smiled and nodded at Tess. "Pick you up at two?"

Once he was gone, Tess did a little barefoot twirl on the hardwood floor. "Eight months pregnant and I still got it!"

I grabbed her up in another hug and kissed her cheek. "Darlin', you could be eighty years old and you'd still have it."

She laughed. "Not like I need a date or anything, but he seemed nice."

"He's very nice. Seems like a good man. Family man, from what I can tell." Her face registered surprised disappointment, so I quickly amended my statement. "He's single. At least, as far as I know. I only mean he's close to his parents and siblings, who live over in Meeker. It's about an hour, hour and a half northwest of here."

She blew out a relieved chuckle that lifted her dark brown bangs. The rest of her hair was up in a messy ponytail that made her look younger than she was. "Not that it matters. I'm hardly looking for a relationship," she repeated, like maybe she was trying to convince herself.

Her words were familiar. Casual denial.

A little bit like the same brush-off I gave myself fifteen minutes later when I stroked myself to thoughts of Finn Heller's fit climber's body under mine as I sank deep inside of him.

It didn't matter. I was hardly looking for a relationship.

8

FINN

I slept poorly after everything that happened the night before. As soon as I got to my trailer, I tried a meditation exercise in hopes of clearing my mind so I could focus on the workday ahead of me. Before I finished my second deep breath, Kix banged into the small space like a herd of trampling hyenas.

"Dude, tell me everything."

I closed my eyes and took another cleansing breath. "There's nothing to tell."

"Uh, that's not gonna fly," Kix said, smacking my shoulder lightly with the back of his hand. "Everyone is talking about it, and I just shared one of the photos in my Insta Story."

I blinked my eyes open. There were photos?

"Shit. I need to call Iris," I muttered, looking around for my phone and remembering I'd put it on silent as soon as Declan had left me alone in the SUV to confront the man with the gun. There were dozens of missed calls.

Iris answered immediately, her voice sounding like it was fueled by espresso. "Finn, babe, you need to milk this. It's PR gold. Nolan's already been on with me this morning arranging with his agency folks to coordinate interviews. The sooner we can spin you as a real action hero, the sooner your new reputation on-screen will be locked."

My hands began to shake. This wasn't a game. It wasn't a public relations stunt. There had been real danger, and a woman had almost been shot. Hell, *I'd* almost been shot. The bullet had gone through the passenger door and hit the base of the center console. If I'd been in the footwell, I would have been hit.

"I don't think that's a good idea," I said.

Iris chuckled. "You pay me to think, babe. You just show up when I tell you, and answer your damned phone when I call."

After she ended the call, I stared at the phone. Kix moved closer. "I know you're upset. Of course you are. It must have been scary as hell. But think of how good this is for your career. Surely you can see that? Man, I'd give anything to be caught at the scene of something like that."

I closed my eyes and tried to empty my mind to keep from snapping at him. My phone vibrated in my hand.

It was my mother.

"Oh honey! I just heard about the shooting!"

I exhaled. "I'm okay."

"Of course you are. You're a Heller, for goodness' sake. I'm calling because Mario says he can get you on *The View*. If so, you have to tell me so I can be there, too."

I bit back another snappish response. My teeth were already sore from grinding together, and I didn't even know who Mario was.

"Gotta go, Mom. I'm on set right now."

I hung up while she was still talking.

As the day progressed, I tried to find time to meditate, but it wasn't easy. There were more phone calls, curious cast and crew visits to the trailer, unnecessary calls to the set and wardrobe that turned out to be more flimsy excuses to get inside information on "the shooting," and even a visit from one of Declan's deputies to take my official statement from the night before. By the time Shelly finally released me from the set, I was exhausted, and I still had a video interview Iris had roped me into.

"Come out with us," Crystobell asked, poking her head into my trailer while the makeup tech was helping me prep for the interview. Her invitation surprised me. "Looks like you could use a drink. Come on. We're just going to the Roadhouse again."

Kix's eyes were wide over her shoulder. He'd wanted to hang with her forever.

"I have an interview..." I began.

"That's okay. I was going to head back to my chalet first for a shower and change of clothes. We'll swing back by the set to grab you after, and I'm not taking no for an answer. Logan is going, too, and it'll be the three musketeers."

Kix's frantic nod was going to send his head careening off into the woods if he wasn't careful.

"Okay, but—"

"Great! See you soon!" She turned and left, almost plowing Kix down in the process.

He stepped up into the trailer with hearts in his eyes. "Fuck yeah. I'm going to need you to take some pics of me sitting next to her for my social media, bro."

I closed my eyes and let the makeup tech finish with my face. "You're all set," he murmured. "Text me if you need a fix before go time."

I thanked him and watched him leave the trailer while Kix gave him a lurid stare. As soon as the door closed behind the tech, I chastised him. "That's skeevy. Don't look at him like you want to fuck him. The poor guy is at work."

Kix laughed. "Are you kidding? He blew me in the makeup tent like two hours ago. Mind your business."

I shuddered. This set was noticeably less professional than any of the other projects I'd worked on for as long as I could remember. Kix's behavior was a reminder that he wasn't really the kind of person I wanted in my life, and I wondered for the millionth time what the hell I was doing remaining friends with him.

You owe him.

The old refrain was getting very tired. He'd had years to find his own path to success, and maybe his behavior on set was part of the reason no one took him very seriously.

No one takes you seriously either, Chip.

I gritted my teeth once more. I was used to being compared to my air-headed, super-chipper childhood role, but hearing it out of Declan's mouth yesterday had been a slap in the face.

Thankfully, I was spared more thoughts about it by a knock on the trailer door. I would withstand anyone's pushy questions about the shooting just to get me to stop thinking about Declan Stone.

"Come in," I called.

The door opened to reveal Declan Stone. Of course.

"H-hi," I said nervously. What did he want? Why was he here? Had I done or said something wrong on my statement? My palms flooded with clammy heat.

Declan's eyes flicked to Kix and back to me. "I came to see if you were okay. I thought... I thought you'd be riding with me again today."

I opened my lips in surprise, and he kept talking. "I mean, obviously it's okay if you don't want to. I just didn't want you to think you couldn't. I committed to—"

"I'll ride with you!" Kix interjected. "I'll do it."

I shot him a look. "Kix, can you excuse us, please?"

He was obviously annoyed at being kicked out of the conversation, but he left anyway, promising to be back after my interview so we could ride to the Roadhouse together.

Once the door closed again, Declan stepped a little closer. "You're going out?"

I shook my head. "I don't want to, but..." *I don't want to be alone either.*

Our eyes locked, and a world of words hovered unspoken between us. Was I the only one who felt them?

I swallowed and tried again. "I—"

Before I could admit my fear, the trailer door banged open and Nolan came in without knocking. "Let's get this show on the road, action hero! Oh." He stopped when he saw Declan in full uniform. "Hello, Sheriff Stone. Is there something we can help you with?"

Declan turned and cleared his throat. The softness in his eyes disappeared as he reached out a hand to shake the director's.

"Just stopped by to make sure the situation last night didn't interfere too much with your production," he said. "I apologize for putting Finn in harm's way. If there's anything I can do to—"

"Nonsense," Nolan said with a wide grin, moving around to clap me on the shoulder. He seemed to be full of energy every time I saw him, like he had trouble sitting still and wanted to be off to the next thing. "You did us a solid. The media coverage alone is worth thousands. We can't thank you enough for allowing our boy here to be a part of a truly heroic moment. Thanks to your department for making sure he came through it unharmed, and I'm doubly glad you and your deputy were unscathed. That poor girl. Hopefully she's alright as well?"

Declan nodded and gave Nolan some platitudes about the young woman's condition, but I could see the tightness in his jaw as he spoke. He didn't love this. And he was in good company, because I absolutely hated it.

Nolan glad-handed Declan out the door with polite apologies that our "very important" interview had to cut his visit short. After one precious moment of eye contact with the strong, dependable sheriff, he was gone.

I followed Nolan to the media tent where everything was set up for the interview. A few minutes before we were scheduled to start, he turned to me to say, "Now's the time to capitalize on the fact you're doing your own stunts. After what happened last night, it will really add to the excitement and danger. I'm impressed with how seriously you took your prep work, Finn. Arranging for the ride-along like that was smart thinking, and your being there when the most exciting action in Aster Valley happened... well, you can't say there's not a little Chip Clover luck in you for real, right?"

His nearby assistant smiled and winked at me at his stupid-ass statement, and Shelly, the show runner, thought it was hysterical. I wanted to remind him that being present for any drunken shooting wasn't good luck. It was bad. But then again, I did consider not getting shot last night to be a stroke of luck, so maybe he had a point.

The interview started before I had a chance to respond. While Nolan greeted the energetic interviewer on the screen, I concentrated on keeping an open smile on my face while I talked myself through a centering mantra.

I am the rock, and the rock is fearless.

"Finn," the reporter said after the standard greetings were over, "we have reports of a deranged gunman threatening you last night in an armed standoff. Can you tell us how you managed to subdue him?"

I blinked at the screen and felt my polite smile falter. "I... I didn't subdue him. The man was apprehended by the Rockley County Sheriff's Department. The sheriff and his deputy are the real heroes."

She gave me the kind of look that said she thought I was being deliberately humble. "Come on now. We've seen the photos of you standing next to the suspect while he's being loaded into the vehicle. It's clear you were more involved in the takedown than you want to take credit for. Why don't you take us through the event minute by minute?"

I hadn't gotten close to Gene Stanner until after he'd been hand-cuffed and read his rights. If I was photographed anywhere near him, it was because I shadowed Declan like a hungry tick right after everything had happened.

"I..." I was at a loss for words. "I didn't..." My media training kicked in, and I remembered who I was. I was an Emmy Award–winning actor who'd been interviewed like this hundreds of times. "I'd rather talk about this production and how proud I am to be bringing Nolan's vision to life. We've been on location this week here in the Rocky Mountains, and I can't imagine a more beautiful setting for filming. Crystobell and Logan have already shot some amazing scenes, and I'm especially excited for the chance to get dirty on the side of the mountain when we shoot the climbing scenes."

Before the interviewer had the chance to bring me back around to last night's incident, Nolan jumped in. "We are thrilled to have Finn on board doing all of his own stunts. One of our goals with *Gold Rats* is to present the action as realistically as possible. That's what the audience expects in a Nolan Trainor film," he said with a zealous gleam in his eye. "Not only will Finn be doing his own climbing scenes, but he'll also be doing his own stunts in some hand-to-hand fighting scenes and our climactic scene involving pyrotechnics and a daring mountainside chase. We're thrilled to have the incredible talent of Finn, Logan, and Crystobell. The three of them are professional, dedicated performers, and they've already spent countless hours training for these challenging scenes."

I smiled weakly and tried to appear like a "professional, dedicated performer," but I didn't feel particularly prepared for a pyrotechnic chase scene. At all. It seemed Declan had been right about the explosion situation, and I'd been left out of the loop. I needed to call Iris as soon as the interview was over and find out what the heck I'd agreed to.

Nolan kept the interview focused on the prep work and filming for the next several minutes, but he finally allowed another question about the shooting the night before.

"Is it true the gunman took a shot at you as soon as he realized who was in the sheriff's vehicle?" Nadine asked.

I opened my mouth to deny it, but I realized I didn't really know why he'd shot at the passenger-side door. Declan had explained it as a wild shot taken at the moment the deputy rushed the suspect, but since I couldn't see what was happening, I couldn't really say.

"I don't think the suspect would have had any way of knowing I was there," I said instead. "I was out of sight. From what I was told, it was a wild shot rather than one aimed at a specific target."

The woman pursed her lips and lifted her eyebrows as if to call me on my humble bullshit again. "The only shot taken during the standoff was aimed at the most famous celebrity in town, and you think that was a coincidence?"

I nodded. "I do. Yes. And I'm not the only celebrity in town," I added with a smile.

She went on to ask me if I'd met other famous residents of Aster Valley like Tiller Raine and Gentry Kane. I told her I'd met them briefly the night I'd arrived since Tiller and Mikey were kind enough to host the cast and crew at Rockley Lodge. "And supposedly Gent and the rest of GUS will be performing at a small music festival while we're here. I'm looking forward to seeing them play."

I continued singing the praises of the charming town of Aster Valley and all it had to offer. Part of the reason Tiller and Mikey had agreed to let Nolan film on location here was to help give the town and the mountain some positive media exposure before they opened the new ski resort. Hopefully, interviews like this helped.

When she finally wrapped up the interview, she left with one chilling question. "Nolan, are you adding extra security to protect your cast and crew in light of the situation Finn found himself in last night?"

Nolan looked into the camera with his serious face. "Nadine, our cast and crew are like family, and we take their security very seriously. We regret Finn was put into such a dangerous situation last night by the very law enforcement group who is supposed to protect us while we're on location in Rockley County."

My entire body stiffened in response to his harsh implication. I opened my mouth to cut in, but he kept talking.

"Obviously we do not blame the sheriff's office for last night's events, but it has brought up the need for us to revisit our security measures even here in a seemingly safe place. Of course, we will provide the best personal security possible to our valuable cast and crew while we are here."

Was he going to assign us some kind of bodyguard? There was no way I wanted someone following me around when the events of last night were so clearly a one-off situation rather than the norm.

Before Nadine could end the interview, I added, "According to the Rockley County Sheriff's Department, the violent crime rate is twenty-eight times lower in Aster Valley than the national average. What happened last night is not indicative of anyone's safety here. It was a single event perpetrated by an unhappy person. I feel completely safe on the streets of Aster Valley, especially under the watchful eye of the Rockley County Sheriff's Department."

As soon as we were off the air, I let out a whoosh of air. I was exhausted from lack of sleep, nerves, and trying to keep smiling while everyone seemed to want to dig a salacious story out of me.

Nolan patted me on the back. "Good job, buddy. I like the humble citizen routine. Very Chip Clover. Works perfectly with your reputation. Keep it up."

I wanted to ask him if he was really going to step up security, but I didn't trust myself not to get into an argument if his answer was yes. Instead, I thanked him and headed for my trailer. Logan and Crystobell were there waiting for me, and Kix was on the phone a few yards away.

"You all set?" Crys asked with a big smile. "Nolan looked happy after the interview. It must have gone well."

I nodded. "I think so. Listen... are you doing your own stunts in the avalanche scene?" I already knew she wasn't doing her own climbing in the one climbing scene she had, so I was curious if the "authenticity" bit Nolan had hyped only referred to me.

She laughed her famous throaty chuckle. "Are you kidding? Darien would kill me."

Darien VanNyke was her agent, but there'd been rumors for at least a year that they also lived together as a couple. They supposedly kept it quiet to maintain her "available" image as a sexy single woman, but anyone in the industry who'd ever seen the two of them together knew she was about as single as a handcuff.

I glanced at Logan. "And you?"

"I do all my own fighting stunts," he said. "But that avalanche shit is no joke. I'm not interested in being anywhere near the pyrotechnics. My cousin lost two of his fingers shooting off fireworks when he was a kid. No, thanks."

Kix ended the call and strode over to us. "If I had the chance to do it, I'd jump on it in a heartbeat. Think of all the ass you could get."

Logan huffed and shook my shoulder. "As if this pretty boy has trouble getting ass back home in WeHo. Not sure he needs his gonads blown off to get whatever dick he wants."

Kix laughed. "Point taken. Maybe you should back out of it, Finn. No point in risking this face."

He reached out to pinch my cheek, but I batted his hand away. I was this close to canceling my plans and returning to my chalet to hide under the covers until my courage returned. But Kix's next words changed my mind.

"I wonder if we'll run into the sheriff and that deputy up at the Roadhouse again tonight. Surely they'll be there having congratulatory drinks, too. Finn can buy them a round in thanks for not getting his nards blown off last night."

The fear in my gut turned to more normal nerves at the thought I might get to see the sexy sheriff again at the bar.

"Can everyone stop referring to my nuts, please?" I muttered, turning to head to the parking area.

There was only one person I wanted thinking about my balls tonight, and god willing, he'd be at the bar.

He wasn't.

After we'd been there an hour and I'd had to spend most of that hour fending off pushy fans, I overheard a server telling the bartender he wouldn't be able to rely on the sheriff's help closing the bar tonight.

"Penny told me he's down to Denver tonight for personal reasons and won't be back until late tomorrow."

After that, my brain went on a fantasy spree thinking up all the ridiculous reasons Declan would have to go to Denver. Did it have something to do with the bacon lady on the other end of the line yesterday? The woman he called honey?

It was none of my business. Obviously. But the realization I wouldn't see him was enough for me to be done for the night.

"I'm headed back to the chalet," I finally told Kix and the others. "I'm beat, and I don't have the energy to pretend to be pleasant for our fans. Sorry."

They let me go without a fuss, probably because I hadn't been nearly as open and talkative as they'd hoped when they'd invited me out, and they understood how hard it was to be "on" when you didn't feel up to it.

I made it back to the chalet without incident and made another attempt at meditation before taking a long, hot bath in the large tub.

After I finally fell into bed, I slept hard. But the nightmares were enough to wake me several times during the night. The following day was just as full of curious cast and crew as the day before, and when I'd gone for a run on the country roads near the chalet, I'd been swarmed by a band of fans from out of the blue.

The craziness went on for two more days until I couldn't find a moment's peace either on set or back at the chalet. I was suddenly everyone's favorite novelty, and the low-lying fear in my gut remained. It didn't make any sense. I hadn't actually been in that much danger at the Stanner property, so why was I so damned scared all of a sudden?

When I got a copy of the contract from Iris and saw exactly what I'd agreed to on this project, I wondered if maybe my fear had come from some kind of sixth sense. But it was too late to back out now. Not if I wanted the Shakespeare thing to happen in my lifetime. And when I asked my mom about it, she agreed.

I felt hemmed in, burdened by the weight of everyone's expectations... and at the same time, really alone.

I finally had an afternoon off and decided to go climbing by myself to find a place where no one else could get to me. I'd researched popular climbing locations in the area before coming to Aster Valley, so I decided to head to one of the most challenging climbs at Slye Peak. The harder the climb, the fewer people to interact with.

When I finally clipped into my harness and felt the rough surface of granite under my fingertips, I closed my eyes and relaxed my body.

I am the rock, and the rock is fearless.

I began to climb, deliberately ignoring the darkening sky in my desperation to escape into solitude.

9

DECLAN

I wanted to kill Finn Heller. Thanks to his interview with Nosy Nadine after the Gene Stanner incident, the media was all over my ass which meant the county council was all over it, too. The opinions ranged from what a great thing it was for our little burg to what a nuisance it was to have to deal with spiteful implications of our ineptitude.

On top of everything, Tessa's first visit with the OBGYN in Aster Valley had resulted in a referral to a specialist in Denver. I'd dropped everything to drive her to the city for some tests. It had been a rough couple of days in which Tessa spent most of the time in tears and I spent most of it wanting to kill my former partner for being the kind of selfish asshole who got her pregnant and then walked away from every sense of paternal responsibility.

Thankfully, the tests came out fine, and we returned to Aster Valley with nothing more than instructions for her to take it easy. It made the decision on whether or not she should stay a very easy one.

"As soon as this damned movie production is gone," I told her this morning over breakfast, "I'll have time to set up the back bedroom as a nursery. Maybe I can swing by the hardware store and pick up some paint swatches and magazines so you can decide how you want it to be."

She looked up from her full plate of eggs, toast, and sausage. "You've already done so much. I don't want to be a burden on you."

"It's not a burden at all. I hope you know that. I'm honored you came to me when you needed to get away."

She leaned back and stretched her feet onto a nearby chair. Her eyes met mine like interrogation lights. "I need you to stop feeling like this is all your fault. I don't regret this pregnancy which means I can't regret being with Nick."

I turned back to the stove to finish cooking my own eggs. "I'm glad. You're going to be a wonderful mother."

"Look at me, dammit."

I squeezed my eyes closed before taking the pan off the burner and sliding the fried eggs onto my plate. Once I was settled across from her at the table, I met her eyes again. "I'm listening."

"I don't regret everything that happened between me and Nick. I need you to hear that and understand it."

I shook my head. "If only I'd—"

"No. I begged you to introduce me to him. When you and I lived next door to each other, I saw him drop you off or come by for dinner or to watch a game with you or whatever. Every time I saw his handsome face, I daydreamed about being with him. You finally agreeing to introduce us wasn't the same thing as forcing him on me, regardless of your damned savior complex."

I gritted my teeth. She was right. She had begged me. But I still felt like if I hadn't brought him around our building, she'd have never found herself in his destructive path. Tessa had moved into the apartment next to mine for security, so she could live in the city but still have someone to rely on like family. We'd grown up together in Encino. We'd known each other for years, and then I'd accidentally hooked her up with a criminal. But she was right. She'd begged me for an introduction, and obviously I hadn't known Nick's true nature at the time.

"Fine," I said finally. "But you need to know I don't feel like taking care of you is a burden. Taking care of my friend and her baby is a privilege. Besides Nick, you've been my closest friend for five years, Tess. I love you, and I want you to be happy and healthy. I want the same for that baby. Let me do this. Let me take care of you right now. We'll figure the rest out later. As you can see, I have plenty of room. When the crazy people from Hollywood aren't overrunning the town, I actually have time on my hands, too."

Her face softened into a smile. "I'm looking forward to it. Shawn showed me around a little, and I really like it here."

Her cheeks turned pink at the mention of my deputy.

"Did you tell him everything was fine with the pregnancy?" I asked, finally tucking in to my breakfast.

She nodded. "He was worried. He kept texting to make sure I didn't need anything. Apparently one of his cousins had to go into Denver for similar tests, and he remembered how stressful it was." She blinked down at her food. "He's very sweet."

I agreed and mentioned just how often he'd asked after her the day before at work.

"He did?" she asked, snapping her head up. "Why? I mean... why in the world would he care so much?"

I rolled my eyes. "Gorgeous single woman looking even more gorgeous thanks to a healthy pregnancy? Golly gee, Tess. I surely don't know."

She reached out a foot to kick my shin. "I know we were kidding around the other day, but nobody wants to date a pregnant woman. Do they?"

I put down my fork and met her eyes again. "I am gay. Really very gay. But even I can see how gorgeous you are. Even I want to take care of you and be there for you. Maybe there's something about seeing a woman so pregnant that calls up our protective instincts. I don't know. But I can tell you this. That man is goofy for you. Penny asked me if she could send over a fruit basket, and Shawn damned near tripped over himself offering to deliver it for her. I don't think Shawn was kidding."

She blushed again. "He asked if he could take me to the movies, and I said no."

That surprised me. "Just because he's interested doesn't mean you have to be. It's okay to say no."

"But... I am interested. I just feel..."

"If you're trying to be loyal to Nick, stop that shit right now. I can't think of anyone who deserves it less."

Tessa shook her head. "That's not it. What if I fall for Shawn and he..."

I finally got what she was so afraid of. "What if he turns out to be an asshole, too? That's something we're always risking when we give away our hearts, isn't it?"

We ate our breakfast in companionable silence for a little while before she spoke up again. "I think... I think I'm going to ask him if he wouldn't mind taking me to Walmart to get some baby things. He said he can help me pick out the basics, and if we have questions, he can call one of his sisters or his mom." She hesitated a beat. "And maybe I'll be able to tell how he really feels about my pregnancy, you know? If he looks uncomfortable or acts weird when faced with the reality of diapers and stuff, I'll know to be more careful."

I glanced over at her with a smile. "I think that sounds like a good plan. And maybe if he passes your test, you can enjoy a nice movie."

She nodded and let out a breath. "That would be good."

We finished eating and cleaned up the kitchen. I kissed the top of her head when it was time to head to work. "Supposed to thunderstorm pretty bad today, so keep your eye on the weather if you go out," I told her before heading out to my vehicle. The sky was deceptively blue, but I'd lived here long enough to know how quickly the storms could come in across the mountains. I hoped drivers stayed off the roads when the rain came. Summer storms caused flash flooding that made for perfect hydroplane conditions.

I got to the department and didn't even make it as far as my office before Penny sent me out on a call. "It's Mrs. Brainthwaite."

"Again? Christ, I thought they'd reached a stalemate," I muttered, reaching for my rain gear just in case I was still out when the rain hit.

"No. It's not the pet store. Her car was stolen out of her driveway."

I headed out to her address and discovered she lived in a little blue house tucked a block behind the Mustache Diner. Before I had a chance to turn off my vehicle, Penny called. "Sheriff, the car was just found abandoned behind the high school. I'm sending Deputy Graham to check it out."

After greeting Mrs. Brainthwaite and taking down a statement that basically amounted to "I woke up and my car was gone," I called Shawn to ask for an update.

"The keys are in it, Sheriff. Nothing broken or disturbed. But there's some fast-food trash in the footwell, so we might be able to check surveillance at the drive-thru."

I glanced back up at Mrs. Brainthwaite. "Ma'am, have you had anyone in doing work here or given anyone access to somewhere you might have left your keys?"

She began shaking her head before stopping mid-shake. "Well, other than Solomon... he takes my car to pick up my prescriptions sometimes."

I thought of the teenaged son of the couple who owned the diner. Solo had always seemed like a good kid, so I hoped like hell he hadn't done this. I nodded and told her the car would be returned to her after processing. I suggested she consider getting a video camera doorbell at the very least to keep an eye on who came and went in her driveway. Then I gave her the number of the young woman in town who helped install them.

Once back in the car, I called Shawn to give him an update on who he might be looking for in that drive-thru footage.

I stopped by the diner to ask Solo about it but learned he wasn't there. His father, Pim, gave me his customary cheeky smile. "Got himself saddled with summer school, actually. The boy takes after me, after all. Failed his literature class. So now he's stuck with Danny Reyes and a summer full of Shakespeare. The kid is miserable."

Bill hollered from the kitchen. "Quit sounding so smug about it. The boy's gonna think you're proud of him, for god's sake."

Pim laughed. "I'm not proud of him when it means I'm the one picking up his shifts. But when he cut out on his homework all semester, I warned him this would happen. He made his bed, and now he's having to lie in it with Danny Snooze-Fest Reyes. Tell me that's not karma."

I almost asked if he knew where Solo had been last night, but thankfully, I stopped myself before opening that can of worms. Instead, I asked how old Solo was.

"Turns eighteen at the end of September. Why?"

That was something, at least. I played it off like I was just making polite chitchat. "So he'll be a senior. Does he know what he wants to do after high school?"

Pim shrugged. "You know how it is. One day he wants to be a rock star, the next he wants to be a politician. The only thing he doesn't want to be is a diner owner, go figure."

Penny's voice came over my earpiece to inform me about a fender-bender in the parking lot of the nearby market. I responded I was on my way before saying a quick goodbye to Pim and Bill.

The next several hours progressed the way they always did when the people of Aster Valley were going about their regular lives. It was busy but not difficult, and I enjoyed keeping my mind off a certain actor who'd been occupying it like a tapeworm for the past several days. Thankfully, the cast and crew were busy on the set because there was no sign of any of them in town. With the weather coming in, even the tourists were indoors instead of hanging around hoping for a celebrity sighting.

Around four in the afternoon, another call came in just as I was shaking off the rain and hoping for a nice hot cup of coffee to perk me up for the last hour or two of paperwork.

Penny's face looked worried as I passed her desk. "There's a report of a lone climber out on Slye Peak."

I froze in place, immediately picturing Finn dangling on the side of the perilous rock face. I forced myself to shake off the image, realizing how ridiculous it was. Surely Finn was on set with everyone else. Besides, an experienced climber like Finn Heller wouldn't solo climb, especially on a day like this.

"They sure the climber is alone?"

She nodded. "The lady said there's a car in the lot at the base of Slye Creek trail. She and her daughter were hiking there and cut their visit short when the rain started. She said it's either the climber or someone else is out on the trail, but she didn't see anyone while they were hiking."

I slipped my rain gear back on and headed out, trying not to feel resentment that I had to go back out in this mess because someone hadn't planned well.

As soon as I rounded the bend on Timberline, I saw the sheer face of Slye Peak. Sure enough, there was a single climber about halfway up the climb. I was too far away to make out any details other than the fact the person was wearing an orange helmet and didn't appear to have more than that, a pair of shorts, and climbing shoes on. Which probably meant it was a man.

Dammit.

I continued on Timberline until I saw the turnoff for the Slye Creek trailhead. As soon as I pulled in, I noticed the McLaren. *Dammit.* I quickly parked my own vehicle and scrambled to change into the old pair of hiking boots I kept in a bin in the back of the SUV, along with several changes of clothes and various other emergency supplies. My duty boots would get trashed on the muddy trail, and I didn't relish spending hours cleaning them up tonight.

I tried not to scream at Finn in my head as I made my way down the trail to the base of the rock face. What the hell had he been thinking? Why didn't he come off there when the rain started? Did he have a death wish?

Was he hurt? Was he even able to get himself down?

By the time I finally got to the climbing area, I was at a dead run flinging specks of mud up the back of my uniform pants and wiping water out of my eyes. He hung there like a dead weight, simply sitting in his harness and letting the top rope hold him. The only reason I knew he was conscious was his upright position.

"Get your ass down here," I shouted. My voice didn't even sound normal to my own ears. "Finn! Rappel, dammit."

He startled and craned his neck to look down at me from where he hung at least four stories above me. "Dec?"

"Get down here. Please. Why are you here by yourself?" I wanted to beg. I wanted to climb up there and grab him. Why did I feel so compelled to look out for this stranger? Why did I care so fucking much about his happiness and well-being? He was nothing to me. Nobody. He was a pain in my ass.

I tried to tell myself it was the same way I'd look out for anyone else in town, but I knew it was a lie. I didn't just want to ensure Finn's safety; I wanted to ensure his happiness and well-being, too.

Right now, he was the sharpest point of my focus and the only thing tethering me to earth. I needed him down here. I needed him safe.

I needed him, full stop.

"If you're gonna yell at me, just leave me alone!" he called down. "I don't need your help. I want to be alone."

"It's storming. Don't be stupid. Get off the rock!"

He didn't move.

"Finn," I said, voice breaking as the rain began to beat down harder. "Please. *Please.*"

The temperature had dropped quickly when the sky had darkened. Finn was shirtless and drenched. Part of me wanted to race back to the SUV and grab as many warm clothes as I could. Why hadn't I thought of it? Why hadn't I brought them out here with me?

I saw a bundle of his things at the edge of the clearing. A backpack with a few climbing chocks poking out of the opening sat next to a pair of running shoes and a now sodden T-shirt.

I stepped closer to the hanging anchor rope dangling from his body all the way to the ground.

Finn said something, but his voice was carried away by the wind and the rain. My heart thundered in my chest as my eyes caught the flash of lightning in the darkening sky to the west.

I opened my mouth to scream at him that he was going to be struck by lightning if he didn't get his ass down on the ground now, but before I could get the words out, I saw him begin to make his way down slowly. It was a long process, removing chocks as he went and shoving them in the little bag at his waist, but at least he was coming down.

"Thank Christ," I said under my breath, wishing I could hold the rope and help belay him safely. I didn't know much about climbing, only a few things from an LAPD outing to a local climbing gym a few years ago.

When Finn finally landed on the ground next to me, I grabbed him by the back of his harness and yanked him close until he was plastered against my front and my arms were tight around his chest.

He struggled to turn in my arms until we were hugging tightly. I never wanted to let him go.

"Fuck," I said into his wet hair. "Why? Fuck. *Fuck.*"

"Dec, I—"

I pulled back and clasped his face in my hands. "What the hell's wrong with you? Why would you go up there alone? Christ, when I thought about you getting hurt, I just... I was so fucking scared, Finn. Why would you—"

He lurched at me, smashing my mouth with his and nearly breaking my nose in the process. I gripped his face even tighter and held him to me as I kissed him back with everything I had. Our tongues tangled, and the hot press of his lips on mine sent sparks shooting into my groin.

I groaned into his mouth as I moved my arms around the slick skin of his back. He tasted like fresh rain and peppermint. His slim, muscular body fit against mine like it had been carved especially for the purpose. Finn stood on his toes to deepen the kiss, and his hard dick brushed against mine.

I sucked in a breath and ground my hips against his, moving my hands down to his ass and pulling him closer even though it made the carabiners and knots on his rigging dig into me, too.

Finn's entire body shook, and after a moment, I realized he was freezing. I pulled back enough to rub my hands up his bare arms. "Come on, let's get you warmed up."

I helped him unclip from the rope, remove his harness, and pack his things. I carried everything for him on our trek back to my vehicle, and as soon as we arrived, I opened the back hatch and sat him on the tailgate to get him out of the rain.

I rummaged through my supplies until I found an old towel and handed it to him. He dried himself off enough to put on the hoodie I handed him next. When I tried to move him around to the passenger seat, he balked. "I have my own car."

"Too bad. We're leaving it here, and I'm taking you home. You're not driving right now like this."

He tightened his jaw, but I could tell he was too worn down to argue with me. I brushed his wet hair back from his forehead, and when his gaze locked on mine, he almost looked... lost. "Please let me take you home," I said more softly. "Please let me take care of you."

He swayed against me without realizing it, and I wrapped my arm more tightly around him for a moment before putting him in the car and belting him in. As soon as I turned on the engine, I set the heat to High.

We drove to the chalet in silence. Finn looked out the window away from me, and I concentrated on driving safely in the wet conditions. I called in an off-duty code and told Penny to mark me as off duty until tomorrow's shift unless something big happened.

When I pulled up in front of the chalet, Finn was practically asleep, curled up against the door in my large hoodie. I walked around to the passenger side and opened the door, pulling him out gently and supporting him as we made our way inside the cabin. It was cold enough now for a fire, so I quickly started the gas logs and sat him on the small sofa before covering him in a quilt and going to the small kitchen to make him a hot drink.

Instead of coffee, I made two mugs of hot cocoa and brought them into the living area. Finn sat up and held the thick mug in both hands as he blew on the steaming liquid with his gorgeous, full lips.

The memory of tasting those lips flashed hot all over me. Finn must have felt my eyes on him because he turned and met my gaze. "Why did you come to Slye Peak?" he asked softly.

"There were reports of a lone climber, and the storm was coming in," I said, even though that wasn't the reason at all. "Why did you solo climb when a storm was forecast?" He wasn't stupid, but at the same time, he was used to California where the weather was more predictable.

"I wanted to be alone. It was the only place I could think of." He tucked his face back into his mug and began to take cautious sips. I watched him stare into the fire as he drank. He looked haunted.

I'd wanted to rail at him, accuse him of playing the victim in front of as much media as he could possibly get, but I could see the truth of it now in his face. He didn't want this. I wasn't sure if he wanted any of this.

I moved closer and reached for his mug, placing it on the coffee table next to mine. "C'mere," I murmured, pulling his body against mine. "Be alone now. Be alone here with me. I won't say anything, and you can just be."

He turned and buried his face in my neck, wrapping his arms around me like I was the last life raft in the wreckage of his life. The thought should have made me laugh. How could this spoiled Hollywood actor have any cause to complain about his life?

I didn't know. And yet it felt like maybe he did.

And maybe he didn't feel like he had the right to admit it out loud.

10

FINN

I lay in Declan's arms and did my best to let every worry melt away. As long as this man was willing to hold on to me, how could I have a care in the world?

But apparently, I did anyway because I opened my mouth to thank him for giving a shit, and out poured a bunch of horrible crap.

"You were right. He's going to do the explosion. And I can't even think about that right now because first, he wants to film me doing a twenty-foot fall down a rock face. And my mom says it's good for my career. And my agent told me I'm contractually obligated regardless of how unprepared I feel. Nolan threw me under the bus during that interview, so if I back out now, I look like a coward. And everyone won't stop asking me what happened the other night, and they all want a piece of me, and no one understands how dangerous it really was, and now..." I thought I was going to choke on my own breath. "And now I don't know what to do, and I feel like I don't have anyone to talk to about all of this."

I felt so stupid, so immature and young. Here was this older man who had years of tough life experience under his belt, and I was back to feeling like naive Chip Clover again.

I whispered an apology into his neck, but he shushed me. "You have every right to be upset," he murmured. "It's a lot, and you're probably not used to having to navigate some of these decisions on your own."

I shook my head. "That's another thing. I'm tired of having everyone else think they know what's best for me."

"No one can possibly know what's best for you," he said swiftly. "Except you."

"Says the man who told me to come down off the mountain," I teased, not really feeling angry about it anymore.

"Mpfh."

To be honest, I hadn't been angry at Declan from the moment he'd run his hands over my cheeks and said he was scared for me. How long had it been since someone worried about me, Finnegan Heller, rather than Finn Heller the movie star, the investment, the cash cow?

I couldn't even remember.

I pulled back and looked at Dec, really looked. He was so damned sexy, with his scruffy beard and those tiny crinkles at the corners of his eyes. His lips were dark red, like maybe I'd bruised them a little with my kisses, and it thrilled me to think I'd marked this man in some way, even temporarily.

"Thank you for caring," I said softly. "Even if it was because of your job."

His nostrils flared. "It wasn't because of the job. You have to know that by now." Declan's words sounded gruff, as if he was forcing them out under duress.

"I thought you had a woman at home," I said, knowing I couldn't allow myself to kiss him again if that was the case. "A pregnant woman."

The edge of his lip turned up. "I do. But it's not what you think. She's a friend. I told you in the car the other day, I'm gay. And single."

I blew out a relieved breath and tucked my face back into the safe warmth of his neck. "Thank fuck."

The vibrating rumble of his laughter made me smile against his skin. His arms felt secure around me before he began rubbing his hands up and down my back, eventually moving them under the hoodie until they were warm and strong on my bare skin.

A whimper escaped me, a desperate sound I couldn't have held back even if I'd wanted to. Declan's body jerked as if the sound I'd made was directly tied to him. Within seconds, we were kissing. Hands were everywhere, and I eventually had enough brainpower to focus my fingers on the buttons of his uniform shirt. Thankfully, Declan had already removed his duty belt, but when I got his shirt open, I realized he still wore his Kevlar vest over a cotton undershirt. I pulled at the wide Velcro straps and pulled the protective vest off him, saying a silent prayer of thanks that he wore it every day even in this small town.

When I finally got the last layer off and revealed his wide, muscular chest covered in dark hair, I leaned in and inhaled the masculine scent of him.

Damn.

Declan's fingers sifted through my hair as he indulged my need to rub my face against the crisp hair on his chest.

"You're so fucking sexy," I said, moving up again to kiss him on the lips. "I want you so much. Take me to bed. Please."

Declan stood, holding me still wrapped around his waist and chest. I let out a surprised whoop of laughter. It felt good. It was the lightest I'd felt in days. Dec's smile was wide and easy. "Which way?"

My heart tripped over itself as I directed him to the chalet's only bedroom. When he placed me on the bed, I shimmied out of the clothes I was wearing and reached out my arms to him. He took his time unbuttoning his uniform pants as his eyes roamed all over my bare body.

"Fuck, you're perfect." His low grumble made my dick even harder.

As soon as his pants were open and he began pushing them down, along with a pair of black boxer briefs, I found myself holding my breath.

His cock was fucking perfection, hanging heavy and full over balls I could almost feel on my tongue. "Let me suck you off," I said without thinking.

Declan shook his head. "Lie there and be still."

Oh god. Oh, what that commanding voice did to my insides. *Fuck.*

I did as he said. Once his clothes were gone, he crawled up my body, dropping small kisses along the inside of one of my legs until he nuzzled against my sac. My breath came fast and harsh in the quiet room.

Please, I thought. *Please put your hot mouth on me.*

As soon as his lips opened and his tongue came out to paint a stripe along the inside of my thigh, I almost fainted. Slick drops of precum escaped my slit, and Declan spotted it immediately. He leaned up to suck the head of my cock into his mouth and groaned after swiping over the slit with his tongue.

I bowed off the bed with a loud cry of relief and continued desperation. He'd barely taken me into his mouth, and I was ready to blow down his throat any minute.

God, I was going to humiliate myself, and I honestly didn't care. At all.

"Suck it," I begged. "More, please."

He met my eyes and pinned me down with the intensity of his gaze. I couldn't look away. I stared at him as he continued to take me apart with his lips and tongue. He wet his fingers at one point and began sliding them over my hole until my thighs trembled with need.

When he finally slid a thick finger inside me and bumped up against the right spot, it was all over. I screamed and arched up into his mouth, shoving myself deeper into his throat as the orgasm took the breath from my lungs and shot numb fire through my limbs.

The aftershocks kept coming as his mouth and finger seemed determined to short-circuit my brain. When I was finally completely spent, he moved up next to me and kissed me sweetly on the cheek. "Fuck, you're stunning. I want to see you come again."

I let out a breathy chuckle. "Fat chance. I might be young, but even I can't rebound fast after something like that."

He gazed at me with an unbelievably adoring expression on his face, something I'd never in a million years expected to see from a man, much less a man like Declan Stone.

It made me feel even more naked than I already was.

"Let me taste you," I whispered.

His eyes darkened. "You sure?"

A laugh bubbled out of me. "You crazy?"

I scrambled up and pushed him onto his back before climbing on top of his larger body and kissing the fuck out of his face. He laughed and ran his hands over me until I moved down and got to work. There was already a sticky smear of precum in his happy trail, and it made me flush with a little pride that I'd turned him on enough to cause it.

I licked and sucked and explored, taking each of his fuzzy balls into my mouth and licking hard across his taint, until sucking his dick down my throat again. While I didn't have much experience giving men head in the real world, I'd spent an embarrassing amount of time watching porn and imagining myself giving award-winning blow jobs once I found a man who wouldn't run and blab to the press about them.

Declan Stone would be the last person on earth to blab to the press about getting sucked off by an actor.

It didn't take long before Declan's fingers tightened in my hair and he warned me he was going to come. I stayed locked on his cock while he came in a hot rush down my throat with a loud cry. It had been so long since I'd done this, since I'd had a mouthful of dick and craved its release, that I wanted to stay down there like some kind of cockwarmer after he came down from his high.

I laid my head on his inner thigh and ran my fingers through the hairs there. His thigh muscles twitched under my touch.

"You're beautiful," he murmured, reaching for one of my hands and moving his lips along the back of it and up my forearm with reverent, open-mouth kisses. "Inside and out. I didn't see it before."

Hot tears threatened to fill my eyes, and I took a slow, steady breath to banish them before they appeared and ruined everything. He already thought of me as a child. There was no reason to prove him right with a crying jag. "Not surprised. I learned a long time ago to play the game."

My admission surprised me—how did this man make me want to admit things I never admitted to anyone?—but it didn't seem to surprise him at all.

"It makes sense. Not sure there are many people in your situation who had an easy time becoming their true selves. When you're encouraged to be someone else from a very early age and rewarded for doing it well... it seems only natural you'd lose the ability to show your true self."

His hand toyed with my hair as I thought about what he said. "True. It's especially hard when it comes from your mother. I was in college before I had the guts to find a therapist to help me work through it. It took two years before I started to realize I'd let someone else dictate my entire future."

"Who's dictating it now?"

The question wasn't pushy, simply curious, but it hit me hard. I moved up and buried my face in his neck again. I didn't even need to say the words. We both knew the answer wasn't me. I wasn't dictating my own future, and that was the true cause of my discontent.

I would have been embarrassed if I didn't feel so easy in his company. It was like a time-out from the real world. It didn't matter what this semi-stranger thought of me. He wasn't critical to my future. I could be myself around him—whatever that meant—and then go back to being the Finn Heller everyone knew and loved when I returned to LA.

But for now, I let myself face the truth.

"I feel like I'm stuck at a crossroads," I admitted softly into his damp skin. "And there are trains coming from all sides."

Declan pulled my face away from him so he could meet my eyes. His smile was gentle and kind. "You know all you have to do is step off the tracks, right? You don't have to pick one to stay on. Step off and catch your breath. You've been working hard for a long time, Finn. You deserve some time to figure things out."

He seemed so sure of himself, so confident that what he said was true, even though it felt about as far away from true as anything.

"You make it sound so easy," I said with a laugh, moving to lie down on his shoulder and snuggle into his side. Declan's arms wrapped around me and held me close.

"No. Not easy. But it is your choice."

He sounded like he spoke from experience, and I was reminded that he had his own story to tell.

"Why did you leave LA? Did something happen?"

It was like seeing the metal shutters come down on the vegetable market shop down the block from my house. With one quick yank, all of the intimacy that had seemed to be growing between us was snatched away.

"I should probably go," he said.

I felt like a vacuum had just sucked the happy, relaxed feeling right out of me. In its place was the sharp sting of rejection.

"Oh."

Declan's arms loosened around me, and he moved to the edge of the bed. "I'm sorry."

Fucking hell. No fucking way. I was not a pity fuck who was going to cry when this man walked out while his taste was still salty on my tongue.

I waved my hand numbly in the air. "Yeah, no. It's... I need to get some sleep anyway. Big day tomorrow."

You called me beautiful. Inside and out. I twisted my tongue between my teeth to keep from saying it out loud like an accusation.

He glanced at me. This time the unspoken words between us were arrows with poisoned tips. "Finn..."

I cleared my throat and plastered on my media smile. "No, it's cool. Thanks for the beej, Dec. I really needed that. Kept me from taking Kix up on his offer. He's fucking good at it but then wants to stick around and talk my damned ear off. No, thanks."

Declan's nostrils flared as if he smelled the lie for what it was, a desperate attempt to downplay how much this had meant to me.

"Happy to be of service," he bit out before standing up and grabbing the pieces of his uniform.

I clenched my fingers into tight fists in the bedding until my knuckles turned white. All I had to do was hold it together for three more minutes until he bolted out of there.

He shoved his legs into his uniform pants and yanked them up, closing them with quick, efficient movements. Sheriff Declan Stone, quick and efficient even in the way he hooks up with men.

Great.

After he left the bedroom to search for his shirts, I rubbed my face in my hands and muttered a curse. But then he came back for one last word.

"Don't fucking hook up with that jackass," he warned, pointing his finger at me. "You hear me? Don't do it."

I felt myself gawp at his surprising command, but before I could shake myself out of my shock enough to tell him he wasn't the boss of me, he'd stormed out and slammed the door to the chalet with one last bossy statement about making sure I locked it behind him.

For some reason, that last bit made me laugh. Even when he was a total controlling asshole, he cared about the safety of the people around him.

Fucking Christ.

At least the laughing kept me from crying like a damned baby.

The following day, I woke up with a newfound desire to stop letting other people's image of me define my own. Over the course of a long, hot shower, I reminded myself I wasn't the spoiled young celebrity Declan thought I was. I also wasn't the experienced stuntman Nolan was trying to convince everyone I was. And I wasn't the social player Kix wanted me to be. Most importantly, I wasn't the blockbuster-seeking actor my mom had raised me to be.

So then who was I, and what did *I* want?

One of the answers came to me by accident.

Instead of wallowing in my recent rejection and eating a bowl of cold cereal for breakfast, I made my way to the diner in town. I was starving after skipping dinner the night before, and I'd been relieved to see Declan had somehow arranged to return the McLaren to me overnight.

When I got to the diner, I shoved my hair under a ball cap and kept my head down, asking quietly for a booth in the back. It was clear the older man who'd greeted me knew who I was, but he seemed to read my mood. "Maybe sit on this side," he suggested casually, pointing to the bench that faced the back wall instead of the one that faced the rest of the diner. I shot him a grateful look and took a seat.

When the man came back with a steaming pot of coffee and a sweating glass of ice water, I smiled in thanks and ordered the big breakfast special. I scrolled through my phone while I waited and tried not to eavesdrop on the teenager sitting behind me whispering furtively into the phone.

"Dude, they'll kill me if they find out I'm failing summer school, too. It doesn't even make sense to have Mr. Reyes for the same damned Shakespeare unit I failed during regular school. If he didn't explain it right the first time, how am I supposed to learn it in summer school? I'm fucked. My dads are going to freak out. They won't let me keep working at the diner if I can't pass this class, and then I'll never be able to buy a car."

My ears perked up when he mentioned my favorite topic. How could someone have trouble with Shakespeare? There were like a million resources online to help.

I wanted to butt my nose into his conversation, but I kept my mouth closed. It was none of my business anyway. I went back to scrolling social media.

The older man delivered my food a little while later, and I realized the kid was back working behind the counter. He was tall and lanky with dark hair and a friendly smile for everyone. It didn't take long to figure out my server was one of his dads. The man beamed at the kid with a kind of affectionate pride I'd always imagined my father would have for me if he'd ever known I existed.

Something about this little family made me feel wistful, and I suddenly wanted to help the young man discover the joy and intricacies of Shakespeare. I hated hearing someone think of it as a chore when it could be so much fun.

I waited until his dad went back into the kitchen before waving my arm to get his attention. The kid came over right away with the coffeepot. "Ready for a refill?"

When I lifted my head, I saw the moment he recognized me. He did a quick blink of surprise before getting his expression under control. "Or can I get you anything else?"

I smiled in thanks for his not treating me any differently. "Actually, I was wondering if I could help you," I said, keeping my voice low. "I overheard you earlier, which I'd apologize for if you hadn't been sitting six inches away from me. I happen to love Shakespeare and have studied the man and his works for years."

The kid's eyes widened. "Shit," he muttered. "Sorry about that. I... probably sounded like an idiot."

I shook my head. "Not at all. It's not easy to learn something if you don't gel with the teacher. And, hell, maybe you won't gel with me either. But I'd like to try. To teach you. If... if that's something you'd be interested in."

He looked too surprised to respond, so I held out my hand. "My name is Finn."

"I know." He shook it without thinking and then quickly added, "I'm Solo. Well, Solomon, but everyone calls me Solo. Pim and Bill are my dads. They own the diner. You probably already know that, and now I'm making a fool out of myself."

I grinned at him. "Not at all. But don't feel obligated to say yes. I know it's weird that I even offered, but... Shakespeare's kind of my thing."

"But you were in that SEAL movie. That was badass," Solo said.

I loved that he immediately went to that rather than my time on *Cast in Clover*. It was a testament to his age.

"One of my lines in that film quoted Shakespeare," I said. "When I'm rallying my team for our final push to defeat the enemy, I say,

'Once more into the breach, my friends.' The actual line is a little different, but that's from Shakespeare's *Henry V*. His body of work was so influential and comprehensive, it's still being used and referenced today. That's why we study it in school. It's one of our culture's secular bibles. Biblical stories like David and Goliath represent concepts in our daily lives regardless of whether or not we're religious. It's the same with Shakespeare. Romeo and Juliet represent star-crossed lovers, irony, and the toxic effects of long-running feuds. It's..."

I tried to think of some way of encapsulating why this stuff was important. It was important to know it, not just to pass a class.

"It's like a shorthand. But it's also a kind of recorded history. You know why we study the Holocaust?"

He rolled his eyes like a typical teenager. "Yes. So history doesn't repeat itself. So we know what happened."

I nodded. "Shakespeare wrote *The Merchant of Venice* in 1596 about Europe's Christians and their problematic relationship with Europe's Jewish population."

Solo looked surprised. "That prejudice stuff was happening back then?"

"Yes. And look at his play *Twelfth Night* and its exploration and commentary on gender identity. He wrote that around the year 1600, Solo. Viola says, 'I am all the daughters of my father's house, / And all the brothers too.' She's dressed as her brother. But here's the thing. Her role had to be played on the Elizabethan stage by a man."

Solo nodded. "I know that much."

"So we have a man playing a woman playing a man. It's a statement on gender and whether or not it can be defined by simply putting on a costume or playing a role. Underneath, the person is who they are regardless of the costume."

"So he... he was into LGBT stuff?"

I wondered if this was what it felt like when a fisherman finally felt a tug on his line. His interest was sparked, and I felt like I'd won a prize at a fair. "Heterosexual and homosexual as terms didn't exist back then. So we have to look at it differently rather than with our modern-day binary language. Did you know he wrote 126 of his sonnets to a young man? But as early as 1640, editors were already changing the pronouns to make them more palatable."

"You really know a lot about this stuff," he said.

Understatement of the century. "When I was thirteen, I realized I was gay. For some reason, the stress of it manifested itself as severe stage fright. I was two years into my role on *Cast in Clover*, and suddenly I was in jeopardy of losing it all. My mom found a performance therapist, and before you ask, yes, there is such a thing in LA. Her name is Roshawna, and she changed my life. But she's a Shakespeare geek. All of her exercises used his works, and by the end of it I had monologues and soliloquies memorized, and I'd caught the bug."

"When, uh... when did you come out? Like... how did you handle all that?"

God, where did I even begin? My pause must have worried him, because he quickly added, "Not that you need to share that with me. I didn't mean to ask something so personal or anything."

I gave him a reassuring smile. "It's fine. I'll tell you what. Agree to give me one hour to help you with your class and I'll answer all of your questions about coming out. Sound good? We can meet up in the park on Saturday morning as long as no one recognizes me and interrupts us."

I knew better than to arrange to meet a teenager in private somewhere, but I wasn't sure what the alternative would be if we got mobbed.

He looked at me skeptically. "What's in it for you? Why are you offering to help me like this? Am I some kind of charity case you're going to..." He seemed to realize how rude the question was. "Sorry, it's just... why would you do this for me?"

I swallowed my usual instinct to keep this geeky part of me to myself. "Teaching someone to love this stuff as much as I do would be pretty damned amazing."

After exchanging cell numbers with Solo, I left the diner lighter than I'd entered it. Sure, there was still the pesky issue of a sheriff running hot and cold on me and a film director bound and determined to put me in harm's way. But at least I had a teaching gig lined up for the weekend.

Chaos reigned on set when I arrived. I discovered we were starting primary filming on some of the climbing scenes sooner than I expected, so I met with the team to walk through the first scene on the ground several times and go over some of the technical issues involved in getting the angles Nolan wanted.

"We'll only have the helicopter for a few hours on Monday, so we'll need to get it shot without too many takes," Shelly said.

I tried not to let the show runner's words stress me out, but when she repeated the warning several more times throughout the day, it was hard to keep the pressure from getting to me.

I found a few spare minutes at the end of the day to ring Franklin and ask his advice on the best way to approach the thing with Solo.

"He said the first thing he needs help with is interpreting the use of the ghost in Hamlet."

Franklin sighed over the line, his snobbish attitude as familiar to me as the "Brevity is the soul of wit" sign that hung crookedly above his desk in his cluttered campus office. "Lord, what fools these mortals be," he muttered.

I barked out a laugh. "Dude, it's small-town high school English class. The teacher probably doubles as the soccer coach."

"Yes, yes, it's going to be a question on the AP exam for all the same reasons. People are idiots. As for luring this kid over to the dark side, consider mentioning *The Lion King* as a modern-day *Hamlet*. That often blows the mind. What else? Oh. The Patrick Swayze ghost movie. The one with the pottery. What's that one called?"

"*Ghost.*"

"Impertinent child," he chided. "So it is. The use of ghosts to deliver messages from the main character to themselves is well-known, but perhaps not put in so many words for a teenager to have realized it before. I also suggest... what's the one with Bruce Willis and the child?"

"*Sixth Sense.*"

"Yes, that one. If he's seen it, you can discuss the use of spiritual communication. However, if he has not seen it, don't spoil the damned thing for him."

I loved that he wanted to protect a stranger from ruining a twenty-year-old film. "Okay."

"And discuss the concept of conscience. Use Scrooge, etc."

When we finished the call, I thanked him profusely for his help and told him I planned on taking him to lunch when I was back in LA in September.

"Promises, promises," he muttered before hanging up. The conversation left me with a big smile on my face. Knowing Frank, he was secretly happy I'd come to him for advice. And he knew he'd be the first call I made as soon as I returned to the city from filming.

I was in such a good mood that I agreed to yet another night at the Roadhouse with the cast and crew. Even though Shelly had arranged for us all to have a private back room this time, it was still a huge mistake. Crystobell had brought a fashion vlogger with her and was busy chatting about clothes, but the vlogger had invited a man I recognized from a release party last year. He'd been on the arm of a gossip columnist.

I made a point to sit between Logan and Kix, but somehow after going to the bar to get refills, Kix had wound up on the other end of the long table talking to one of the fans Shelly had invited into our room as a special treat.

The gossip columnist dude moved around to take Kix's abandoned chair. "I'm Jado," he said with a flirty grin. "And you're goddamned adorable up close."

"Thanks," I said with my media smile. "I think I remember you from the Rampart release party."

He nodded enthusiastically. "That party was wild, man. I barely remember it."

Logan leaned over and spoke low in my ear. "Shelly is going to let a few more fans in here. That okay with you?"

It was so nice of him to ask, I immediately agreed like an idiot.

Jado laughed and leaned against my shoulder. "Man, that night was sick. You were there with... gosh, I can't remember now. Who were you with?"

I'd been there with Iris's assistant, Dawson, because he'd begged for an introduction to one of my co-stars.

"What do you do, Jado?" I asked, as if he hadn't been talking about the party.

He laughed again and nudged my shoulder harder. "I work in online marketing. It's not as boring as it sounds, I promise."

I didn't care. I didn't care about any of this. I was at a private party with some of the world's biggest celebrities, and all I wanted to do was go home and pull out my well-worn copy of *Hamlet* so I could think up exercises for Solomon.

"That's great," I said instead. Thankfully, the fans Shelly invited into the room quickly surrounded us, begging for selfies and autographs. For once, I was happy to engage with anyone and everyone in Aster Valley who wanted to meet me, but I quickly realized doing this in the evening at a place that served alcohol wasn't the best idea.

Many of the fans were getting handsy.

I made my way over to Shelly and told her I needed someone to help keep people from getting in my personal space. She laughed. "I thought you were joking when you expressed security concerns to Nolan."

I opened my mouth to ask her what the hell she was talking about since that wasn't at all what had happened, when Jado came up behind me and slid his arms around my front like he had rights to my body. I quickly pulled him off me and lifted an eyebrow at Shelly.

She dropped her smile and nodded. "I'll call the sheriff's office and see if we can't get—"

"No!" I blurted before she could finish. The last thing I wanted was Sheriff Stone coming out yet again to find me surrounded by fans like an idiot. This was my fault. I should have known the private room wouldn't make a difference, and I'd even said yes to inviting more people into it. "Not necessary. Actually, I've got those climbing scenes in the morning, so I'm going to go."

She nodded and agreed that was probably a good idea considering my call schedule the following day.

When I turned to make my apologies, Jado begged me to stay for another drink. I politely declined. After finally pushing my way out of the bar and into the clear night, I noticed Jado jogging up behind me.

"Please god let me come home with you. Let me blow your mind. I'd give anything to suck you off."

My stomach turned over. I didn't feel physically threatened by him at all, but I'd also heard enough horror stories not to be naive about interactions with fans.

"No, thank you. I really need to get some sleep."

"At least let me have your number so we can arrange another night," he said with that same flirty smile.

I shook my head, wondering if I should tell him to try it on with Kix since Kix was usually up for anything. But I didn't want to be responsible for Kix saying something stupid that might end up online, so I kept my mouth shut.

"Good night," I finally said, wishing I had a standard set of keys instead of this useless Senturion key on my wrist.

Thankfully, he didn't follow me to the car. I drove away with shaky hands and a familiar feeling of being terrible at the public-facing side of this business. Even though Roshawna had been a miracle worker in helping me tackle my acting nerves, I'd never felt fully confident in front of the public again. Maybe it was a side effect of growing up. Maybe all young children had nerves of steel and lost them at some point along the way.

Regardless, the drive back to the chalet was filled with second-guessing and negative self-talk, the exact opposite of the way I'd begun the day. No. Unacceptable. I reached for my phone to connect it to the car so I could play some cheer-up music on the way up the mountain, but the phone slid out of my hand and tumbled to the floor beneath my feet.

I swerved a little but quickly gave up on retrieving my phone in order to concentrate on the curvy turns.

Blue lights instantly flashed in my rearview mirror.

Fuck. Fuck, fuck, *fuck*.

11

DECLAN

Another night, another callout to Matt's bar because of the cast and crew of that damned movie.

I almost allowed the responding deputy to deal with it on his own. Almost. But then the dispatcher had described an occupancy hazard in the private function area, and I'd decided to make sure the crowd was dispersed without incident, a task that would work much better with more than one of us.

But as soon as I'd pulled into the bar's parking lot and seen the flash of that blue sports car peeling out into the night, I'd turned right around and followed it as if the McLaren itself held a leash attached to my own neck.

I would simply make sure he got home okay. That was all.

It definitely wasn't because I'd been missing the man since I'd walked out of his chalet the night before. Or that I'd been obsessing about him messing around with that stupid sidekick of his. Or that every time I'd closed my eyes the night before, I'd replayed the hurt expression that had flashed over his beautiful face before he'd locked his emotions down, and hated myself for becoming another person he had to put on a front for.

After radioing the other responding officer to let him know he was on his own, I settled in to follow the sports car up into the hills toward Rockley Lodge.

My plan went out the window the minute I saw his car almost drive off the road. Was he driving drunk? On these roads? Did he have a death wish?

I immediately turned on my lights and pulled him over. Once he was parked in a pullout that normally boasted a picturesque vista, I got out and approached the driver's door.

"Step out of the vehicle."

He turned to me, defiant and angry. "Are you fucking kidding me right now?"

"Don't make me repeat myself."

Our eyes locked for a few beats before he huffed and opened the door. As soon as he stepped out of the car, I wanted to pull him in my arms and thank every god in existence that his car hadn't careened over the edge and tumbled into the valley. Instead, I began interrogating him.

"How much have you had to drink tonight?"

Finn's eyes narrowed. "None of your damned business."

"You were driving recklessly. Answer the question."

He crossed his arms in front of his chest, those arms whose ink had tasted warm and sweet against my tongue just last night.

"Fine. I had four drinks."

Was he insane? He was too slender to handle that much alcohol and think he could still drive. "F-four drinks? What the fuck were you drinking?"

He leaned forward and hissed at me. "Ginger ale, asshole."

The words caught me by surprise, so I couldn't help but parrot them back at him. "Ginger ale?"

"Yes, but since you seem to think I'm a liar, I'm sure you don't believe me."

"I..." I didn't know what to say. *I'm sorry* seemed too pathetic.

Finn threw up his hands. "Go ahead and field test me. *Again*. Just like the other night in the parking lot. Go on. I dare you."

I wanted to drop to my knees and beg his forgiveness. "You swerved."

He let out a breath and suddenly looked tired. "My phone fell on the floor by my feet. It surprised me."

"I thought..."

He gritted his teeth. "I know what you thought."

"No. *No.* I thought you were going to run off the road, off the side of the fucking mountain, Finn. My heart..." *My heart almost died in my chest.* I pressed a hand over my name tag. "My heart skipped a beat. I..." My breath came faster just thinking about it. The mangled metal would have been completely inadequate to protect his fragile humanity.

Finn's face softened. "I'm okay."

"I'm sorry."

Now his face widened into a smirk. "Woah. It's a miracle, ladies and gentlemen."

"I was wrong. I'm..." I wanted to say more, to keep him there on the side of the mountain talking to me. Where I could touch him and feel the warm breath from his lips, smell the coffee and woodsmoke scent of him. But it wasn't my right. "You're free to go."

Finn's eyes flashed back and forth between mine like he was studying me. Possibility sparked in the air between us. Finally, he seemed to deflate. "Fine. Good night, Sheriff."

He turned to go, but it felt like maybe my solar plexus was tied to his because I followed right after him. "Wait."

He flicked a hand in the air over his shoulder. "It's fine. You already apologized. Go home, Sheriff."

"Stop calling me that," I ground out. I hated him thinking of me as my office and not as a man. Of all people to reduce me to my job, he was the one who stung the most.

Finn spun around. "Why? That's what you are. That's all you apparently want to be to me, right? You made it perfectly clear last night. I'm nothing to you. And you're a big fat liar. You called me beautiful, Declan. 'Inside and out,' remember? And then you fucking left me naked and alone like a goddamned whore. But it's fine. I'm used to being used. It's the story of my fucking life. Just so we're clear, *Sheriff*, I don't need you. I never did."

He got into the McLaren and sped off before the oxygen returned to fill my lungs. His shaking voice betrayed his words as lies, and it was like he'd stripped me bare and left me bleeding on the side of the road. Why did I feel this insane connection to him, and why did part of me think I'd gotten him all wrong?

It was like there were two parts of me battling each other. One thought this kid was a spoiled dilettante I needed to protect my heart from, but the other... the other saw this incredibly strong and fragile man who hid his damned light under a bushel. A kindred soul who was afraid to let anyone see the real person underneath the mask in case the rest of the world found him lacking.

I scrambled behind the wheel of my SUV and sped off after him, hoping like hell it wasn't too late to rip the bushel away and bask in the light of the real Finn Heller.

When I pulled up beside his car in front of the chalet, I saw a man on his front porch. Finn got to him first and confronted him.

"What are you doing here? I didn't invite you here." Finn looked both exhausted and annoyed. I'd begun to get a feel for what he must go through on a regular basis. I remembered him telling me last night that everyone wanted a piece of him. He'd sounded so alone. And so tired.

And I'd left him like he was nothing. Like I, too, had only used him for what it would get me.

I felt like an ass. I had to make it right, but first I had to get rid of this player.

The stranger was all smiles and hands in the air. "It's cool, bro. I could tell you just needed a little privacy, and I respect that. I figured I'd make it easy on you by showing up here. Crys's people hooked me up with a ride and told me which of these little buildings you were in."

I put my hand on my weapon and walked over. "There a problem here?"

Finn looked at me with reluctant relief. His chin began to wobble, but he did his best to hold it together. "A simple misunderstanding. Jado is going to call a ride to take him back to wherever he's staying."

Once the man saw my uniform, he did an awkward kind of double take and held up his hands again. "Look, man, I don't want any problems. I just thought..."

Finn said, "He's not here for you. He's here to get me to sign some papers about the incident the other night. But still. You need to go."

Jado nodded his head. "Of course. No problem. Catch you later. I'll just... walk out to the road and wait for a ride."

"Be careful," I couldn't help but add. "Come back if you have any problems getting home safe."

He shot me an appreciative smile and headed down the drive. I turned back to Finn. "Please give me a few minutes of your time," I said in a low voice. "Then, if you want me to leave, I'll leave."

He blew out a breath and nodded before leading me into the chalet. After he kicked off his shoes, he turned on the fire and threw himself down on the little love seat, pulling the quilt around his shoulders like he was cold.

I closed and locked the door behind me before taking the chair next to the small sofa. I clasped my hands between my knees and leaned toward him, fighting every desire I had to touch some part of him and make a physical connection.

"I'm not used to trusting people," I began. "It's not an excuse, but... I, ah..." God, I felt like a fool. *Dec, get your shit together.* "I've never had this feeling like... like I needed another person so desperately for no apparent reason." I gestured to my gut. "Like if I didn't find a way to... to be with you, to touch you, to find out more about you, I might just lose the fucking plot. I panicked, Finn. I'm so fucking sorry. Please. Please give me a chance to make it up to you."

As I spoke, his eyes filled with tears until they ran unchecked down his cheeks. My heart squeezed tight enough to steal my breath away, something that seemed to happen a lot around him. I didn't understand it, but I was tired of trying to figure it out. I just wanted to hold him and stop fighting against the need to rationalize it.

"Please come here," I whispered. "And let me hold you. That's all. Just that would be enough."

He uncurled from the quilt and climbed over into my lap, tucking his wet face into my neck and wrapping his shaking arms around me. "I'm so tired, Dec," he said.

"I know, baby," I said softly against his hair. "I can see that. And I'm so sorry I made it worse."

I stood up and carried him to bed before pulling both our clothes off until we were down to our underwear. We slid under the covers and came back together in a twist of limbs. Finn fell asleep while the sheets were still cool against our skin, and I held him for a long time, thinking back over everything he'd said.

And everything I'd said.

I'd exposed my feelings which left me feeling raw, but I'd also seen the truth of his own feelings, how the harsh smack of my rejection had hit him after I'd told him he was beautiful. How could I have done that?

I pressed kisses against the top of his head and murmured my apologies even though he wasn't awake to hear them. For those few moments in the dark calm of the summer night, I let myself wonder if there was any kind of future an almost forty-year-old sheriff could possibly cobble together with a twenty-four-year-old superstar deep in the middle of a high-profile acting career.

It was impossible. How could I even daydream about it? I wanted nothing to do with LA ever again, and Finn would never want to leave it.

I ran my fingers through the longer hair on top of his head, feeling the silken locks slide along my skin. What if I could give him a temporary reprieve from the demanding life he lived back home? What if I could be a safe haven for him for just a little while?

At some point I fell asleep and was awakened later to the insistent press of a hard dick against my stomach. I reached down and stroked it, pulling a sleepy groan out of Finn that made me smile.

"Feeling a little better?" I mumbled into his hair.

"Mm. Feeling a big sheriff in my bed," he said, running hands over my chest and shoulders as he shifted to lie on top of me. He was warm from sleep, and I wanted to hold him there and drink in the sexy feel of him for a little longer.

"You're definitely making things bigger," I admitted, pressing my own dick up into his.

Finn seemed to remember the seriousness from earlier because his playful, sexy mood suddenly disappeared, and his weary expression returned. "Are you just here to—"

"No. Whatever you were going to say, please don't say it," I urged. "I get why you'd think that, but... no. I want to be with you right now, even if there's no sex involved."

He narrowed his eyes. "Are you saying you don't want sex?"

I suddenly found myself caught in a trap. If I said I wanted him, he might think I was only using him for sex. If I said I didn't want sex, well, then I'd be a fucking liar.

I opened my mouth to respond but had no idea what to say. Of course I wanted sex with him. Who wouldn't?

Finn began giggling. "The look on your face right now."

Brat.

I rolled him over until I was on top of him, pressing my own hard shaft into his inner thigh. "Are you saying *you* don't want sex?" I growled before leaning in to suck on his earlobe.

He sucked in a breath. "N-no. Not saying that. Not saying it at all. I want the sex. All the sex."

I moved to his mouth and tasted his lips. They were full and sweet, and when I felt them curve into a smile against mine, I felt an odd little flip in my gut.

I reached down and shoved his underwear away until I could grip his dick and stroke it again. He was manscaped in a fussy way like some of the men in LA I'd hooked up with. I tried not to imagine who else had seen him like this. The thought of it made me want to snarl and snap.

Finn fumbled into my own shorts and clasped my cock until we were jacking each other off and panting into each other's mouths.

"Lube," he said on a gasp, rolling away to grab a tube from the nightstand. "Here."

I slicked my hands up and grabbed both of our cocks together, staring down at the sight of them rubbing hard against each other. The edge of his tip caught against mine with every stroke.

"Fuck," I groaned. It was quick and hot, a slick frot that had us humping wildly into my grip until both of us cried out and came in my hand.

When I finally caught my breath, I let out a laugh. "That was embarrassingly fast."

Finn closed his eyes and grinned, clearly enjoying his afterglow. "It would have been faster if I'd let myself peek at my dick in your big hand."

I kissed his forehead and pushed up so I could clean my hands off and find a washcloth for his stomach. While I waited for the sink water to heat up, I looked at myself in the mirror. My hair was a rat's nest, and I had beard burn across my neck and chest, but both of those paled in comparison to the big dumb grin on my face.

I wanted to give that sweet, sexy man the world. But he was a multimillion-dollar movie star who was used to having everything he wanted, right? A bouquet of flowers or a candlelight dinner would seem... trite compared to the things he'd probably gotten from other lovers.

Are you trying to woo him now? What is this?

I rinsed and wrung out the cloth before turning off the water. Maybe not woo him, but I wanted to give him something to let him know the vulnerability wasn't one-sided. He'd let me see a tender side of him, and he deserved to see the same from me.

As soon as I walked back into the bedroom and saw him there, I realized one thing I could give him.

12

FINN

Declan looked different when he came back into the bedroom. Determined.

"You asked me why I left LA," he said, reaching out to run a hot cloth over my body with gentle strokes. "And I kind of... avoided answering."

"You shut down tighter than a stiff screen door."

I watched him return the cloth to the bathroom before joining me in bed again. My body still felt languid and easy from the orgasm, but his words woke me up.

"I don't like to talk about it," he said, as if that hadn't been obvious. "And part of me assumed you probably already knew why."

"Why would I know why you'd moved to Aster Valley? I've known you less than a week." It didn't make any sense. "And every time I've asked you, you've bolted."

He sighed. For some reason the implication I should have already known about it made me feel jittery and nervous, like I'd somehow been involved in a situation I was completely unfamiliar with.

"I thought maybe you'd googled it. People do," he said wryly. "I was a witness in the department bribery scandal. I'm sure you heard about it. My ex-partner was involved."

I lifted my head up to look at him. "Partner as in..."

He shook his head. "Partner on the force. Not lover. Nick turned out to be one of the officers who'd accepted bribes from high-profile... people... in exchange for not charging them for crimes."

I sat up. "You're kidding? He let people bribe him out of charges? What kind of cop does that?"

Declan's forehead crinkled in confusion. He sat up, too, and pulled the bedcovers over him as if he didn't want to be naked for this conversation. "The corrupt kind. The kind who think justice only applies to poor people. The kind who cater to..." He met my eyes and clamped his lips together before saying, *people like you.*

I felt my heart rate tick up. "I didn't hear about it." And that was the truth. "When did it happen?"

He looked like he didn't believe me. "New Year's. Several house parties were busted for drugs. When no charges came from all the police activity, Internal Affairs did an investigation. Now does it ring a bell?"

Now his tone was straight-up disbelieving, and I felt like I was being accused of something. "No, why... why would I know about something that happened while I was out of the country? I don't understand. You're acting like I had something to do with you losing your job."

"You weren't out of the country on New Year's. Yours was one of the house parties busted."

I stared at him. Now it was my turn to look incredulous. "Are you fucking kidding me? I was in England. For six weeks working on... working on my graduate degree."

He was the first person I'd told outside of Franklin and the students and professors in Stratford. It was my secret indulgence, something I feared being judged for if the world discovered silly Chip Clover fancied himself a student of something *serious.*

Declan still looked suspicious. "Why do you sound like you're making that up?"

"Because no one knows about it, dammit! Because it's my little secret. The treasure of my fucking heart. So go ahead and make fun of me, okay? I snuck off to Stratford-on-Avon to study the bard and told everyone I was vacationing on a private island."

His eyes widened in surprise. "Why wouldn't you tell anyone you were taking Shakespeare classes? Wouldn't that be seen as a boost to your resume or whatever an actor calls it?"

I let out an ugly laugh. "No. Not me. People would think I was a joke."

Now Declan's face was as stormy as the weather outside. "You're not a fucking joke. But at least that explains your alibi was legit."

"Alibi for what? What are you talking about?"

"One of the New Year's parties we busted was at your house in Santa Monica. There was extensive drug use, property damage to a neighbor's house, and one instance of a guest driving drunk. No charges were made, and it was discovered that responding officers had accepted a large cash payment from someone claiming to be your representative."

I wanted to laugh. This story was ludicrous. I had left a set of house keys and my alarm code with Kix because he'd been worried about a fan who'd gotten a little too close, and he could confirm there'd been no party. But how was it possible that no one had ever breathed a word of these accusations to me? Not Iris, not my publicist, not Kix himself?

Declan wouldn't invent something like this, though, and I could tell that my ignorance made me sound guilty.

Heat flooded my face, and I began to panic. "It wasn't me, Declan. You need to believe me. I have my travel receipts if you need to see them, and you can contact the head of the program—"

He reached out and took my hands in his. "Shh. Okay. Okay. Slow your breathing down, sweetheart."

I couldn't calm down. This didn't make any sense. "Why didn't anyone say anything to me? Why didn't someone contact me when I got home? I don't... I don't understand."

"The department probably didn't reach out because they were too busy dealing with the internal shit to realize they'd never spoken to the actual homeowner in your case. If someone had posed as your representative, that would have been enough. But if you weren't there... was the house burgled?"

"No. I... gave the keys to a friend." I swallowed and looked at him. "I need to find out what happened."

I could tell he wanted to ask the name of my friend, but he kept the question back. Instead, he went on to tell me about some of the bigger busts that night that happened at much higher-profile residences.

"They had plenty of evidence of the corruption from those busts and the history of bribes that came out of woodwork afterward to worry about the smaller busts like yours. Believe me, a few people doing coke and ecstasy at a house party paled in comparison to the house full of heroin and prostitutes. And one of them had surveillance footage of actual police officers participating. So, no. Yours wasn't the one anyone gave a shit about in the end."

"Except you," I pointed out.

Declan sighed. "Yeah. But only after I met you."

"No wonder you thought I was an entitled dick."

His eyebrows lifted, and his eyes danced. "No, that was because of the valet thing. And you telling me you'd 'look out for' me."

Realization dawned. "You already thought Finn Heller was someone who bribed cops, and here I was offering you money to do my bidding."

He nodded. "That's about the long and short of it, yeah."

I couldn't help it; I started laughing. I laughed so hard I almost pissed myself. At one point, Declan started laughing, too, and we fell against each other in a pile of ridiculousness. One thing led to another, and our lips and hands found each other again. The laughing turned quickly to a kind of desperate sexual grappling. We fought for domination and flipped each other over and over until we damned near fell off the bed.

"Let me have you," he said against my mouth. We were sweating and panting, leaving trails of beard burn all over each other's skin. "Please. Please let me inside you."

I groaned and nodded, hoping like hell I had a condom somewhere in my toiletry kit. I hadn't come to Aster Valley expecting to have sex, but I usually... *My wallet!* I usually kept one in my wallet in case someone offered me a blow job and I found myself in a position to accept.

I pulled myself away from him long enough to scramble out to the living room and find my wallet in my backpack. Once I returned with the condom, I grabbed the lube from the bedside drawer where I'd used it to jack off countless times already to thoughts of the sheriff's stern looks and strong body.

After handing the condom to Declan, I snapped open the lube and began to prep myself. Declan's eyes glazed over as he watched. "Fuck, that's hot," he said, reaching for the lube so he could help. As soon as his fingers were involved, I lay back and lost myself to the feel of him. The thick press of his fingers stretching me was enough to make me hard and dripping again despite my massive orgasm earlier.

I couldn't believe Declan Stone was going to fuck me. I'd fantasized about it but never thought it would actually happen.

When he finally leaned over me and pressed his covered cock to my hole, I sucked in a breath.

"You're shaking," he said.

"Please don't change your mind," I blurted. "I don't think I'd survive it." I tried to give him a cheeky smile to soften the echoing sound of desperation in my voice, but he stopped it with a hard kiss.

"Not a chance."

When he stretched me open with his thick cock, I arched back and squeezed my eyes closed. His arms were propped under my knees, holding them back and keeping my legs wide open for him. I normally would have felt exposed, but with Declan I didn't. I trusted him. He seemed like the kind of man who would take care of the people he had sex with.

"Look at me," he said through clenched teeth. "Sweetheart, open your eyes so I can see you're okay."

When I opened them, they were embarrassingly wet. I clenched my jaw in defiance, but I didn't see any judgment or pity on his face.

"You're fucking gorgeous," he said softly. "Sexy and sweet, hot and responsive. So fucking tight. Christ." He hissed the last part and squeezed his own eyes closed for a beat. "You're gonna make me shoot off too fast."

I reached out and cupped his cheeks, pulling his face in for more kissing. With every stroke in and out of my body, I felt more and more overwhelmed. This wasn't like any of the hookups I'd had before. My heart felt like it was some kind of emotional expanding foam and it was going to grow right out of my chest and ruin everything.

When his dick hit at just the right angle, I cried out against his lips and arched back again. "Just like that, *fuck*. Dec, just... just like that."

He thrust his thick dick into me, brushing that spot until the orgasm pulsed through me in a sudden rush. I grappled for my dick to get the most out of my release, and I vaguely noted the sounds of his own grunts and cries.

We ended up in a sweaty, jizz-covered heap, limbs tangled and hot breath skittering across each other's skin.

A stupid joke popped into my head, and I couldn't hold back a laugh.

"What?" he asked, smirking at me.

"You'll think I'm crass."

"I'm the one who had my fingers in your ass a few minutes ago," he reminded me.

A low pulse of an aftershock tried spurting more cum out of me, but it was no use. My balls were empty.

"I can see why people are so keen to bribe the LAPD now."

A beat of silence fell heavy between us, and I regretted the joke immediately. But then a second later, Declan grabbed my pillow and slammed it into my face before jamming his fingertips against my ribs and tickling the fuck out of me.

When we finally calmed back down, Declan padded out to the kitchen to get us some water. When he came back, I blurted out something that had been bothering me. "Who's the pregnant woman?"

I regretted it instantly. It was none of my business. Besides, he'd assured me he was single. And gay. It wasn't jealousy, exactly. Maybe it was simple curiosity.

Mm-hm.

"Remember I mentioned my ex-partner on the force? Tessa was Nick's girlfriend. Unfortunately for her, she wasn't the only one. And when she found out, she broke things off. It wasn't until after he was busted in the Internal Affairs investigation and arrested that she realized she was pregnant. At that point, she couldn't really give him another chance, even if she'd wanted to. He pled out, but he'll still serve a long stint."

I thought of my own single mother and how desperate she'd been. How alone she'd been.

"I'm sorry, Declan. Is she doing okay?"

He nodded. "Nick signed away his rights. I'd told her I'd be there for her if she needed anything, so when the media tracked her down and made things difficult for her, she decided to get out of LA for a while."

"That was nice of you, taking her in like that." I tried not to feel even more soft toward him than I already did. He wasn't a soft man. Just because he showed kindness to a friend, didn't mean I needed to drool at his feet. I cleared my throat and prepared to start the awkward postcoital goodbye sequence. "Will you please stay?" I asked instead, startling myself as much as him.

"Are you sure?"

I bit my lip to keep from begging. "Mm-hm."

His face relaxed into a smile. "I'd really like that. Let me text Tessa and let her know I'm staying out."

I forced myself to get up and brush my teeth, if only to give him a little privacy. When he joined me at the sink, I nodded to the prepackaged toiletry kit that sat in a welcome basket on the vanity. "I think there's a complimentary toothbrush in there if you want it."

We brushed our teeth side by side. I couldn't help but sneak glances of his muscular form in the mirror. A dark, furry trail led down his stomach to his groin, and his soft cock swung gently against his thigh as he shifted his weight from one foot to another. The muscles in his ass flexed as he turned to rinse his mouth in the sink. My eyes ate up the muscular curves of his back and shoulders and the dip of his spine. Two shallow divots marked the top of his ass, and I pictured myself pressing thumbs into those spots as I thrust into him. His ass would be tight and hot around my dick, and his grunts and groans would fill the room with—

"Your teeth are probably clean enough by now," he murmured.

I glanced at his eyes in the mirror to see him smirking at me. My own reflection was ridiculous. Toothpaste foam ran down my chin, and my eyes looked glassy.

"Ungh." I rinsed my mouth out and grabbed a towel. "You're killing me."

"Pretty sure it's the exhaustion. Get in bed. Otherwise, I'm going to ask you to deliver on the promise those eyes are making right now."

"I want to fuck you," I said simply, even though he was right. I was tired enough to want to fall asleep in the cold, wet sink if it meant not moving another muscle.

He let out a soft chuckle. "I would like that, but I'm not sure my ego could handle a man falling asleep midfuck."

I opened my mouth to argue with him that if I had his ass, there was no way I'd fall asleep midfuck, but before I could get the words out, he grabbed me around the waist and half carried me to the bed.

I fell asleep quickly against the solid warmth of him. Most likely there was a smile on my face the entire night, but when I woke up and found myself alone in the chalet, the smile threatened to melt away.

He was gone.

What exactly had that been between us? A one-night stand? The beginning of something with the possibility of more?

And what did I want it to be?

I started a pot of coffee in the kitchen and forced myself to put thoughts of the sexy sheriff behind me for the day. I had a hectic schedule, beginning with shooting climbing scenes all day and prepping for Solo's tutoring session this weekend.

The shooting went by in a happy blur. The weather was perfect for the three climbs, and there were no equipment problems to speak of. Kramer, my climbing trainer, was there overseeing safety protocol, which gave me extra confidence to focus on the acting over the technical climbing details. Nolan was thrilled with the results, and I finally felt like my role in the film was back on track.

Even though I didn't have a spare moment to myself to do more than daydream about the sheriff, I floated into the weekend on cloud nine. Declan hadn't called or texted, and I forced myself not to contact him either. I didn't want to come off as needy and desperate for a repeat, even though that was exactly how I felt.

I was embarrassed by the story he'd told about my house being involved in the LA cop scandal. I needed to find out what the hell had happened, but Kix was suddenly too busy to talk to me. I knew it was because of our busy shooting schedule, but it still rankled that something so critical could have happened at my house and been kept from me. My relationship with Kix was complicated. Finding out about New Year's hadn't helped.

Late Saturday morning, I put on the most nondescript clothes I had—a navy blue T-shirt and faded jeans—and topped it off with a battered gray ball cap I'd gotten at a climbing event years ago. It was one of my favorites from the stash I always traveled with. As trite as it sounded, a simple ball cap and sunglasses really did go a long way toward hiding my identity when I was in public. I had distinctive hair, longer on top and short on the sides, and if I covered it up, one of the most recognizable aspects of my appearance disappeared. If I used makeup to cover up my freckles, another one disappeared. If I really wanted to go unrecognized, I covered my green eyes with brown contact lenses.

Today, though, it was just the clothes, hat, and glasses. People in Aster Valley already knew I was in town, so a true fan wouldn't be fooled by any of it. I made my way to the park and found Solo waiting for me on a picnic bench situated well off to the side and away from the central gazebo and playground. The summer sun slanted down on his back as he sat hunched over his paperback and spiral notebook.

"Hey," I called as I approached. "Ready to nail this stuff?"

He turned to me and looked resigned. "Not really. If I sucked at it last spring, and I'm sucking at it now, I pretty much know how this is going to go."

"*Be not afraid of greatness. Some are born great, some achieve greatness, and others have greatness thrust upon them,*" I quoted. "That's from *Twelfth Night.*"

He looked at me blankly.

"Never mind," I said quickly. "Just know I'm here and ready to thrust greatness upon you whether you believe in yourself or not."

A reluctant smile curved the edge of his lips. "I appreciate it. Really. It's pretty cool of you to offer to help me."

I took the seat opposite him at the table and began asking him questions about ghosts and ghost movies. He looked a little confused at first but quickly began talking about horror movies I'd barely heard of. I held up a hand. "Slow down, I don't watch horror movies."

"So then what were you expecting me to talk about? Scooby-Doo?"

"Do you know who that is?" I had no idea they still showed that to kids.

Solo rolled his eyes. "Yes. Jeez. Everyone knows Scooby-Doo."

"Good. So then you know about the ghosts there and how they were usually fake. The villain used them to move Shaggy and the gang where he or she wanted them, right? Sometimes the ghosts even tried to get the gang in trouble."

Solo nodded.

I continued. "That's how Shakespeare used the ghost in *Hamlet.* To get Hamlet where he wanted him to be. Only, not physically. The ghost egged him on toward vengeance."

I began explaining more about the ghost's role in convincing Hamlet to seek revenge. When Solo's eyes glossed over, I stood up and pulled him away from the table. "Here, let's act some of it out. It might make more sense that way."

He looked around as if there were a dozen high school friends waiting in the bushes with their phone cameras pointed his way. "I'm not very good at acting..." he said.

I shot him a glance. "How many times have you acted in something?"

He rubbed his face with his hands before offering me a sheepish grin. "Point taken. Fine. But I don't see how this is going to help."

"*Though this be madness, yet there is method in 't,*" I quoted, flipping through Solo's copy of *Hamlet* until I came to the part I wanted. We took turns reading through some of the sections. Solo stopped here and there to ask questions, and I answered them as well as I could without getting too deep. But then he surprised me.

"So, it's kind of like the ghost is in purgatory until he gets his stuff handled, and Hamlet is also kind of like... in a purgatory, too, since he's—"

"Yes!" I yelped, unable to withhold my excitement at the lightbulb that had gone off in his head. "Exactly."

His grin grew wider. "So in a way... the ghost is a reflection of Hamlet's own mind."

I sighed and held the paperback to my chest. "My work here is done. But not really, because I'm sure Hamlet's ghost isn't the only topic your teacher is covering, right?"

Solo's smile faded. "Nah. Next week we have a test on the themes of action and inaction. And I'm not great with themes."

"Not great *yet*," I corrected, handing him the book back. "Believe it or not, it ties into the concept you already discovered. Purgatory is like indecision, right?"

His eyes opened wide with surprise again, and I wanted to throw my head back and laugh with satisfaction. I loved this stuff so much.

"You're smarter than you look," Solo said before realizing how his words had sounded. "Shit. I'm sorry, I didn't mean it like that."

Rather than give him an easy out, I challenged him. "How did you mean it?"

His eyes flicked away in embarrassment. "It's just... I don't know. That show you were in... you play this eager kid. Like a puppy. And then when your character gets a little older, he's moody and shit. I guess I thought you were like that. Not into brainy stuff like Shakespeare and studying things in school."

"I get that a lot. But I'd encourage you to remember that actors are not their characters. Natalie Portman went to Harvard. Wentworth Miller went to Princeton. Hell, Emma Watson went to Brown. And people still think of her as a sassy little witch."

I'd caught a spark of interest in Solo's expression when I'd mentioned the gay actor from *Prison Break*. It reminded me I'd promised to tell him my coming out story.

"Do you want to talk about anything else today or save it for tomorrow?" I asked so as not to push him if he wasn't in the mood.

He glanced at the time on his phone. "Nah, I gotta go help my dads at the diner for lunch. Rain check?"

"You got it."

"Hey, Finn?" Solo asked, suddenly looking less sure. His toe scraped through a patch of dirt, and his thumb tapped out a beat against his hip.

"Yeah?"

"This was good. Today. The Shakespeare stuff. Thank you. Also... I was wondering if maybe a couple of my classmates could join us tomorrow?" He hurried to add, "I mean, if I made them swear not to tell anyone about you? It's just that they're struggling, too, and this really helps."

I hesitated. If I started teaching a group of kids Shakespeare in the park, there was no way it would go unnoticed. My agent would love that kind of media attention, but I'd always kept my Shakespeare stuff close to the vest.

Before I could respond, Solo said. "That's okay. Don't worry about it. Sorry I asked. I totally understand not wanting to—"

"That's fine," I said before I could change my mind. "But make sure they know to keep it quiet. And I find out any of them are more interested in me than in Shakespeare, I'll boot their asses out. Fair?"

His grin split his face, punching in a dimple in his young face. "Totes. No worries, man. Thank you."

He jogged off before I could change my mind, which was probably for the best. The idea of teaching a group of people made me more nervous. As if it was more than just helping a kid with his homework. This would be more like teaching a class, something I hadn't done outside of a little bit of student teaching during my grad program.

I'd loved it, though. Every single minute.

And now I was doing it for real. I felt the familiar excitement of tackling a new challenge.

Action and inaction. Themes I was familiar with from *Hamlet* and my own life. I thought of the sexy sheriff and the action I wanted to take with him. *All* the action.

But he'd been the one to leave without a word. Without so much as a note or text. If anyone needed to take action here, it was him.

I was beginning to recognize I was in a kind of purgatory myself.

So I forced myself to focus on the task at hand which was prepping a *Hamlet* lesson and pretending I didn't ache for the handsome sheriff of Aster Valley. He was nothing to me. I neither wanted nor needed him. I had plenty of other things to occupy my mind and heart. Like my work. My efforts with Solo and his friends. The challenging climbing scene I'd be filming on Monday.

There was really no time for sex with Declan Stone anyway. Besides, he really wasn't all that good at it. It had been fine. *Fine.* No different than sex with anyone else. I didn't need someone who wanted nothing to do with me. Who saw me as a pain in the ass and a spoiled brat. I didn't need a handsome man bossing me around in my own damned bed.

The lady protests too much, methinks.

13

Getting called out of a warm bed with a hot man pressed tightly against my chest was agony. The morning I'd awoken at Finn's place to the insistent buzz of my phone, there'd been a near-fatal car accident out on the highway toward Steamboat. I'd raced there directly and had spent hours dealing with all of the horrible aspects of a devastating multi-car accident with multiple injuries.

After all of the victims had been taken home or to the hospital, we'd had to spend even more time managing to collect evidence while also diverting traffic. I'd practically crawled back to the office and spent the rest of the day and evening dealing with the paperwork. That night I'd fallen into bed without even a word to Tess. She'd heard about the accident from Shawn and had simply pressed a homemade sandwich and bottle of lemonade into my hands before urging me to eat it in a big bath before climbing into bed.

I'd slept like a brick.

But the following day was even crazier. Crystobell Edmund had booked a magazine photo shoot on the shore of Hungry Lake, which was a couple of miles outside of Aster Valley but easily accessible via a walking path from town. The tourists walked, biked, or drove there to watch the leading lady strut around in couture gowns and skimpy halter-top bikinis for the photographer.

It was clearly the best of both worlds for the actress. She was able to preen for her adoring public and earn money for the shoot itself. In addition, the film people probably loved the extra media attention it brought. Her adoring fans had their phone cameras out and were no doubt posting like crazy to social media with hashtags like #ComeToAsterValley and #DriveSheriffStoneCrazy or #WhoCaresAboutBoundaries or simply #FreeSideBoobHere.

Deputy Graham and I worked crowd control for several hours while I tried my best not to crane my neck in hopes of a Finn Heller sighting. No luck. It was a Saturday, which may or may not have meant he had the day off. Maybe I'd hear from him that evening, or maybe I'd get called out to Matt's bar again to drag the sexy actor out to the parking lot one more time.

But that didn't happen. I didn't hear from him, and when I was inevitably called to Matt's bar that night, I managed to ascertain there'd been no Finn in the bar all night.

On Sunday, I was grateful to be off the duty roster. Tess and I went to the diner for breakfast where we ran into Gent and Winter. They invited us to join them at their booth since the place was packed, and I enjoyed the chance to introduce Tess to the famous singer and his husband.

I was midbite when Gent casually mentioned setting me up with a friend of his who was coming into town the following week.

"He's one of our backup drummers and cool as hell. I remember you mentioning mountain biking was one of the reasons you chose Aster Valley, and he rides, too. I thought maybe the two of you could hook up for a ride."

Instead of choking, I forced myself to swallow and take a sip of coffee. "Oh, uh..."

Tess snorted and leaned forward as if to impart a secret on Gent and Winter. "I'm pretty sure he's seeing someone already. In secret."

I turned to her. "Not... not really."

Now it was Winter who snorted. "You don't sound convinced."

My cheeks were hotter than the fresh coffee Pim had just poured me. "I mean, I... there's someone who..."

I was being ridiculous. This wasn't middle school. But at the same time, I had no idea what Finn was to me right now. A hookup? A date? A figment of my desperate imagination?

I liked him. A lot. But I also valued his privacy. It wasn't my place to tell anyone what Finn was up to in his private time. I knew from living in LA that those details were often treated like currency.

Gent caught my eye. "A *no, thanks* is good enough for me."

I swallowed and tried to calm down. "No, thanks."

Winter's eyes twinkled. "Not sure that's good enough for me, though. I want the scoop."

Gent elbowed him. "He clearly isn't ready to talk about it, babe."

"It's just that... I'm not sure..." I realized how stupid I sounded. Gent had mentioned a bike ride. I could do that. "Actually, if you make it clear it's not a setup or anything, I'd still be up for showing him around the local trails."

Tess looked happy at the idea. "You could use some fun. You've been working so hard lately. I only wish I could go, too. Remember when you took me to Portuguese Bend?"

We talked about biking for a little while. Gent and Winter expressed interest in trying it out, so we agreed to go as a group the following Friday on my day off. I couldn't help but wonder if it was something Finn would want to do as well or if he was even allowed to engage in action sports outside of climbing while he was actively shooting a film.

We lingered a long time over coffee and good conversation, but after Tessa's third trip to the ladies' room, I realized she would probably rather walk around than continue being trapped in the booth with us.

The weather was perfect with the typical deep blue sky and warm sunshine Colorado was known for. When we stepped outside the diner, Tess closed her eyes and turned her face to the sun. "God, I love it here," she murmured. "No hazy smog. No horns honking or sirens blaring."

After saying goodbye to Gent and Winter, I looped Tessa's arm through mine and led her toward the market stalls set up in the park in the middle of town. While Saturday mornings in summer were for fruit and vegetable stands, Sunday afternoons were for local crafters.

We meandered through the stalls, stopping here and there to look more closely at various items. Tessa picked out a few baby items, and I bought a small watercolor painting of the sunset painting the granite face of Slye Peak in vibrant reds, oranges, and yellows.

While standing in line at a table selling cold drinks, I glanced across the park at a cluster of teenagers laughing in a cluster under a large shade tree. I recognized Solo from the diner and one of the underage girls I'd kicked out of the bar the other night. But I also saw a man with very familiar body language.

Finn.

My heart sped up as I watched him gesture wildly. His face widened into a huge grin, and he looked... happy. The happiest I'd seen him yet. The kids around him seemed to be riveted to what he was saying, and something about it was different from the fan inter-actions I'd seen him have in town.

"Sheriff?"

I blinked and turned back to the line I was standing in, only to find there was no longer a line. Karen Vetter stood looking at me in anticipation. "Can I get you a cold drink? All proceeds benefit Rockley High athletics."

I swallowed and nodded, stepping forward and reaching for my wallet. "Two bottles of water, please." I glanced over at Finn and the fans surrounding him. "Actually, make that six bottles of water. Thanks, Karen."

"Anytime, Sheriff." She stacked the bottles in a little pyramid for me, and I took them in my arms after handing her the cash.

I found Tess sitting at a nearby picnic table talking to a young mother with a baby. I handed her a bottle of water, offered another to the woman sitting with her, and pointed to Finn. "Be right back."

I wandered over to the group, taking my time in case Finn shot me a *fuck off* glare. My feelings still stung from not hearing from him the past couple of days, even though logically I knew I wouldn't have had time to see him.

The phone works both ways, asshole.

There'd been several times since leaving his warm body the other morning when I'd pulled out my phone to message him, but I'd let doubting voices in my head get the better of me. There were a million reasons this beautiful celebrity wouldn't want anything to do with a boring small-town sheriff, and I wasn't quite sure I could handle catching feelings for him just in time for him to roll back out of here in his fancy sports car, never to be seen or heard from again. Not only that, but I still wasn't sure I could trust him. I'd spent almost twenty years learning over and over again how duplicitous some of the players in LA could be. So many of them were out for themselves or all about their image. They'd do anything to get special treatment, including pretending to be someone they weren't.

Finn's laughter turned to an uncontrolled giggle when one of the teens said something that set everyone off. He was radiant. Even though he had a ball cap on over his stylish hair, I could see the sparkle in his bright green eyes. His lips were pink and wide with laughter, and his perfect white teeth made him look like a model. As he threw his head back, the sun snuck under his ball cap and lit up the spray of freckles over his nose, and I thought right then and there I might actually *hurt* when he left this town without me.

I didn't have words for how he made me feel. Like I was a flat paper bag and he was the *pop-pop-pop* of corn kernels bursting inside. He made me feel warm, excited, full of... something.

I sucked in a breath. Finn turned his head at the sound and caught my eye. Was it possible for a man's face to light up even more? Holy fuck, I was gone for him. I'd come to Aster Valley and fallen for a Hollywood star. This wasn't the way my life was supposed to go.

I cleared my throat and held out the remaining water bottles. "I, uh..."

The teens turned to look at me. Finn took his sweet time sauntering closer. He moved like liquid sex in faded jeans and his plain T-shirt.

I felt sweat pool under my arms and behind my neck.

"Are those for me?" he asked softly.

I swallowed. How could I speak without telling him that I wanted him, that he was perfect, that he was somehow irrevocably *mine*?

I nodded instead.

He took the top two bottles and turned to hand them to Solo, who'd walked over to say hello. "Thanks, Sheriff Stone," Solo said. "Acting's hard work."

I blinked back at Finn, who scraped his teeth over his bottom lip. "I'm, ah... working with these guys on some... stuff." He handed out the rest of the bottles except for one, taking the final water and cracking it open. He took a big slug without ever losing eye contact with me. "What are you up to today? No uniform must mean a day off?"

I looked down at the rumpled hiking shorts I wore. My favorite T-shirt topped off the lazy-ass look with its six-year-old fundraiser logo half-gone from wear. "I look like I belong under a bridge," I muttered.

Finn reached out and put a hand on my chest, directly over my heart. I wanted to lean into his touch and sigh with relief, but I forced myself to remain still. "You look like someone I'd like to haul under a bridge," he said even more softly.

I glanced at him in surprise before looking around to see if we were being watched. Finn started to pull his hand away, but I quickly clapped it to my chest again and squeezed just for the briefest moment before letting it go.

There was nothing left to do but make a big, giant fool of myself. "Uh, I thought... um... uh..." Jesus Christ, how did people do this dating thing? I swallowed and tried again. "I'd like to... ah..." My heart started thundering with embarrassment. I tried to recall some of my law enforcement training. *Steady on, Sheriff.*

Finn's eyelashes fluttered like they, too, were laughing at me. I didn't blame them.

"Dec?"

"Mm?"

He leaned in and deliberately brushed his nose across my cheek until his lips touched my ear. I squeezed my eyes closed and tried to remember a public park boner could get me fired. "Will you please come over tonight so I can suck your—"

"Finn!" Solo called, making me jump back and reach for my sidearm. I quickly shook it off and shot a glare at Finn for distracting me. He only grinned proudly and shot me a wink.

Solo called over again. "We gotta finish before I'm due for my shift at the diner, remember?"

I gathered my wits about me and finally got my head out of my ass. "Let me make you dinner," I offered quickly, before he left to finish... whatever it was he was doing with this group of kids. "I'll text you the address, okay?"

He nodded. "You sure?"

I clenched my jaw for a moment, debating about whether or not to share my thoughts with him. Fuck it. I stepped closer and lowered my voice. "I'm not just interested in the sucking, okay?"

The playful grin melted away as his eyes met mine. He nodded. "Yeah, okay. It's... yeah. Good. I... same."

I reached for his hand just long enough to rub my thumb across the back of it. The sounds of snickering from the group of teens met my ears, but I ignored them. "Seven o'clock."

When I returned to Tessa, she gave me a knowing look. Thankfully, she waited until we were in the car before beginning the third degree.

"You and the Clover kid."

"His name is Finn," I said a little too peevishly. "Sorry."

"It's okay. I just didn't realize you were quite so..." She lifted her hands up and wiggled all her fingers in the air. "With the feelings."

I shrugged. "Not sure there can really be feelings there, but... yeah. I... yeah."

She made all kinds of squishy sweet noises like she was watching puppy videos. "What do you like most about him?" she asked next.

"He's feisty but vulnerable. I can tell he's fighting to figure out who he is underneath all the expectations on him."

Tessa studied me. "Sounds familiar, huh?"

I glanced at her. "What do you mean?"

"You forget we grew up together. I know your family. I know what it was like for you trying to figure out who Declan was outside of all those highbrow Stone brothers."

She was right. It hadn't been easy telling my father, a renowned oncologist at Cedars-Sinai, that I wanted to join the LAPD right out of high school. In fact, he'd been so angry, he'd made me a deal. Get a college degree first, and then if I still wanted to become a cop, he'd support me.

So that's what I'd done. And it had damned near killed him to watch me put on the uniform and put myself at risk every day. When I'd told my parents I was moving from the LAPD to a small county sheriff's office in Colorado, they'd celebrated. "The distance is a small price to pay for your life," my mother had said over and over at the big family dinner she'd thrown. "And if we have to buy a share in a private jet service, then so be it."

Leave it to my mother, who'd inherited a fortune from her own parents, to mention hiring a private plane as if it was as easy as arranging for an Uber.

My brothers, on the other hand, had been supportive despite the same worries. Two of them had followed my father into medicine, another had gone into investment banking, Patrick had become an attorney, and I'd become a police officer. And I'd never regretted it. Not once. Not even when I had to testify against my fellow officers. Maybe, in fact, especially when I had to testify against my fellow officers.

"Not everyone has such a supportive family," I said. "I was lucky."

She made a pensive sound and looked out the window. I remembered too late that hers was one such family. Her parents had insisted on marriage when she'd told them about the pregnancy. "Shit, Tess. I'm sorry. I wasn't thinking."

She shook her head. "No. It's fine."

But it wasn't, and we both knew it.

It started with a sniffle. Before I knew it, she was crying full-on. I whipped the SUV into my driveway and slammed it into Park. "Christ."

She waved a hand through the air. "Pregnancy hormones. Ignore."

"Not possible," I told her before coming around to her side of the car so I could pull her out and hug her as tightly as I could with a giant beach ball between us. "C'mere. I'm so fucking sorry."

She cried even harder and clung to me as tightly as she could. "I just wish... I just wish I had someone like Finn."

It took me a minute to realize she meant she wished she had someone like *I* had Finn. Not that she wanted a man like Finn. I knew she wanted someone to be there for her, care for her, and love on her the way she deserved. Assure her everything was going to be okay.

I brushed my hand over her hair. "Aw, sweetheart. You will. I know you will." I didn't add that I didn't *have* Finn. It wasn't important. She simply didn't want to go through the scary pregnancy and delivery, not to mention parenthood, alone. And there was only so much I could offer her in the way of support.

After getting her into the house and settling her on the sofa with her favorite blanket, a glass of milk, a bag of fresh cookies we'd picked up at the vendor stalls, and the next episode in a sci-fi show she was into, I returned to the kitchen to look through some of my cookbooks. I'd forgotten to ask about any dietary restrictions he might have during a film shoot, so I decided to stick with something relatively light and healthy just in case.

When I was almost ready to head to the market to pick up the necessary items, the doorbell rang. It was Shawn Graham, looking sheepish.

"Hiya, Deputy," I said with a grin, happy to see a face that might make Tess feel better. "How can I help you today?"

He was holding a small handful of wildflowers tied with ribbon. "Oh, uh... is Tessa here?"

I was so happy to see him, I decided to mess with him a little. "Are those for me? You shouldn't have."

He whipped the flowers behind his back. "Back off, Sheriff. You're not pretty enough for flowers."

I let out a laugh. "Please tell me Truman Sweet didn't see you picking flowers on the highway. He'll file a formal complaint, and then I'll have to jail my own deputy for destruction of public property."

He stepped past me when he caught sight of Tess on the sofa. "No, I actually bought these from a stall he had at the market today. It was either wildflowers or a bottle of smoked paprika." His face softened as he handed the flowers to Tess.

She frowned and met his eye. "I'd rather have had the paprika."

His face fell so fast, I laughed again. "She's messing with you."

Tess flashed Shawn a teasing grin, and I let out a sigh of relief. She was going to be okay. I'd make sure of it.

I turned and headed out the door to the market. When I returned, I showered, shaved, and changed into nicer clothes. Nothing fancy, but at least these shorts weren't wrinkled, and the T-shirt had been replaced with a short-sleeve button-down. When I walked back into the living room, Tessa whistled, and Shawn, who was snuggled up with her watching her show, threw me a thumbs-up. I rolled my eyes and continued into the kitchen.

"Am I making enough for four?" I called out a few minutes later. "Shawn, you're welcome to stay and eat with us."

There was no response. When I wandered back to the doorway between the kitchen and living room, I saw Shawn kissing Tessa softly with a gentle hand behind her head. I cleared my throat just to watch Shawn jump away like a guilty teen.

"You staying for dinner?" I asked again. "I have plenty."

Tess glanced between Shawn and me before murmuring something to Shawn and getting up to follow me into the kitchen.

"After Finn gets here, I'm going to, ah... go for a sleepover at Shawn's." She held up a hand. "And before you jump to any conclusions, I'm only doing this to give you and your man child some privacy."

I held my tongue long enough to fake a serious nod. "So generous," I murmured. "How can I thank you for sacrificing yourself this way?"

She punched me hard in the gut with a small fist. "Asshole." Then she turned and walked out of the kitchen to continue her snuggle on the couch while I gasped for breath through my laughter.

14

FINN

Why was I nervous? It was just dinner. And sex.

Please baby Jesus, let there be sex, and lots of it.

I reached out to ring the doorbell and tried not to notice my hand shaking. Great. I was going to look like the young kid he already thought I was.

But when he came to the door, Declan made me feel the opposite of childlike.

"Fucking Christ, I want to strip you naked and tackle you to the ground right here." His voice was low, so I was the only one who could hear it, but the look in his eyes broadcast the sentiment to anyone looking.

I gulped.

"You look amazing, Finn," he continued. "Thank you for coming. I swore to myself not to treat you like a piece of meat, and now here I am with my steak sauce out and my knife sharpened."

"Yes, please," I managed to get out before he grabbed the front of my shirt and hauled me in for a kiss. I almost lost my footing, but Declan's other arm wrapped tightly around my waist to hold me firmly against him. I made a sound of desperate appreciation into his mouth and surrendered to the power of his possessive mouth.

I loved this side of him. I wanted more of it.

"Let the poor man breathe, Declan," a woman's voice called from inside the house. "I want to meet him before you suck all the brain cells out of him."

Declan let me go, but before I could wobble away, he grabbed the sides of my face in his large hands and kissed me again. Then again. "I missed you," he said gruffly before finally letting me go. My heart skipped at his words. I wanted to remind him he'd been the one to leave, but since he'd given me such a warm welcome, I wondered if the point was moot.

My head spun with excitement and a fair amount of confusion, but I definitely knew I wanted to meet the friend of his who'd come to stay with him.

I took a minute to catch my breath and will my dick to deflate before stepping around Declan and introducing myself to the couple in the living room. A timer went off in the kitchen, and Declan muttered a quick apology before rushing after it.

The woman was beautiful, but in a natural kind of girl-next-door way. She had her blonde hair back in a ponytail, and her face was bare of any makeup. Her blue eyes watched me intently as I came closer.

"I've heard so much about you, Finn," she began with a genuine smile. "I'm Declan's friend Tessa."

I was almost positive she'd dropped the f-word in there to send me a message that she was no threat to whatever designs I had on the handsome sheriff. While I appreciated it, I also felt deep in my bones Declan's own sense of honor would keep him from ever being unfaithful to anyone he was with. Assuming, of course, he was with someone. Which of course he wasn't.

"Nice to meet you." I glanced at the deputy I'd already met. "Deputy Graham. Nice to see you again."

He reached out a hand to shake. "Call me Shawn, please. It's nice to see you, too. Glad you're doing okay."

"I should say the same to you since you're the one who was injured that night at the Stanners' place."

Shawn's hand came up to feel for the cut that was already healing. "No big deal. Tess fixed me right up." He shot a smile at Tessa that suddenly clued me in to the situation at hand. These two were interested in each other. I wondered how that would play out when Declan's friend was at least eight months pregnant with another man's baby. Hopefully Shawn wasn't an asshole.

Tess glanced at the deputy. "Would you mind grabbing the bag I packed? It's on my bed."

He jogged off immediately to do her bidding, and she looked after him for a beat with a goofy look on her face before turning to me. "I won't be back until late tomorrow morning. Meanwhile, ask Declan about mountain biking and magic tricks."

I opened my mouth to ask her what she meant, but Declan came in, wiping his hands on a kitchen towel. "Sorry about that. I forgot I'd left the oil heating in the pan. Would you like some wine?"

Suddenly, I was nervous again. "What are you having?"

Tessa clasped her hands together in front of her chest and made a little sound of contentment. "Have so much fun. I'll get out of your hair. Call me if you accidentally set the house on fire. Shawn can probably hook us up with some hot firefighters."

Shawn entered the room with a bag over his shoulder. "Hey. No need for all that. I'll fight your fire."

Tess and Declan exchanged an eye roll before Tess leaned up to peck Dec's cheek. "Night."

She gave me a quick hug before following Shawn out the door. When they were gone, I followed Declan into the kitchen. It was cozy and clean, modern and updated but not too fancy. Something about it put me at ease. I took a seat on one of the stools at the kitchen island. "She seems great," I began.

Declan opened a bottle of wine and poured two glasses before sliding one over to me. "Yeah. She is. I've known her since we were five. We went to school together the whole way through, then she lived in the apartment next door to me the last few years in LA. That's how she met Nick."

I sensed a story there, but I wasn't in the mood to talk about his ex-partner right now. "What's with her and the cute deputy?"

"You think he's cute?" Declan didn't look at me when he asked the question, but I could tell he cared about the answer.

"I meant cute as in puppy dog cute. He's goofy for her. And just so we're clear, earnest young do-gooder isn't my type."

He finally met my eyes. "Then what is?"

Part of me wondered if my answer would change the direction of our evening from one path to another. I chose my words carefully.

"Calm, mature do-gooder with a tendency to get bossy in the bedroom."

Heavy heat filled the air between us like a muggy summer evening on a bayou. It was hard to take in a full breath, and the air felt both alive and oppressive.

"Noted," he finally said with that familiar deep voice that seemed like it was in absolutely no hurry.

He went back to fixing dinner, leaving me shallow-breathed and restless. I watched the planes of his back move. Unfortunately, the shirt he wore covered his ass, so I couldn't stare at that, too. When he turned, I was able to catch a glimpse of his tanned, muscular fore-arms. I'd never felt quite so light-headed from lusting after a man. What was it about him that turned me into a hormonal lust bucket?

Maybe I needed to steer my thoughts away from sex.

"Tessa said to ask you about mountain biking," I began. "Is there a story there?"

Declan turned to smile at me. "Nah. It's just a hobby of mine. One of the reasons I picked Colorado instead of another big city. There are some great trails around here."

"How did you get into it if you're from LA?"

He turned his back to me before answering. "I grew up in Encino. Topanga State Park was practically in my backyard."

Encino. How the hell did he wind up as a cop if he'd grown up with that kind of money? "Oh," I said stupidly. The old feelings of being the poor kid came rushing back. It had been a long time since I'd been that insecure schoolboy in thrift store clothes and the church charity backpack. Free lunch at my school was a choice between a peanut butter sandwich or a bologna one. I never wanted to see either kind again as long as I lived.

"What area did you grow up in?" he asked. It was the natural progression of this kind of conversation.

I considered lying. But I was a grown adult who'd made good. And my mother's situation back then had been a result of her own desperation to leave her borderline abusive parents. Those years of free lunch had also brought our freedom from them. And I'd worked my ass off to make sure I'd never had another free lunch again.

"Watts."

I watched carefully for his reaction. The muscles of his back stiffened, but he continued stirring the food in the pan. It smelled like a delicious veggie stir-fry, and the scent of it suddenly made me realize how hungry I was.

Declan didn't say anything until he was finished with the dish and had plated two deep pasta bowls with rice and the stir fry. After setting the dishes on the kitchen table where he'd already set two place settings, he reached for my hand as if to lead me from the kitchen island to the table.

Only, instead of leading me, he pulled me into a tight hug. His voice was gruff when he finally spoke. "Fuck. How the fuck did you get out of Watts?"

I was beginning to notice his language deteriorated when he was experiencing strong feelings. Knowing he felt that way, that he was worried about me in a way instead of judging me, made my shoulders fall and my breathing steady. I held him just as tightly.

"My mom. She busted her ass to get us out of there."

He pulled back and met my eyes. "It wasn't the show, the acting job?"

I sighed. "Yeah. It was. But I never would have gotten that opportunity without her taking me to as many casting calls as she could find."

Declan's jaw tightened around words he wanted to say but didn't. I could probably have guessed them, so I was relieved he held them back. I didn't want to hear about how horrible my mom was for using her child that way. I'd heard it a million times before. Hell, I'd *thought* it a million times before. But it was an easy criticism to have now that I was richer than god and could barely remember the disgusting smell of that shared bedroom in the house in Watts.

"That explains some things," he said at last, letting me go so we could begin eating.

His words got my hackles up. "Like what?"

Declan shrugged, reaching for the open wine bottle to refill our glasses. "Your loyalty to your mom. Your commitment to acting."

I could tell there were more things he would have added had he not been parsing his words. I wondered at them.

"I owe her everything," I said.

He pursed his lips and stared down into the steaming dish of savory vegetables. "I would imagine you've set her up for life financially."

"Of course. The first thing we did was buy a house." I thought of that first house and the look on her face when the real estate lady had handed my mom the keys. Looking back on it now was almost comical. The house in Mar Vista had been a little three-bedroom ranch house with a postage stamp yard. It had seemed like we'd won the lottery.

"You must have been proud," Declan said gently.

"God, you can't even imagine," I admitted. "It was like seeing the weight of the world lift off her shoulders. That house had a fenced yard out back, and Mom let us get a dog. She insisted on naming him Clover because as far as she was concerned, everything we had we owed to that show."

"And you."

I looked up from the bite I'd just taken of the stir-fry. "Hm?"

"It was also owed to you. They wouldn't have given you the role or the paycheck if you hadn't been good at it."

My face flooded with heat. The food was spicy, so I fanned my cheek with my free hand. "I guess."

Declan studied me for a minute before asking an odd question.

"What did you call the dog?"

"I just told you. His name was Clover."

His lip curved up in a sly grin. "That's not what I asked."

I looked away and took another bite of my food. After chewing and swallowing, I muttered, "Henry Higgins."

I refused to meet his eye. I didn't want to know if he got the reference, and if he did... whether or not he understood my connection to it.

"Mm," he said before going back to his own dinner portion.

Silence sat heavily between us. I'd never met an awkward silence I couldn't fill.

"I felt..."

Declan put his fork down and held up a hand. "Before you say anything, I want you to know I would love to hear it. However, you do not need to explain anything to me or talk about anything you don't want to. I always want to know what you're thinking, and I'd love to learn more about you, but you don't owe me any explanations." He watched me for a beat before continuing. "I judged you that night, Finn. The night you sped up in your fancy car representing everything I'd happily left behind in LA. I know now that was on me. I judged you instead of getting to know you. I'd like to fix that."

I stared back at him. Had anyone in my life ever wanted to get to know the real me? The one who didn't love chasing fame or worrying about public perception? And was it possible he meant it?

Plenty of people in my line of work had warned me away from trusting new people. I knew better than to spill secrets to a stranger. But Declan was... was different. He was the kind of man who practically radiated honor from his every pore.

"I felt like I was never good enough," I admitted. "I had no training, no experience. They'd cast me based on my looks and the fact they could sign me super cheap, at first anyway. Then they had to put up with the results which was a kid who didn't know what a gaffer was or a grip. Or any number of lighting and direction terms. I was constantly being told I was doing it wrong, and I felt like..."

"Eliza Doolittle."

I nodded and let out a little huff of laughter. "Exactly."

Declan grinned. "And poor Henry got all your backtalk and complaints."

"But he never spilled any of my secrets. Henry Higgins was the best friend a lonely gay kid in Hollywood could have ever had. I remember when my agent was negotiating the contract for the fifth season of the show, I demanded permission to allow Henry in my trailer on set." I laughed at the memory. "They were all stunned. I'd never demanded a single thing. Ever. My mom was horrified. She told me to let it go, but I stood my ground."

"Don't mess with a boy and his dog," Declan teased.

"Did you have a dog growing up?"

He nodded. "Several. My mom had a Great Dane named Poe, who wouldn't give the rest of us the time of day. My brothers and I had a motley crew of dogs over the years, but my favorite—my heart dog— was a corgi basset hound mix named Goose. She used to sleep on the pillow above my head."

I had a hard time picturing a lanky, awkward teen version of Sheriff Stone with a little dog curled on the bed above his head.

"Have you thought about getting a dog here in Aster Valley? Seems like you have enough land for it. My agent cautioned me against getting one since I don't have a yard and I travel a lot. But you have plenty of land and presumably don't travel."

Declan studied me again. It was becoming a little eerie. Like maybe there was an entirely different conversation going on between us in his head. Finally, he spoke.

"Do you have enough money set aside to last you and your mom the rest of your life?"

I stared at him in shock. What the fuck was he asking me? Had I gotten him all wrong? Was he interested in my money more than my childhood dog stories?

"I don't see how that's any of your business." I stood up and grabbed my almost empty dish, quickly taking it to the kitchen sink and rinsing it off before trying to remember where I'd set down my keys. I needed to get out of here. The man had just tripped my creep-o meter in a big way.

Before I could turn away from the sink, the sheriff's big body boxed me in from behind. "Slow down," he said with that infuriatingly calm tone. "Let me explain why I was asking before you go off half-cocked."

I shrugged out of his hold. "Get off me."

He stepped back and held up his hands. I made my way over to where I'd kicked off my shoes. There was a bench by the door. I quickly sat down and shoved my foot in the first shoe.

"I was getting around to asking you why you do it. If it's not for money, which I have to think at this point it's probably not, then why do you keep doing something you hate?"

I froze. My heart pounded in my chest like cops were banging on the door of a drug bust. *Police, open up.* I glanced at Declan.

"I don't hate it," I said automatically.

His face stiffened into a resigned disappointment. "Okay. Then please accept my apology for implying otherwise. Would you like a piece of pie?"

He sounded so distant all of a sudden that I wanted to scream and possibly cry. *Open back up, dammit.*

"I don't," I called at his back as he moved toward the kitchen.

"I heard you the first time," he said casually, like it was no big deal. Like it was something other than the live grenade he'd left me holding with the pin pulled.

I wanted him to put the pin back in my grenade. I wanted it so badly. I'd been carrying this pocket-sized bomb for such a long time. I'd gotten so used to carrying it, I'd forgotten all it would take was one person curious enough to pull on the metal loop.

"I don't want to talk about my fucking feelings," I called out. "Or... or work. Or... childhood fucking dogs, dammit! I don't want to make small talk with you. I..." My breathing came faster. Need crawled under my skin, but I wasn't clear on what exactly I needed. "Can't we just fuck? Can't I come here, eat a nice meal, and just... get naked with you? I'd rather have your dick than your psychoanalysis."

I sounded like a brat. Ungrateful and rude. I knew that. But he was holding my pin, and if I didn't do something to distract myself from the grenade I was holding, I was going to drop it and destroy everything.

Declan appeared in the doorway between the kitchen and front room. He looked as calm as ever. Like my angry words hadn't affected him at all.

"Go upstairs to the bedroom on the right and strip down to your underwear. Lie down on my bed and think about a white piece of paper. That's it. Just a white piece of paper. Nothing else." With that, he turned around and returned to the kitchen like he'd just instructed me on how to take the trash out.

I left a Finn-shaped cloud of dust behind me as I raced toward the stairs. Finally, we could stop talking and simply fuck.

15

DECLAN

I took my time cleaning up the dinner dishes and putting the left-overs away. The puzzle pieces of Finn were starting to snap together one after the other, and I finally felt like I could see glimpses of the person he was underneath all the pretense.

He was terrified and lonely. Exhausted and unsure. He'd been trying to navigate this life as a grown adult since the age of ten, if not younger. He'd been the primary breadwinner in his family at an age most kids were learning how to throw a baseball or ride a bike. Thanks to his young mother, he'd been the man of the family long before he'd been a man at all.

Finn Heller needed to let go. He was holding this crazy life together with paper clips and string, and it was wearing him down to the bone. Something had to give, or there wasn't going to be a Finn Heller left underneath the Hollywood celebrity profile much longer.

He was begging for help, only... he didn't realize it. Everything he did seemed to be for other people's happiness. What did he do for his own? And how could I help him see he deserved to start living his life and making his choices for his own happiness instead of everyone else's?

When I finally made my way upstairs to my room, I found him

dead asleep as I'd suspected, sprawled out like a sexy half-naked starfish on my bed. I loved seeing him there among my things. His body was the hottest thing I'd ever seen, but his face in sleep was... breathtaking. The freckles scattered across his nose. The sooty eyelashes brushing his cheeks. The full lips completely relaxed instead of pursing in concentration. I wanted to kiss him and hold him, protect him from the harsh, judgmental world he lived in.

So I did exactly that. I carefully moved him under the covers and stripped myself down before joining him. I pulled him against me and held him close, pressing kisses into his clean hair and murmuring my gratitude that he'd felt comfortable enough to let himself fall asleep in my space with only a little help from the simple meditation I'd given him. But he'd seemed so tired lately, I wondered if there was something else to it than merely exhaustion from work.

My mother had called it "burning the candle at both ends." Was that all this was?

Dark smudges lay hidden beneath his lashes, and his skin looked unnaturally pale. Was he eating enough? Sleeping enough?

I stayed awake for a long time, reviewing the things I'd learned about Finn so far.

He'd been working in secret on a graduate degree involving Shakespeare. He certainly didn't need a graduate degree in anything to continue on his current career path. Unless... unless he wanted to transition into directing or producing? He was still so young, though, and his experience seemed to be mostly television. He had several movie credits to his name, but they'd been either teen flicks, the SEAL movie, a family holiday movie, or the Hallmark romance-type ones. Nothing even remotely like a Shakespeare film.

And why keep it secret? What was he afraid of?

Suddenly, I remembered what he'd called his Shakespeare program. *"The treasure of my fucking heart."* It was the one thing he kept just to himself. Something for him and him alone.

Solomon and his friends had been holding paperback copies of *Hamlet*.

"No wonder you looked so damned happy," I murmured against

the warm skin of his temple before pressing another kiss there. God, he felt good in my arms. In my bed. I wanted to keep him there forever. Let him rest and then wear him out again. Over and over again.

I reached for my phone on the bedside table and searched one-handed for articles about Finn. I'd been avoiding looking him up online since he'd come to town, but now I was desperate to know more. It only took a few minutes before I was disgusted on his behalf. The invasion of privacy, the ridiculous speculations about his personal life, the insistence he was a one-note, that he only knew how to be Chip Clover and couldn't act his way out of a paper bag, forgetting or ignoring completely that he'd actually won an Emmy Award for his guest appearance on *Saturday Night Live* at the age of sixteen in addition to the Emmys he'd won on *Cast in Clover*.

I had to laugh at myself. It had only taken a week or so for me to go from thinking he was the most spoiled actor on earth to defending not only the man himself but also his acting skills.

"Wha's so funny?" Finn slurred against my chest.

"You're good at what you do," I admitted sheepishly.

"Drooling?"

I brushed his hair back so I could see his eyes. He was adorably sleep-dazed, but he had more color in his face now. "No, acting."

He leaned back and narrowed his eyes at me. "How would you know? You didn't even know who I was at first."

It was time to come clean. "That's not entirely true."

Finn scrambled to sit up so he could face me. I missed the warmth of his skin against mine, but the view was spectacular. His hair was a rumpled nest, and his face was pink where it had been pressed against my chest. "You've watched my stuff?"

My face was probably pink, too, if the heat in my cheeks was any indication. "Is there anyone alive who hasn't seen *Cast in Clover*?"

I sounded like an ass, so I quickly continued. "Yes, I've seen it. All million seasons. I also watched the Hallmark movie. The gay one you did for them."

His face lit up, making my stomach swirl a little. "You saw me in *The Holiday Hiccup*?"

I nodded. "You were so fucking hot in that movie, I'm surprised Hallmark released it. I..." My face heated even more. "I may have ah... used one of those scenes as inspiration when I jacked off that night."

Finn moved over to straddle me. Our cotton-covered dicks brushed against each other before he settled his ass on my thighs. I clutched at his hips before running a hand up the sexy bumps of his abdomen.

He grinned. "Tell. Me. Everything. What scene? And if you say Derek Wooten was hot, too, I'll have to school you on what an ass he is in real life."

I licked my lips as the image came screaming back into my mind. "No. Not him. You. It was... god. You were sitting on a bench in the snow. Your cheeks were pink from the cold, and your eyes were bright. You... you had this crinkle between your eyes."

Finn's face softened. "I was worried about my little sister. She was lost in the woods, and I couldn't find her. My parents were going to kill me if she didn't come back by Christmas dinner."

"You looked lost and so fucking sweet. Then you shifted on the bench, and I saw the outline of your huge fucking dick." His jaw dropped, and I started laughing. "I pictured stripping you down, throwing you over the back of that bench, and railing you right there in the snow with my hand around that big cock."

"Oh my god, you pervert! There I was worried about poor Polly, and all you could think about was getting your dick wet."

He was so damned cute, I couldn't hold back the bubble of laughter at his indignant pout. "I think her name was Molly. How worried could you have possibly been if you didn't even know your own sister's name? Besides, I was offering you a comfort fuck. Like a special kind of Saint Bernard. Offering dick aid in the snowy woods."

Finn snorted and tackled me, throwing me backward on the bed. We laughed and wrestled around until I'd wrapped my bigger legs around his and pinned him to the bed. One of my hands held his wrists above his head, and the other grasped the front of his neck gently.

"I want you," I breathed. "I've never wanted anything more."

We were both panting from the exertion. I could feel the flutter of his heart beating beneath my fingertips. His eyes flared at my words. "You offering me dick aid, Sheriff Stone?"

I leaned in and licked along his collarbone with the tip of my tongue. "You seem like a man in need," I murmured against his damp skin. "And I'm here to protect and serve."

Dropping open-mouthed kisses down the center of his chest, I moved slowly down his body. As soon as I released his wrists, his hands came down to thread through my hair. "That feels incredible," he whispered.

All I wanted was to make him feel good. To make him feel like the most important person in the world. He was used to being in the limelight, but that wasn't at all the same thing as being treated as special just for being himself.

When I got down to the band of his short navy blue boxer briefs, I noticed several spots of precum had soaked through, making the fabric even darker. The sight of it made me grab my dick and squeeze. Fuck, he made me desperate for him. Just the sight of that bulge behind the blue cotton had me salivating.

Finn's fingers tightened in my hair as I nuzzled my face in his junk and inhaled. I reached around and grabbed the elastic band over his ass, yanking the underwear down until he was naked underneath me. There was his tidy little patch of pubic hair that made me want to laugh, as if his fancy Hollywood stylist would consult with him on even this part of himself.

I traced the shape lightly with my fingers. Goose bumps came up on his inner thighs, and I dropped down to kiss the tender skin there before sucking one of his balls into my mouth. His gasp filled the room, quickly followed by a groan as I worked my tongue around it. After licking and sucking and exploring for a little while, I lifted my head up to meet his eyes. They were glazed over, and his cheeks were flushed blotchy red. His hair was still a mess, and his lips were wet.

Fucking Christ.

I lurched up to take his mouth in mine. His fingers grabbed my head and held me tight to him for the kiss. His legs wrapped around my back as if he didn't want to let me go. The feeling was completely mutual. This man had breezed into town and bewitched me out of the clear blue sky.

I hadn't been expecting him. I wasn't, in fact, ready for anything like him. But here he was, and something inside of me was begging me to hold on tight with both hands.

"Want you inside me," he mumbled without stopping the kiss. "Need it. Need you. Please."

I kissed him for a few beats longer, enjoying the soft sweet taste of his mouth. But I finally pulled away and leaned over to grab a condom and lube from my bedside table. "Do you want to top me?" I asked, hoping like hell he'd say no. It wasn't that I didn't want to bottom for him—I did. I wanted to do everything with him. But right now, I wanted to bury myself so deep inside of him, I ached with it.

"Not this time. Is that okay?" he asked. Sweetest man ever.

I heaved a silent sigh of relief and nodded. "More than." I noticed a crinkle of worry between his eyes. "Hey." I drew my thumb along the crease. "What's going on?"

He swallowed and opened his mouth to say something, but no words came out. Then he tried again. "This isn't... this isn't a casual hookup for me, and I just..." He turned away from me and blew out a nervous breath. "I guess I just wanted you to know that. I don't... have sex often. I mean, I... sometimes have people blow me or whatever. Like, casually... *Ugh.*" He groaned and closed his eyes, shooting a hand into his hair in frustration. "This is so embarrassing."

I gently removed his hand from his hair and placed it on my chest. "You can tell me anything."

His face flamed deep red. "Never mind."

I shook my head. "No. Tell me what you're thinking or this doesn't go any further. If you can't trust me with your thoughts, you probably shouldn't trust me inside your body."

Why did I sound like an after-school special? I tried to soften the bossy-father tone. "Please, Finn. I want to know what you're thinking and feeling. And just so you know, this isn't casual for me. It hasn't been from the very beginning. I can't see how anything between us could be more than temporary, but it definitely doesn't feel casual to me."

The tension seemed to bleed out of him, and he smiled weakly up at me. "That's how I feel, too. Exactly. I just didn't want you to think..."

"That I was one of a million people you let into your bed. Into your body."

He bit his bottom lip and nodded. "I don't trust people easily."

It made sense. Anyone lucky enough to get Finn Heller into bed might be tempted to turn it into an opportunity, especially if it was a onetime thing.

"I hope you know you can trust me," I said as sincerely as I could.

He flapped his hand in the air between us. "Pfft. If there's anyone who's definitely not going to talk to a reporter about me, it's you. I'm not worried about that."

"Then what are you worried about?"

Finn met my eyes, and I suddenly knew the answer to my question. He was afraid of rejection. He was scared I was going to walk away. Again. The realization and the vulnerability in his eyes made my throat tighten.

"I'm here. I'm not leaving. You're not leaving. I promise." My words were thick and rough. "I promise."

"You said last time—"

I cut him off because I couldn't stand to hear it. "I... I got a call out, and then... things got crazy. And my head... I second-guessed myself, Finn. I..."

"Before that. You left. After I asked you about LA."

The memory of that conversation set my teeth on edge. "I thought you'd had that house party. I told you."

"You could have asked me about it."

True, but that would have required a level of maturity I hadn't had after he'd sucked me into a mind-melting orgasm. "You said you'd hooked up with that smarmy sidekick of yours."

Finn's face relaxed into a smirk. "I lied."

"Thank Christ," I said in a whoosh of breath before I could stop myself.

His grin turned even more smug. "I don't mind a jealous sheriff. It's kinda nice, actually."

I scowled at him. "It's not nice for me. I felt sick when I thought of you with that poser."

He laughed. "Poser? The eighties called, they want their sick burns back."

Finn's grin was irresistible. I leaned in to nip at it. "I was born in the eighties, punk."

"Old man alert," he said on a laugh. I kissed him some more until we were back to panting and humping against each other.

His body was perfect, all smooth muscles and unblemished skin. *Unblemished skin.* I blinked. "Where are your tattoos?"

He furrowed his brow. "What tattoos? Oh, my arms? Those are temporary ones for the film. They'll put a new set on tomorrow."

I stared at his bare arms, trying to reconcile the concept of temporary tattoos to the ink that had made its home on his skin all week. "Wow, that's... that's incredible. I thought they were real."

"Not good for business, as my mom says. Takes too much extra time in the makeup trailer. Honestly, I think they only decided to give them to my character because I look like such a child. I'm not believable as a cop without some kind of hint of danger. Not sure the floral motifs are great for that, but they don't pay me to have opinions about such things. One less item for me to have to make a decision about."

I lifted up one naked arm and began kissing along the pristine skin, enjoying the few freckles scattered here and there that were only visible this close up.

I didn't want to talk about the film anymore. I didn't want Finn Heller *the actor* in bed with me. I wanted Finn Heller the sweet, semi-insecure man who picked the zucchini out of his stir-fry to eat first and who made a little *mmm* sound every time he took a sip of cold water.

"Lie back and let me make the decisions for a while," I said. His eyes were molten, a rich, dark green that said so many things without saying a word. As Finn's body relaxed into the bed, I continued exploring his skin with my mouth and hands.

With every pass of my lips and fingertips, his dick got harder and his breathing shallower. By the time I slicked up a couple of fingers and began toying with his ass, he was making sounds that went straight to my cock. He was tight and hot, just like the other night when I'd been inside him, but something about this time was different.

We knew where we stood. There were feelings involved. Even if this didn't turn into anything other than a temporary fling, it was more than a one-night stand. More than a meaningless hookup with a stranger.

"Tell me what you like." My voice sounded rough with need. I needed to be inside him, but I also needed to make it good for him.

"I like..." He swallowed. "I like it when you hold me down. I like it when..." He closed his eyes as one of my fingers brushed against just the right spot inside him. "Oh god. Dec. Don't make me use my brain right now. Just fuck me. Hard."

I flipped him onto his stomach and yanked his hips up, knocking his legs apart with one of my own. One of my hands pressed between his shoulder blades to tell him to keep his face down before I grabbed both of his wrists and placed his hands on the rails of my headboard. "Hold."

His long fingers gripped the slats with white knuckles as his entire body shuddered beneath me. I brushed my hard dick through the furrow between his cheeks and enjoyed every bit of the resulting groan out of him.

"I want to hear you," I murmured behind his ear. "I want to hear you beg and scream for me. I want to hear how much you like having your hole stretched out on my cock. Do you understand?"

He shuddered again and nodded. "Yes," was all he said.

"And you will tell me to stop if anything hurts or is uncomfortable."

"Yes."

I leaned up and pressed a long kiss to the side of his head, inhaling the now familiar scent of his shampoo. "Good boy."

The noise that came out of Finn's throat made my dick jump against his ass. He liked the praise. *Noted.*

I pressed my dick against his ass again and again and enjoyed Finn's attempts to push back against it despite his limited range of motion.

"Not yet," I murmured against his back as I kissed down his spine. I moved my fingers back to his hole and played with his rim, running my thumb in circles but never pressing inside. It made him crazy with need. His breathing shallowed even more, and his whimpers came closer together.

"Dec. Declan. Dec," he chanted. "Please. Now. Need. Please."

His voice was slurred against the bedsheet where his head was turned to the side. His cheeks were flushed, and his eyes lay closed. The sooty eyelashes I loved so much fluttered against freckled cheeks.

"You're so fucking beautiful," I told him for the millionth time before finally pressing my thumb inside him.

He arched and keened. I quickly replaced my thumb with two long fingers so I could find and rub his gland. With my other hand, I reached around to stroke his cock and noticed it was already leaking like crazy.

"I'm going to come," he warned.

"No you're not," I said as sternly as I could. I grasped the base of his cock and squeezed. "Stop now."

"Oh god. Oh. Oh goddd."

Finn was writhing beneath me, prickly and restless from being edged, when I finally suited up and pushed inside him with my dick.

"*Fuck,*" I groaned. The feeling was indescribable. I lay over his damp, warm back and wrapped both arms around his front. My lips found the side of his neck, and I sucked on a spot while I tried not to come right away. "You feel... Baby, fuck. I've never... god. I can't..."

I didn't have words for this. I felt drunk and high. Anchored and untethered all at once. One of Finn's hands had let go of the bed rails to clutch onto the hand I had pressed against the center of his chest. Our fingers formed a tight twist like a desperate pretzel.

It was a moment more intimate than I could ever remember having with another person in bed.

"Please don't leave," he said. I wasn't sure if I'd misunderstood him. Did he mean leave his body? This bed? I didn't have the brainpower to figure it out, even when he said it again. "Stay. Please."

As if I was going anywhere.

I made a tentative thrust, and we both groaned loudly. Thank god Tessa had left for the night. There was no way I could stay quiet when I felt this amazing.

"More," Finn breathed.

I moved my free hand up into his hair, using it to move his head so I could kiss him on the mouth. He made a hungry sound when my lips met his. We kissed and fucked and kept clinging to each other's hands like shipwreck survivors until I'd shoved him so far up the bed, his head had to tilt to keep from banging against the headboard.

I needed more. More of him. More time inside of him. Closer. I needed... I needed to be closer to him. I pulled out and grabbed him, flipping him onto his back and yanking him back down the bed. Then I bent his legs up until his knees were next to his ears, and I thrust back into him, locking eyes with that dark green intensity.

Finn screamed and threw his head back as my dick hit a good spot. He begged for more. Harder. And I gave him everything I had. I hooked my arms under his shoulders and held on tight until his leaking dick finally shot all over his belly and he shouted my name to the roof.

"You're so fucking good," I grunted, thrusting a few more times, enjoying the last tight squeeze of his body before my own orgasm slammed into me. I groaned and shook, pressing my release as deep inside him as I could, despite knowing the condom was there. When my orgasm subsided, I tried not to crush him. I supported most of my weight on my arms and kissed him gently on the cheeks, the eyelids, the forehead, the lips. I murmured words of praise and gratitude, unsure of whether or not he could hear and process them or if he was in his own little afterglow world.

"You're so fucking beautiful. Responsive. God, you make me feel so good. Your body is amazing, and the noises you make... Finn... fuck. You're... so fucking sweet. Thank you."

His green eyes were clear when he met my gaze. I'd never seen a more heavenly sight in my entire life. He looked like a damned angel, fucked out and boneless in my bed.

"Can we go again?" he asked with a straight face.

I probably looked like a suffocating fish before a smirk appeared on his sexy-as-fuck lips and clued me in to the joke.

I pinched his ass. "Yes, tiny newborn baby, *you* can go again. I, on the other hand, will need a Gatorade, a vitamin B shot, some physical therapy, and possibly a bump of coke to go again anytime soon."

His laughter was magnetic. He looked so damned relaxed and happy, I almost wanted to pat myself on the back. Mission accomplished. If all it took to make him this way was fucking him into next week, sign me the hell up.

I leaned down to kiss his laughing mouth, which turned into a longer make-out session than I'd intended. When we were done, we were both covered in cum and lube.

"Come on," I said, hopping up and reaching for him. "Shower time."

I stared at him like a pervert as he walked in all his naked glory to my bathroom. His body was fucking amazing, which wasn't surprising considering his livelihood, but was still something I wasn't quite used to. After I started the water, I pulled him in for more kissing. It got pretty handsy until I realized steam was fogging all around us.

I adjusted the water and led him into the big tiled shower stall. It wasn't anything fancy, but it was big enough for two, and the water pressure from the large rain-style shower head was amazing. Finn groaned as he stepped under the hot spray.

After taking my time washing every square inch of him as diligently as possible, we were as desperate to come as we'd been half an hour earlier. I jacked us off with soapy hands as I growled dirty words into his ear. Finn clung to me to keep from sliding to the floor in a boneless puddle, and I had to practically pour him into bed after drying him off with a fluffy towel.

"Sleep," I told him when I caught him fighting the pull of the soft bed and comfortable sheets.

"Don't want to wake up again and find you gone," he admitted softly.

I brushed the floppy damp hair back from his forehead. "I promised you I wouldn't leave. And if I get called out on an emergency, I'll wake you and tell you what's going on, okay? I promise."

He reached up and ran a fingertip down the center of my forehead to the tip of my nose. "You're not real. None of this is real."

Finn's voice was soft and sleepy. It tugged at my heart. I leaned in and nuzzled his neck. "Sleep. I'm worried about you. You seem worn-out."

He lifted an eyebrow as if to ask, *Whose fault is that?* "Tomorrow we film the tyrolean traverse scene at Tempter's Chimney. My climbing trainer isn't going to be there for it, so I'm worried. That's all."

"You've filmed those kind of scenes before. In *Cast in Clover* season like... eight, I think, you did a tyrolean traverse over that raging river..." I let my words die off as I realized what I'd just accidentally revealed.

Suddenly, Finn Heller was wide-awake. He bolted upright in bed and poked me with a pointer finger right in the sternum. "Spill it, Sheriff McLying-Liarpants. Every single detail. And don't you dare leave anything out."

I played stupid. "Spill what? I already told you I'd watched it."

His grin was nearly feral. "I didn't realize you'd watched it enough to know specific episodes! You little faker. Acting like you had no idea who I was. I almost believed you, too."

I sighed and threw myself back on the pillow dramatically. "Everyone knows who you are. That doesn't mean—*mpfh*!"

He jumped on top of me and slammed his mouth down on mine, kissing me with renewed enthusiasm. My lips were damn near chapped at this point, and my balls were definitely done for the night. But god, his body felt good on mine, and my hands didn't mind another exploration session. We kissed and made out for a while longer before he pulled away laughing.

"Sheriff Clover-Fan. Who knew? Me. I knew. You absolute faker. I still can't get over it. Tell me what your favorite parts were. Wait. Let me guess. You liked it when I got arrested for breaking into the school to steal my science paper."

I huffed out a laugh. "Served you right, punk."

Finn raised a teasing eyebrow. "The cop sucked me off in my trailer after we filmed that scene."

Suddenly, it wasn't funny anymore. Finn must have seen something change in my face because he put a hand to my chest. "Woah. *Woah*, big guy. I was joking. He flirted with me and tried to kiss me. My mom walked in and interrupted us. Then she threatened to call the real cops on him even though we were both legal. Calm down. Besides, he was an actor. Not an actual police officer."

I sighed. "I'm making a mental list of people I need to punch. Except I'm obviously not going to punch anyone. But I can give them a very stern look." I gave him my stern look to show him I was serious.

We fell asleep laughing in each other's arms.

And it was so fucking good. I never wanted it to end.

Which meant I was terrified.

16

FINN

When I arrived at work on Monday morning with a belly full of bacon and eggs Declan had made just for me, I felt like I was carrying the world's most exquisite secret. I'd had mind-blowing sex with Declan Stone. Sheriff Stone had held me in those big burly arms of his all night long. He'd called me beautiful again and again. He'd told me I was sexy, and he'd worked hard to make me feel good over and over and over until I felt like a puddle of sticky honey begging for him to lap me up.

Declan Stone was a generous and diligent lover. And he had a big fucking dick that felt—

"What the fuck?"

I spun around and nearly dropped the two paper coffee cups I'd picked up on my way through town. Tomo, my makeup tech, had a thing for a caramel latte but rarely treated himself to it since he was saving up for a nicer apartment back in LA.

Kix stared at me like I'd turned into a green, scaly monster since I'd seen him last.

"What? You almost made me drop my coffee," I said, moving up the steps of the trailer.

"Is that a hickey on your neck?" Kix asked with a dramatic gasp. "Like, from a human other than yourself?"

He followed me into the trailer, and I tried to hide my smug grin. Tomo was already in there waiting for me. I could hear him chatting with someone. As soon as I stepped fully inside the trailer, I saw who he was talking to.

"Mom?" I squeaked.

"There you are. I was worried sick. Come here and give me a hug." She moved toward me in a cloud of familiar perfume. I handed the drinks tray to Tomo and wrapped my arms around her slender frame.

Lola Heller had always been a gorgeous woman by any standard, but now that she had plenty of money and lived an easy lifestyle, she was even more lovely. Part of me thought it was simply a matter of growing into her beauty, but maybe it was something else, something more mundane like a high-quality skin care regimen. Either way, she was undeniably beautiful, and she turned heads wherever she went.

She was also charming as hell. My mother could talk anyone into anything and make them think it was their idea. It was both a blessing and a curse.

"What are you doing here?" I asked when she finally pulled away. Her hands clutched my arms as she gave me a mother's assessing once-over. Her eyes immediately spotted the mark Kix must have seen, because they narrowed for a split second. Thankfully, she kept her opinions to herself about it.

"Iris called and said you might like having me here for the next few days because of your call schedule."

I stared at her, unblinking. My agent was behind this? "Why would I need you here?"

She waved a hand in the air. "I didn't say need, honey. I said want. You know how you get when the call schedule gets demanding. I guess she was a little worried you're not taking good care of yourself. And I can see now she was right. You look like you've barely slept. Have you lost weight?"

I was suddenly unreasonably angry. When Declan had gotten

close to the subject of my mother last night, I'd felt defensive. My mom had busted her ass to get us away from her toxic parents. She'd done everything she could to support and protect me from people in the industry who might have taken advantage of me along the way. In fact, she'd spent my very first paycheck on a lawyer to protect me, to protect *us*, from predators in the business.

But now that she was here, I saw so much of her through a new light. I was twenty-four years old and my mommy had just shown up at my workplace to "manage" me. It was untenable. I was horrified.

For some reason, I wanted to call Declan and ask him how I should handle it, but that only made me feel less in control of my own life. I didn't need anyone. I needed to handle my own shit.

"Kix, Tomo, would you mind giving us a few minutes, please?"

After they left the trailer, I turned to my mom. "I can't have you here. Thank you for your concern, but you have to see how inappropriate this is. I'm no longer a child actor, Mom. You can't just show up on set when I'm working."

"Iris told me you'd refused to bring Alix to Colorado with you. Why?"

I pictured my personal assistant, a young woman I couldn't imagine living without most of the time. She'd become one of my closest friends over the three years she'd been working for me. But I hated being seen as a diva on set. I didn't like showing up with "people."

"I gave her a few weeks off," I explained. "She went to Maine with her parents and siblings. I guess they have a house there or something."

She frowned. "Honey, you can't expect to be able to manage a starring role like this without some support."

"I've done it before." I didn't add that I'd done it many times before. "Also, I have plenty of support on set, and I have Kix here for moral support."

It sounded as lame out loud as it had sounded in my head. Besides, I still needed to ask Kix about the house party at New Year's.

"I'd feel more comfortable if I stayed at least for a few days. We can catch up and have a few nice meals. I'm sure you aren't eating well. You always forget meals when you're filming."

She wasn't wrong, but I'd made a strong effort to manage my nutrition this time around since so many of the scenes involved physical exertion. Plus, I had a trainer working me out every day to keep my physique in top form for the shirtless climbing scenes.

I knew asking my mother to leave would be akin to waving a red flag in front of her, so I tried another tack. "Mom, I think a nice dinner out sounds great. There's an upscale steak place in Steamboat Springs. It'll take us less than an hour to drive there, and you can check out the shopping."

Her face relaxed into a smile. "That sounds perfect. Ken Whittier has a place in Steamboat. I've always wanted to check it out."

I gestured toward the door of the trailer. "I'm going to have someone show you to my chalet so you can relax until I'm done with the shoot today, alright? Get some rest and take your time getting ready. I'll be there to change clothes after five."

She nodded and leaned in for a kiss to my cheek. "I missed you. Thank you for not telling your old mother to get lost."

I couldn't hold back a snort. "You're the last person I'd describe as an old mother, and you know it."

She grinned. "You fell for my trap. You're so easy."

I laughed and told her to stop fishing for compliments. When she finally left, Kix and Tomo came back in. Tomo got right to work, preparing me for the first shoot while Kix asked me what was up with my mom showing up on set.

"You know how she is," I said without elaborating. "I'm going to take her out to a nice dinner tonight and hope she gets bored enough to leave tomorrow."

Kix made himself comfortable on the sofa while I sat in the straight-backed makeup chair by the kitchen counter where Tomo's kit was laid out.

"Now will you tell me about the hickey?" Kix asked with a knowing grin. "Tell me it wasn't that sexy firefighter. I licked him first, so he's mine. Forgot his name, though. Shame."

I shook my head. "Not a firefighter." If I wanted the entire cast and crew of *Gold Rats* to find out about my private time with the sheriff of Rockley County, I'd spill the beans to Kix. Since I didn't, I kept my trap shut.

"Who, then? You didn't even come out with us last night."

Tomo's ears were like a cat's. They seemed to swivel toward the juicy details. The man was quiet as a mouse, but he heard all the best gossip on set. Thankfully, I'd never heard him repeat any of it.

"Did you go to the Roadhouse again?" I asked, trying to get him to forget about my mysterious hickey-maker.

"Don't change the subject."

"If you don't want to talk about that, then let's talk about New Year's," I suggested calmly, as if I'd mentioned planning a trip to the grocery store.

Kix glanced at Tomo and then down at his lap. "Yeah. A bunch of us went to the Roadhouse. Logan flirted with this hot set of twins. I thought they were going to suck him off right there in the booth. Someone said they were barely eighteen, though, so he freaked and left early."

I watched him from the corner of my eye, trying not to move my face as Tomo did his work to cover up my freckles for the camera. "Mm-hm."

Kix glanced at me and then away. "We can talk about New Year's another time."

I stared at him for a minute, but he didn't look back. I started to get a sneaking suspicion that there wasn't a misunderstanding about the NYE thing. That the misunderstanding was me still trusting this guy.

Tomo moved silently around me. His long fingers brushed various products across my skin to make me look sweaty, bruised, and dirty until he finally declared me ready for my first call. With one last glance between the oddly silent Kix and me, he left the trailer.

Kix opened his mouth, but I didn't have time for this conversation. It was going to be a shitshow. Besides, I was already pushing the schedule, and I hated being late for a call. This morning's first scene was the tyrolean traverse, and it would demand all of my attention. "Not now," I muttered, ducking into the back room of the trailer to change into the clothes the wardrobe assistant had left for me there. It consisted of a filthy red tank top with several rips in it and a pair of khaki cargo pants in the same state. This scene came after my character had already raced through the woods, fallen down a ravine, and scrambled across a boulder field. Thankfully, the pants were deceptive. They looked like tight-fitting cotton cargo pants, but they were actually made from a stretchy material that allowed me to climb better than regular pants would have.

Without my climbing trainer there, the rope work was being managed by two production assistants who'd been hired specifically for their climbing experience and ability to help with the technical aspects of these scenes.

I still didn't trust them the way I trusted Kramer. He'd been overseeing my climbing for years, but his mother was having a medical procedure and he needed to be back in LA helping her through it.

We'd planned for this, but it was still a departure from the routine. It still meant the rope work for the tyrolean had been set up by PAs who weren't necessarily expert at it.

When I arrived at the location of the shoot, I greeted the two PAs with a smile. "Hi, Sara, Bo. How are you two doing today? Are we ready to traverse this bad boy?"

The first scene involved my character realizing that when he rescued Crystobell's character, he'd need a way to get her across a deep ravine. He had to assume she might be hurt or unconscious, and even if she wasn't, her character didn't know how to rock climb. The scene entailed my character setting up the tyrolean traverse as quickly as possible. These action scenes had a sense of urgency to them since my character was racing against the clock to get Crys's character out of the mountaintop cave before it detonated.

The first part of the scene went smoothly. I set an anchor at the top of the eastern cliff and rappelled down one side of the rock face to the floor of the ravine below. The sun was shining, and the helicopter noise drowned out the nervous thump of my heart. I got in character and focused on the scene.

I am the rock, and the rock is fearless.

My muscles were warm and loose by the time I hit the ground and hustled over to start the climb up the western face of the ravine, pulling the trailing rope with me that I would anchor at the top to create the first part of the tyrol. Because there wouldn't be a top rope in this scenario, I had to lead climb which took longer since it involved placing anchors as I went. The problem came when Nolan kept shouting, "Cut!" and insisting I speed up the pace to increase the sense of urgency in the scene.

He was standing in the bucket of a cherry picker several yards away from me with the DP, Director of Photography, Joel Wilson.

"There's only so much I can do," I insisted, wondering why the hell he couldn't fix some of this in postproduction. There would be simple ways to edit these scenes to make it look like I was going the speed he wanted.

Joel said, "I'd rather him place fewer anchors. It would look less secure and increase the tension."

"It wouldn't just look less secure," I insisted. "It would *be* less secure."

Joel ignored me. "Let's get a shot of him falling back so one of the anchors has to catch him."

Nerves jangled in my stomach. I was hot and thirsty now, and the sun that had been lovely and warm was beginning to make me irritable and itchy.

While they discussed it, I triple-checked the anchors in reach. If I was going to test them, they had damned sure better work. The most solid cam in reach could still fail if the momentum from my fall placed enough force on it to crumble the rock around it. These weren't meant for deliberate falls. They were oh-shit-last-chance fail-safes.

I moved down and added another nut near the cam below my chosen one and quickly created a "sliding X" anchor with some ropes to self-equalize or spread the weight and risk between two set points.

The lower cam and the newly placed nut together would be more secure as a backup in case the main cam failed. I quickly climbed back up to the main cam and waited for the decision I knew was coming.

"Let's do the anchor fall," Nolan called. "Joel is right. We can use it in post to make up for the lack of tension in the pace of the climb."

Joel called out some direction, and we proceeded to shoot my "fall" for three takes. Thankfully, the main cam held for all three falls. By the time I'd pulled myself back onto the rock after the third take, my muscles were screaming and my body was bruised.

"Okay, climb the rest of the way up and let's get to the next part of the scene," Nolan called. I couldn't help but laugh. He made it sound so easy.

I would have asked for a ride in the cherry picker, but it didn't go that high, and it would have taken me longer to unclip than it did to climb to the top of the ridge.

Once I was there, I quickly tightened the ropes and created my second tyrolean anchor. Thankfully, we had a hidden bolt in the rock, so I only had to make it look like I was using a sketchy boulder as an anchor. As soon as the ropes were ready, I prepared to clip in and pull myself across the high traverse to the other side.

And that's when everything went to shit.

The wind picked up, and the ropes began swinging. The helicopter got too close and made it worse. Trying to pull myself along the ropes was hard enough in perfect conditions, but trying to do it with the ropes swinging in the wind was damned near impossible. I advised them to stop the shoot due to the worsening conditions but got an immediate *no*. Nolan and Joel looked positively orgasmic at the resulting film and told me to take off my helmet again. I'd known there would be times on the climb I'd have to remove my helmet since my character lost his in one of the falls, but with the conditions like this, it was a stupid risk.

I was angry and bitter at the situation I'd gotten myself into. I felt guilty for not looking out for myself better in the contract, and I vowed to fire Iris for allowing this to happen, too. No one should be out here without a helmet on rope work that hadn't even been installed by climbing experts. Production should have brought in a replacement for Kramer to oversee this shoot. Moreover, no one should be on ropes in these conditions at all.

But all of that was pointless to worry about. The more time I hung there suspended over a deep rocky ravine arguing about the conditions, the more at risk I was for an accident.

I pulled off my helmet and lowered it to the cherry picker on one of the ropes I had dangling from my rigging. They'd use it to send the helmet back up to me after getting the shot.

After running my fingers through my hair to get rid of helmet head, made moot with the next gust of wind, I called out for them that I was ready. When I heard the call to start, I grabbed the rope and pulled hand over hand with as much muscle as I could, gritting my teeth and fighting the wind to get to the other side. I focused on nailing the shot in one take. Thankfully, I did it. As soon as Joel yelled, "Cut," I grabbed for the ropes one of the production assistants tossed me to clip in for some extra protection before climbing up onto the ridge and detaching from the tyrol.

That's when the next gust of wind hit me square in the chest and tumbled me right off the edge again. I scrambled to grab for the tyrolean ropes, but they hit the back of my hand at top speed as I tumbled past them. Thankfully, the new anchor rope attached to my harness caught, and I swung quickly against the side of the ravine, scraping my face, my bare shoulder, and my elbow against the rough granite. The nasty metallic screech of the carabiners and chocks on my rigging being caught between my body and the rock face made my teeth hurt.

I hung there for a second, stung and shocked while the adrenaline flooded my system, and I vaguely heard the screams of the production assistants at the top and the director and DP down in the cherry picker.

Fuck, that had hurt.

I closed my eyes for a minute to catch my breath. My body jerked upward as Sara and Bo began hauling me back up by the ropes attached to my harness. The twin looks of horror on their faces made my stomach drop, reminding me just how close I'd come to falling to my death. If they hadn't given me the extra protection of the top ropes...

"Get the jeep," Bo called to Sara, all business now. "The hospital is on the north edge of town. I have it in my phone."

It was on the tip of my tongue to tell them I didn't need the hospital, but I was afraid if I opened my mouth, my voice would break. I was a trembling mess, but I'd be damned if I'd let it show.

I didn't say a word, only climbed back onto the ridge with Sara and Bo's help. Bo pulled off the zip-up hoodie he was wearing. "You're shaking. Probably shock. Put this on."

I winced as I tried to put my arms through the soft sleeves. Blood splotched the fabric, so I made a mental note to replace the jacket for him. He was right. I was freezing suddenly.

After getting the jacket over my tank top, I turned to follow him to the jeep but noticed the set medic racing toward us in another vehicle. She jumped out of the SUV and hurried over to me with her big kit bag. "You're fine. I saw it happen from down below. Looks like a few abrasions, that's all."

Bo and Sara exchanged a look. "He's bleeding from his shoulder pretty badly," Sara said.

The medic flapped her hand like it was nothing. "I'll take care of it. We'll get him patched right up. From the looks of it, he didn't even hit his head. Isn't that right, Finn?"

I blinked at her. At first I thought she was being oddly cheerful to keep me from panicking, but now it seemed like she was being deliberately obtuse.

I tried to remember if I'd hit my head or not. "Well, no, I don't think—"

"He might need stitches," Bo said. "On his shoulder."

My legs felt like noodles. I wanted to sit down. "Can someone please call..." I stopped talking. Asking for Declan was stupid. I hadn't even meant to say it out loud. He wasn't anything to me, and he sure as hell wasn't someone I could claim in any kind of public way.

"His mom is here," Sara said to Bo. "We should call her."

"No," I said, sitting down on the hard ground and putting my face in my hands. I was so fucking worn-out. "Do not call my mother. Trust me."

Another vehicle came speeding up, leaving a plume of dust in the air as it stopped. Nolan and Joel hopped out. "There he is. You're fine," Nolan insisted. "Just a bit knocked around by the breeze up there."

He eyed the two PAs. "Not a word of this gets out. Do you understand? Nothing happened here. Just a scrape or two. That's to be expected while filming a rock climbing scene."

Bo and Sara looked at me with the same surprise as they'd had when I'd almost tumbled to my fucking death in the ravine. I nodded my agreement with the director. It wouldn't do anyone any good for word to get out there'd been an accident on set.

Suddenly, the medic's reaction made sense. I remembered a rule about mandatory accident reporting. It was only necessary when the on-set injury resulted in a trip to the hospital. No wonder they'd hired such a laissez-faire medic.

I reached for Bo's hand to help me back up. "Take me back to my room, please," I said before turning to the medic. "You can treat me there after I have a shower."

Nolan sputtered. "We have two more scenes to film today."

I did my best to look at him as steadily as possible. "You may, but I no longer do."

His nostrils flared, but he didn't argue with me. I managed to hold it together until Bo helped me climb into the back seat of the jeep, and then I asked in a cracking voice, "Can I please use your phone?"

17

DECLAN

I was writing up a report from the third instance of Mrs. Brainth-waite's car being borrowed without her permission when Penny's voice came over my intercom.

"Personal call on line one. Sounds important. Came through 911."

As I reached for the phone, I glanced at my cell phone which didn't show any missed calls or messages. None of my family members would have called in like that. Was it Tess? Had something happened?

"Sheriff Stone," I said.

"Dec?"

Finn's voice sounded strange. I stood up and reached for my phone and keys.

"What happened? Where are you?"

"Can you meet me at the chalet, please?"

"I'll be there in ten. Where are you? What happened?"

He sniffled. "I'm fine. I'll, um... I'll tell you when I see you? Every-thing's fine. I promise."

"Stay on the phone with me," I said before glancing up at Penny. "I'm taking lunch, okay? Call Shawn in if you need extra hands on deck." I knew he'd cover for me if need be, and I'd do the same for him. The more time he spent at our place with Tess, the more I was beginning to think of him as a friend rather than just a coworker.

Penny nodded and made a note in her computer that I was off duty. I strode out of the building and straight to the SUV.

"You still there?" I asked.

"Mm-hm."

"You okay?"

"Yeah."

"Okay. You have a clean piece of paper in your head for me?"

When he spoke, I could hear the smile in his voice. "That was a trick. I looked it up on Google. You were trying to get me to fall asleep."

"You caught me." I turned out of the parking lot and headed straight for Mikey and Tiller's property. The only thing that kept me from turning on lights and sirens was hearing Finn's voice on the other end. Clearly, he was alive and well even though I could tell something had happened.

"I need to warn you my mom is there," he said, returning to the serious and unsure tone from earlier. "And she's..."

"Mothers love me," I said, lying through my teeth. The only mother who loved me was my own. I'd never really met any others in this kind of situation. "Don't worry."

Was that why he was upset? Because his mother had shown up?

Suddenly, I remembered today was the day he was filming a dangerous climbing scene. "Baby?" I asked without thinking. "Were you hurt on set?"

"Mm-hm."

Clearly, he was around other people he didn't want to say much in front of. I gritted my teeth.

"But I'm okay. Just a little banged up. In fact... you don't need to... I, ah, shouldn't have called. It's okay. I didn't mean to interrupt your workday."

"You didn't," I said, lying again. "It's fine. I promise. Shawn's off today and can cover for me if they need someone."

I finally turned onto the road that led up the mountainside. "Almost there."

"Dec?"

He sounded small and scared. Tired and alone. It was killing me. I had to force myself not to slam the accelerator down to the floor. "I'm here."

I heard the sounds of his arrival. Car doors opening and people talking. Finn's voice was muffled as if he held the phone against his chest while he spoke to someone. It didn't matter. I was almost there.

When I pulled onto the Rockley Lodge property and turned down the road toward the chalets, I was surprised to see Mikey unloading a suitcase from his vehicle in the distance. He'd gone to Houston for the preseason with Tiller, but maybe he'd decided to head back early. I knew from hearing Tiller talk about it that his preseason schedule was brutal. It likely didn't leave much time for Mikey.

Either way, I was relieved to see Mikey back here to oversee the cast and crew who'd taken over the lodge. There'd been a callout already for violating a late-night noise ordinance, and I knew Tiller and Mikey were sensitive to their reputation in town. If they wanted the town's support for their lodge and ski resort plans, they'd need to keep their neighbors happy.

All thoughts of the happy couple disappeared when I pulled up to Finn's chalet and saw a large bloodstain on the back of the hoodie jacket Finn had on. A handful of people swarmed around him, and I noticed a woman getting out of an SUV with a large orange EMT bag. What the fuck had happened?

As soon as the woman saw me, her eyes widened in concern, and she made a beeline for me and plastered on a big smile. "Oh, Officer... Sheriff. Everything's fine here. I'm not sure who called you, but it's completely unnecessary."

Finn turned his head and met my eyes. His hair was a windblown mess, and his face was pale. A wide scratch like road rash painted his cheekbone, and he held one of his arms close to his body. He looked dead on his feet to the point I feared he'd tip right over and crumple to the ground.

After ignoring the EMT, I strode over and nudged a young man aside so I could assess Finn's injuries. Before I had a chance to give him a good once-over, he stepped right up against me and wrapped his arms around my waist before leaning his head against my chest.

"I'm sorry," he said almost too quietly for me to hear.

Damn it felt good to hold him. "What for?" I snuck my hands up the back of his jacket and shirt to feel the warm skin of his lower back. His entire body was shaking.

He let out a derisive laugh. "Claim... *Hugging* you in front of these people. I just..."

He didn't need to say it. I could tell he just needed someone. Someone he could trust. Someone just for him.

Knowing his mother was here and he'd still called me made me both angry and sad for him. "It's okay. If you hadn't called, I would have been upset when I found out. And I don't ever mind you hugging me whenever you want or need to."

His body seemed to relax slightly, and I remembered how unsteady he'd appeared. "Come on. Let's get you inside." I kept an arm around his waist as I led him into the chalet. His mother was ensconced on the sofa surrounded by magazines, an iPad, a Starbucks cup, and a cashmere scarf-blanket thing half draped over her legs. She was on the phone.

"Oh, there are people here. Gotta go, darling." She ended the call before realizing Finn was injured. "What in the world?" She stood up and came over to him, fluttering her hands around him as if unsure where to touch. If she decided to touch anywhere, I was probably going to make a rude noise.

I moved past her and guided him into the bedroom and then the large bathroom before closing the door in her face with a murmured, "Give us a minute."

When I turned to Finn, I could see him tense his jaw. I thought he was going to snap at me about being dismissive to his mother, but that's not what he said at all. "I shouldn't have gotten you involved. I really am sorry. It was a moment of weakness."

I leaned in and kissed him as gently as I could. He made a whimpering noise in his throat and leaned in for more. His body was plastered against mine so tightly, I had a hard time taking in a full breath. My hands landed on his ass and squeezed before I remembered why we were there.

"Fuck. Stop. We have to stop. You're hurt. Let's get you cleaned up, and then that medical person can take a look at you."

When I pulled back, I noticed Finn's eyes were full of tears, and he was leaning his head back in hopes of keeping them from spilling.

"Shit," I murmured, pulling his head down and wiping them away as carefully as I could with my thumbs. "Did I hurt you? Fuck."

"No," he breathed. "You didn't hurt me. I needed... I wanted... just... thank you for coming here."

This man. He wasn't at all the cocky actor I'd taken him for at first. He was so fucking vulnerable and incredibly lonely. I was beginning to see his need to be loved like a beacon, shining brightly for all the world to see.

But nobody fucking saw it at all.

Except me.

My back teeth ground together. "You can call me anytime. Do you hear me? Anytime. You are never a burden to me or my schedule. *Never*. Now... what happened out there?" I busied myself getting a washcloth under some hot water so I could wash him off.

"I was doing the tyrolean traverse high above the floor of the ravine. The wind picked up, and I told them we needed to wait for the conditions to improve before continuing. But the helicopter was only booked for a few hours, I guess..." His forehead crinkled. "Wait. Wait. Where was the helicopter? They're not supposed to fly in wind like that, and I don't remember... fuck. They weren't there! They weren't fucking there when the wind picked up. So who... who the hell was filming other than Joel in the cherry picker?"

I didn't follow half of what he was saying other than to grasp the point that this film and the people in charge were assholes who clearly didn't give a shit about looking out for one of their main stars. Even if they didn't care about Finn, they should have cared about their reputation. It didn't make any sense for a high-budget film to run that way.

"Did you fall?" I asked, wondering how that was possible if he was at Tempter's Chimney. It was a canyon with two giant rock faces squared off opposite each other. As he spoke, I carefully wiped the dirt and makeup off his face.

"I fell off the edge, but Bo and Sara had given me top ropes to tie into. The ropes caught me, but I swung against the rock pretty hard when it happened."

I couldn't even imagine. Picturing him slipping off the edge of one of those tall ridges made me prickle with nervous sweat.

I dropped the cloth into the sink and pulled him into another careful hug. "I'm so fucking glad it wasn't worse," I breathed into his messy hair. He smelled like the outdoors: sun, sweat, dirt, and the tang of metal. "Thank fuck you're okay."

Someone knocked on the door. "Finn? Honey? The set medic wants to take a look at you." Finn's mom sounded worried.

"Give us another minute," I said, trying not to growl at her. "Please."

I redoubled my efforts to clean him up and realized the cut on his shoulder was still bleeding into the cotton jacket.

"Let's get this off and put you under a quick shower. You'll feel better, and then the EMT can bandage you up."

After helping him bathe and dry off, I slipped into his bedroom to find him some clean, comfortable clothes. I could tell his mom wanted to go into the bathroom, but I shot her a look. "He's not dressed."

Her nostrils flared, but she nodded. As soon as I had clothes from his dresser, I returned to the bathroom and helped him into clean boxer briefs and some athletic pants. I left the T-shirt off so the EMT could bandage his shoulder and arm abrasions first.

When I reached for the door, Finn stopped me. He was back to being his fresh, freckly self, and I took a minute to drink in his beautiful face and sexy body. Even with the scrapes and bruises, he was stunning, and my heart thumped with the certainty that I wanted him to be mine. Not just today or this week or even this month while he was in Aster Valley, but somehow... somehow I wanted him for much longer than that. Until he got sick of me and forced me away from him.

It would never work. I knew that. He lived in LA, and I lived in Colorado. But the bone-deep need to care for him and make sure he walked through the world feeling loved and appreciated was a part of me suddenly.

"I'm not leaving," I said, in case he was going to apologize and try to release me again. "I don't care what you say. I'm not leaving here, and I'm not leaving you. At least until you're feeling steadier." I couldn't deny I was needed at the office. As soon as I could get him settled and resting, I'd probably have to head back in.

The edge of his mouth curled into a soft smile. "Good. I don't want you to go yet. I decided to be selfish and keep you. But I'm really hungry. Would you mind finding me something to eat while the medic does her thing? I would ask the PAs to grab me something, but they were pretty spooked when I fell, and I'm not sure I trust them to go into town without spilling the beans to someone."

I let out a breath and nodded. "Of course. I'll call the diner. Sometimes the owners' son will deliver if they're not too busy." I remembered he knew who Solo was. "I never did ask you what you and Solo were doing at the park that day."

His radiant smile returned, reminding me of how happy he'd been in the park. "I'm helping him and his friends learn Shakespeare. He said if he doesn't pass his summer school class, his dads will make him quit the diner. I think he's saving up for a car."

When I opened the bathroom door, his mother rushed over. "Oh, my poor baby!"

I leaned over and pressed a kiss to the top of his head. "I'll be back. Any special requests? I'll get enough for a crowd."

He shook his head and mouthed thank you as his mother and the EMT quickly ushered him away from me.

When I called the diner, Pim answered and admitted they were too busy for delivery. I placed a large order of burgers and sandwiches and headed out to pick them up. On the way back to town, I called Tess to give her a quick update so she would know where I was and why Shawn might get called in.

"As long as Finn's okay?" she asked.

"He's just a bit banged up. I think it terrified him, though. He looked pretty spooked, and so did the two production assistants who saw it happen."

"Why doesn't he use a stunt double? It doesn't make any sense." I appreciated her concern and completely agreed. But I also understood how he'd gotten himself into his predicament. He'd been treated like a child for so long, and rock climbing was one of the activities that made him feel competent. To be an accomplished rock climber and let someone else film your rock climbing scenes would be hard to bear.

"It's a long story. Everything okay with you and the baby?" I asked her.

"Yep. This little monster is on a salad kick which is probably a good thing. Tell Finn if he wants a couch potato buddy to watch movies with, I'm his gal."

"I will. Call or text if you need me, okay?"

"Declan?"

"Yeah?"

"You don't have to be everyone's person, you know."

She knew how hard that would be for me to hear regardless of how right she was. "What if I want to?" I teased her. I knew she didn't mean to imply I shouldn't be there for Finn. She was more selfless than that.

"I'm just saying, I'm okay for a while. Go be with Finn. He needs you. Besides, your friend Truman brought over a basket of fresh veggies from his garden and asked if I wanted to come hang out at his spice shop this evening. He's doing some kind of seminar on homeopathic stuff for preggos and new parents. He said it's a good place to connect with other Aster Vallians who are... what did he call it?... 'harboring a fugitive.'" Her laugh rang out and made me smile. "I forgot to tell you that. I died laughing. He's freaking adorable."

When I arrived at the diner, I quickly ended the call and made my way inside to pick up the food. Solo was finishing packing everything up at the front counter.

"Hey, Sheriff," he said with a smile. "Your crew at the station are going to love you today."

"I'm off duty," I said. "Taking it to Finn and some folks up at the lodge."

He glanced over where Pim was busy taking someone's order. He lowered his voice. "Ah. Well, tell him I said we're on for another session on Wednesday night."

"I'll let him know. Hey, Solo? You've been doing some odd jobs for Mrs. Brainthwaite. Any chance you know what's going on with her car?"

He looked at me in confusion as he swiped my credit card through the machine. "What do you mean? Is it acting up? I'm not really good with mechanical stuff about cars."

"No, nothing like that. I keep meaning to ask you about this. Her car has been taken out of her driveway several times and left around town. She said sometimes she loans it to you..."

Suddenly, Solo's face widened in fear. "Sheriff Stone, you have to know I would never, *ever* use her car without permission. I promise."

I shook my head and tried reassuring him. "No. Sorry. I didn't mean to imply you took it. I was only wondering if there'd been a misunderstanding or anything."

He pursed his lip for a minute while my receipt printed out. He slid it with a pen over for my signature. "Are you sure... I mean... she's kinda getting up there. And sometimes she gets a little confused? I wonder if maybe she's forgetting loaning it to someone else or... I don't know. But I told my dads about a time earlier this summer when she called me the wrong name. They said it sometimes happens when you get older, but it seems like it's happening more and more."

Shit. I was going to have to figure out how to handle a delicate situation. But I was glad Solo didn't have anything to do with the joyrides. When Finn had mentioned him wanting a car, I hadn't known what to think.

"Okay, I'll handle it. Thanks." I picked up the big bags of takeout containers. "And tell Pim and Bill thanks, too."

"You'll tell Finn about the... thing?"

I nodded. "Promise."

When I got back to the chalet, it was a damned circus. I handed most of the food bags to the PAs and told them to take everyone outside to the picnic tables and hand out the food. I recognized both the director and the show runner right away.

It took all of my self-control to put on my diplomatic mask. "Nolan, Shelly, nice to see you again."

Nolan's eyes widened comically, and he turned to Shelly as if to ask her what the hell the sheriff was doing there. She shrugged and kept her eyes on me.

"Sheriff, what can we help you with?" she asked.

I held up the remaining bag of food. "Burger delivery for the leading actor. Aster Valley is a full-service town."

While they stood there trying to figure out what the hell I'd meant, I slipped past them into Finn's bedroom.

"Please stop, Mom," Finn was saying, pushing her hand away where she seemed to be doing that mother thing of putting the back of her hand against his forehead. "I don't have a fever. I'm fine. I just want some peace and quiet for a little while. Can you please—"

He noticed me standing by the door, and his lips curved into a smile. His face had a bandage on it, and I noticed another on one of his elbows. He'd managed to get the T-shirt on and was partway under the covers in his bed. His hair had partially dried into a mismatch of brown waves.

"Hey," I said. "Still hungry?"

Finn sat up a little and swung his legs over the edge. "Starving. Let's go eat at the table in the kitchen. I don't want to get food in the bed."

Things were awkward between Finn's mom and me before Finn realized we hadn't exactly been introduced. "Declan, this is my mom,

Lola Heller. Mom, this is Declan Stone, the sheriff of Aster Valley."
His eyes sparkled at me despite how tired he looked. "And my friend."

I shifted the food to my left hand and reached out my right to
shake hers. She was obviously hesitant, maybe unsure of why local
law enforcement was on the scene.

"Nice to meet you, ma'am," I said. "Excuse the uniform. I came
from work, but I'm not here in any official capacity."

She seemed to relax at my words and consented to a handshake.
The three of us moved out to the living area of the small chalet and
sat at the table. Nolan and Shelly still stood in the open space and
stared at me like I was a bomb about to detonate. I ignored them and
began unpacking food for Finn.

He looked a little better, but seeing the bandages pissed me the
fuck off. I wanted to speak my mind, ask in a loud obnoxious tone
why the climbing supervisor hadn't been on set for one of the most
challenging technical climbing scenes of the entire film. But it wasn't
my place.

As Finn had said, I was a friend.

And I had to trust him to manage his own career the way he
saw fit.

Until his mother didn't freaking shut up.

"I'm sure you'll feel better in no time," she said, fluttering around
him and pushing healthy side items toward him while surreptitiously
moving the unhealthy ones away. Fries were replaced with cut-up
fruit, and potato chips were replaced by a side salad. It was a routine
she seemed to do without even thinking of it, and other than a small
frown between Finn's eyes, he seemed to go along with it.

"Finn, dear, I know the little mishap shook your confidence," she
continued. "The best thing for you to do is get back on the horse.
Nolan says you have at least another scene to film this afternoon. I
say we get you fed and—"

Finn didn't even glance at the director when he calmly said, "I
won't be shooting another scene today unless Kramer himself shows
up and suggests I should. Otherwise, everyone will have to be content
with moving those scenes to tomorrow."

I remembered Finn telling me about his relationship with his climbing coach. Kramer was a man Finn respected and admired. He trusted him.

Nolan stepped forward. "We're shooting the cave explosion scene in a couple of days. There's not much time—"

Finn's eyes widened in surprise. "That scene isn't on the schedule until later this month. We haven't even blocked it yet."

Nolan glanced at me and thought for a minute before nodding. "We've made some changes, but don't worry about that right now. We'll work it out. Shelly will clear you for the rest of the day, and we'll see you in the morning. Get some rest. Sorry you had a rough time of it out there today. Good work. You're a trooper."

If looks could kill, I would have to arrest Finn for aggravated homicide right now, but thankfully both the director and show runner said their goodbyes and departed the chalet. I saw Shelly talking to the PAs and the set medic out the window, and before long, all of them seemed to have taken off. Just when I thought Finn might have a quiet enough environment for some true rest, the McLaren came screaming into the drive, leaving a cloud of dust in its wake. The blond-haired sidekick hopped out and raced toward the chalet.

"Holy fuck," he said, pushing the door open with a bang. "The websites are reporting a near-fatal climbing accident on set with Fi..." He saw Finn comfortably munching on his cheeseburger. Finn's eyebrow lifted. The kid at the door clutched his chest dramatically. "Oh Finn. I didn't see you there. I figured you'd be in bed. Thank god you're okay. What happened? Tell me *everything*. I came to get it straight from the horse's mouth."

Finn's face paled. "The media have it? But Nolan insisted on keeping it locked up tight."

I stood up and began cleaning the takeout containers from the table. "You don't need to worry about it. You only need to be concerned with getting some rest. Maybe your friend can get the story from Lola while I help you get settled in bed."

Hopefully my tone had sent the message this wasn't up for discussion. No one said a word as I carefully helped Finn up and led him to the bedroom before shutting the door.

"Sorry about being an ass out there," I mumbled. "But that guy is only looking for the scoop so he can tell everyone he got it from the horse's mouth."

Finn's eyes were oddly intense as they met mine. "I liked it. I liked you taking charge. You know how I feel about seeing that side of you, and it's kind of nice to be... protected. Feel free to take charge of me anytime."

I narrowed my eyes at him and pointed to the bed. "Don't tempt me, Finnegan. Get under the covers."

He smirked at me but did as I said. When he slid beneath the sheets, he let out a groan of happy relief. "God this feels amazing."

I sat next to him on the bed and ran my fingers through his hair. "I want you to sleep for a while. Ignore those two. Ignore your phone. I need to go back to work for a couple of hours, but then I'll come back and see how you're doing, okay?"

He nodded his head and settled deeper into the bed. "Thanks again. I feel better now. Sometimes I think watching you be confident and a little bossy makes me feel like I can do it, too."

Finn laughed a little as he said it, but I didn't think he was joking. I was proud of him for insisting he was done for the day, for knowing his limits and making them clear, but I still got the sense he was surrounded by vipers who were bound and determined to control him for their own various agendas.

Sure enough, after kissing him goodbye and closing the bedroom door behind me, both his mom and the sidekick approached me.

"Sheriff," Lola began, "I'm not exactly sure what your role here is, but I appreciate your help. Poor Finn simply gets overwhelmed sometimes. You can hardly blame him when he has so much responsibility on his shoulders. He just wants to do a good job. His drive to be the best sometimes gets the better of him."

I couldn't get an accurate read on Finn's mother. Sometimes I thought she was opportunistic and manipulative. But then I remembered her original circumstances and wondered if she was simply the product of an insecure upbringing and desperate circumstances. I'd yet to determine what her relationship with Finn would look like if he were to decide to give up acting. Would she accept it? Would she resent him? I wasn't sure.

"I think it was the dangerous weather conditions on the mountain that got the better of him today," I said. "Hopefully it was an oversight on the crew's part rather than dangerous business practices."

She waved her hand through the air in dismissal. "Nolan is one of the best. Finn is lucky to be on a Nolan Trainor project, and he knows it. This kind of film can make his career, and how fortunate he gets to do the kind of rock climbing scenes he loves. Any other director would have insisted on a stunt double, but Finn wouldn't hear of it."

"He refused a stunt double?" I couldn't help but ask.

Lola's eyes flickered away, and I kicked myself for pushing it. It was none of my business, and I had no interest in arguing with the woman closest to Finn's heart. But it annoyed me to hear her imply it had been his choice. His choice had included having his climbing instructor there to oversee everything, something that hadn't happened today.

I backed off, but only a little. "Hopefully, they'll have a climbing supervisor on set for any future climbing scenes. I hate to think of him out there with no climbing expert to back him up."

Kix spoke up. "Bo and Sara are climbers. That's why they were hired as PAs."

I held my tongue. Those two, while nice and attentive, were practically children. And if they were trying to get a foothold in the film industry, they would never in a million years stand up to someone as influential as Nolan Trainor.

I nodded and reached for my wallet. "I'll swing by later to check on him. In the meantime, here's my card. Please call or text my cell number if you need anything."

Before I got to the door, I stopped and turned around to pin Kix with a stare. "Any idea how the websites found out about what happened on the mountain so fast?"

Kix glanced at Lola, and in that split second, I came to my conclusion about Lola.

She was opportunistic and selfish. Kix had come here looking for *her* version of the story because he knew the media had gotten it from her. He'd thought Finn was asleep which meant he'd come in talking to Lola, asking *her* for the story straight from the horse's mouth.

"I see," I said carefully before glancing back at the bedroom door where sweet Finn lay sleeping. While I didn't want to leave him here with these two assholes, I needed to check in at work and follow up on a few things so I could come back here and spend the evening with Finn. My job was still relatively new, and I couldn't risk being seen as a sheriff who was just as wowed by the Hollywood celebrities as half the people in town were.

But that didn't mean it hurt any less to drive away from him. I was only halfway down the mountain to town when I realized I would do just about anything to shield Finn Heller from more pain.

And three days later, that included putting my job at risk.

18

FINN

There was something magically healing about sleeping in the arms of the sheriff of Aster Valley. Or maybe it was simply being in his big bed at his blessedly peaceful and silent house.

We'd left the chalet bedroom for my mother and escaped to Declan's house the night of the accident. I'd never been more grateful the chalet only had one bedroom.

Being at Declan's place made me feel almost like a normal person. His home was nothing fancy, a rental he was in for a year before making the decision of whether and where he might want to invest in his own place. I hadn't been in such a homey place in a very long time. My own place was modern and cold, decorated by professionals my mom had hired in case I was ever interviewed there for a magazine spread.

It only took a few hours that first night before I'd changed into comfy pajamas and joined Tessa to watch an old BBC show called *Doc Martin*.

"This is nice but..." I began.

"Slow as shit?" she asked, reaching for the bowl of baby carrots on the coffee table. "I'm no longer allowed to watch shows that raise my blood pressure. It was either this or *Gilmore Girls*, and I can't handle parent/child relationship stories right now without snot-crying."

"Don't get me wrong," I said, reaching for the other bowl that held pretzels. "I like this. It's nice. I'm a big BBC fan." I took a bite of the pretzel and made a retching noise.

"Those don't have salt on them," she said. "I meant to warn you."

"They taste like..." *The pretzel equivalent of* Doc Martin. "Saltless pretzels," I finished lamely.

"Complain to your boyfriend. They were his idea. He took my high blood pressure personally."

My boyfriend. I quickly turned around to see if Declan had overheard her. What would his reaction be to the label? What was my reaction?

Soul-deep longing.

When I realized he was still in the kitchen cleaning up from dinner, I cleared my throat and took a sip from the glass of ice water Declan made sure I always had available. "I've never had a boyfriend before," I admitted.

Declan had once muttered that I was the king of the slow-pan, but I had nothing on this woman. Her head turned slowly to gawp at me.

"You, Finn Heller, Hollywood heartthrob and world's most eligible bachelor, have never had a boyfriend?"

I shot her a look. "I've had dates. I've had hookups. That's not the same thing as having a boyfriend."

Tessa studied me. Even though she looked tired, she was absolutely gorgeous. I could understand why some straight men had a thing for pregnant women. There was something about her that made me want to be close to her. Maybe it was a biological need to protect her or something, but I felt the same warmth of affection when I looked at her that Declan must feel.

"Why didn't any of your dates turn into boyfriends?" she asked.

"Let's see... first there was Kix, who I didn't want to date because he felt like more of a brother to me." Not a very good one, but the kind you were competitive with, annoyed by, and low-key didn't like.

"Then there was a guy named Dalvin, who wanted me to call him Dungeon Master Dalvin. Which is fine. I'm not kink-shaming or anything, but it wasn't my thing. Then I dated a guy named Lex, who tipped off the press about where we would be so they could capture our date on film. Then... oh, Drew Hilliard from that reality show. He was actually super sweet until I discovered he had a girlfriend. And then there was—"

Tess held up a hand. "I get it. You date assholes."

Declan had been in the middle of walking into the room when he heard her and froze midstep. His eyes bounced to mine.

"Not you," I said quickly. "You're not an asshole."

Tessa started laughing while Dec's brows furrowed. "Uh... thanks? You set a low bar, Finn."

I sighed. "I have a regrettable history with men."

Dec's eyes widened, and I cursed, reaching out to grasp his hand. "Not you. Jesus. I blame all of this on Tess."

He grinned and joined me on the sofa, snuggling close until I was practically sprawled on top of him. "That's what I like to do, too."

Tessa threw a pillow at him.

It took all of five seconds for me to fall asleep to the opening sequence of the next *Doc Martin* episode. At some point Declan must have helped me upstairs because I woke up in his bed, not only refreshed, but also remarkably horny for someone who'd been used as a human battering ram the day before.

Declan's sleepy, grumbly voice began bossing me around immediately, which only made me hotter.

"Lie there and be still," he began. As if I was going to argue with him.

"Pillow princess mode, activated," I promised, stretching against him like a cat before clasping my hands behind my head. "You know, my dick feels a little tender from my accident. I think it needs—*holy mother of Christ!*"

His mouth was hot and wet. Declan's strong fingers grasped my hips to hold them still while his mouth sucked all the brains from my... brains.

"Oh fuck," I said, panting and throwing my head from side to side. I clenched my fists, not knowing if grabbing his head and shoving it closer to my groin would be a violation of the "be still" command.

"Settle down," he warned.

I whimpered. My toes were stretched out, and my heels crawled up the bed to give him more room between my legs. Declan's tongue was everywhere. My balls, my dick, my inner thighs. I was embarrassing myself with a kind of keening, begging noise, but it only seemed to ramp him up and double down on the suction.

"Want you to come," he said against my shaft. "Choke me with it. Come down my throat."

If his purpose in talking dirty was to get me to finish already, mission accomplished. I shouted and arched up, feeling the tight press of his throat around me as I rammed myself deeper inside him. Fuck, that was hot. My brain jumbled and fritzed until the only thing left was his damned white piece of paper. While I was still jerking with the aftershocks, Declan knelt up over me and jacked off above my face, painting me with his release several strokes later when he came with a long, deep groan.

We stared at each other.

"Holy shit," I breathed.

He reached out and thumbed my cheek before licking his own cum off his thumb. My heart thundered in my chest, and my dick perked up a tiny bit.

"Holy shit," I said again.

Declan's grin was dirty and smug. "You like that?"

I closed my eyes and leaned back into the pillow with a groan. "You're so fucking hot. I could seriously come again right now if I wasn't so fucking relaxed and lazy."

The deep rumble of his laugh made me smile. I loved hearing him make a happy noise. He seemed to carry such a large mantle of responsibility, it was nice to see him take time for his own enjoyment.

"You're hardly lazy," he said, climbing off the bed and reaching for my hand to pull me up after him. "In fact, you're probably dead set on going back to work this morning. Tell me I'm wrong."

He didn't seem particularly peeved about it. Declan was an adult. He understood about work commitments. He was the sheriff of an entire county.

"You're not wrong. What about you? Are you on duty today?"

"Yes, but you'll call me if you need me. Understand?"

"You're not the boss of me."

He turned and speared me with a look that went straight to my balls. "Is that right?"

Please, oh, please, be the boss of me, Sheriff Sexypants.

"Well, ah... fine. But only because who else am I going to call if I get into trouble? The cops. It's always the cops. That's just smart planning. It has nothing to do with you being my boyfr... *friend.*"

That wasn't awkward. At all.

Declan's eyes were intense in a way I couldn't interpret. It left me feeling strange like I didn't know where to put my hands.

I coughed a little bit, tried not to trip over the air in the room, and stumbled into the bathroom in search of Dec's large shower. Maybe it would make a good hiding place.

Instead of following me into the bathroom, Declan turned around to answer his ringing phone. I heaved a sigh of relief. While I felt very refreshed and renewed from two hearty meals and a good night's sleep, I didn't exactly feel up to having a conversation about what "this" was between us.

I was halfway through washing myself when Dec's naked body stepped into the space and crowded against me. His dry, warm skin felt delicious against my wet body, and I leaned into him without thinking. Seeking comfort from him was as natural as breathing. I may have felt awkward about talking about my feelings, but I didn't feel the least bit uncomfortable touching him and giving him free rein to touch me the same way.

Declan reached over my shoulder for the shampoo bottle. "The department called. I have to go in for a meeting this morning after I run you back to the chalet. The county council wants to discuss a last-minute public event that will need crowd control and extra security."

He'd mentioned the county council before. "Do you report to them?"

Declan shrugged. "Not officially. Officially I report to the citizens of the county. But when I accepted the position, I suggested adding county council oversight to the department to help prevent another situation like they had before. The sheriff abused his power which is pretty easy with elected positions like this. They're going to try to make it official in the next county election. Meanwhile, it's a professional courtesy thing since it was my idea in the first place."

He was a good man. I wondered if he wanted to continue being the sheriff enough to run for re-election. I made a mental note to ask him about it when we had more time together.

But that turned out to be a joke. For the next two days, we barely had enough time to breathe, much less see each other. I was dealing with my mother's unannounced visit and an overflowing call sheet trying to make up for scenes that I hadn't shot the day of the tyrolean traverse, and Declan was suddenly inundated with plans for the county event, which turned out to be a big *Gold Rats* meet and greet in the center of town after we wrapped filming in Aster Valley.

On the third day after waking up at Declan's and saying goodbye to him in a rush of us needing to get to work, I had just arrived at my set trailer when a production assistant delivered the day's call sheet.

I blinked at it in shock. Right there in black and white, it showed a reshoot of the entire tyrolean traverse scene.

The weather was completely sunny and clear, but the call for that scene was right after lunch when afternoon thunderstorms were more likely to roll in.

Stop assuming bad weather when there is none forecast.

I checked the weather app on my phone and saw nothing concerning in the forecast.

Still. There hadn't been high winds predicted the other day either. That kind of shit simply happened at altitude. Weather wasn't nearly as predictable in alpine areas.

"Why do you look like you've seen a ghost?" Mom asked before taking a sip of the fancy coffee she'd sent someone to fetch for her from town. I'd already told the PAs to ignore her requests, so if they chose to do her bidding, that was on them.

"I have seen a ghost," I muttered. "The ghost of climbing scenes past."

I made my way to the door of the trailer, but she called me back. "Wait. Wait. Explain what's going on."

I glanced at her. "I told you the only way I'd allow you to come to the set was if you didn't interfere. Do you remember that?"

"I'm not interfering. I'm trying to stop *you* from interfering. You have to trust your director, darling. If he wants a scene shot again, that means he didn't get the film he needed. You know how this works, Finn. Without just the right shots—"

I finished the old line with her. "The film goes from wow to meh."

It was a mantra she'd hammered into me a thousand times since reading some director's biography years ago.

"Mom, stop interfering in my career. I mean it. I'm not ten years old anymore. Do you know how it makes me look to even have you here on set with me? Remember how we talked about the importance of rebranding me as an adult actor?"

"I believe the term I chose was action hero," she said, crossing her arms in front of her chest. "And they don't think of me as your mother. They think of me as your business advisor."

I barely contained the eyeroll. "No, they don't."

I turned back to the door, intent on finding Nolan's assistant to ask about the need to reshoot the scene, but the same PA who'd delivered the call sheet appeared again. "We're switching things around because of weather concerns. Here you go." She shoved a new call sheet into my hand and took away the old one. This new one showed the tyrolean scene first up this morning after makeup and wardrobe. Great.

At least we'd get it out of the way while I was still fresh. I studied the sheet some more and noticed a blocking session for the cave explosion scene later this afternoon. I was nervous about the scene now that I knew they'd be using real pyrotechnics, but at the same time, I hoped to finally have some of the stunt coordinators on hand to direct me in how to deal with something I was unfamiliar with.

I'd never been on a set with so much seeming disregard for protocol. But in order for the film to get approval for the pyrotechnics, hopefully they'd had to prove compliance with all necessary safety protocols.

I shot Declan a text.

Me: *I might have to cancel dinner. We're going to be blocking the cave scene until late.*

Declan: *I thought you were doing that this morning. Is it going to take that long? Maybe it's a sign they're being cautious.*

Me: *No. They pushed it back because they want to re-shoot the tyrol.*

The three dots appeared, disappeared, and reappeared several times before Declan's response came through.

Declan: *10-9*

I squinted at the screen and realized it wasn't the same thing as a 10-4. After pulling up my handy police code cheat sheet, I noticed a 10-9 was a request to repeat previous transmission.

I clicked the button to call him instead.

"Tell me you're pulling my leg," he said without greeting me.

"I wish."

"Why? Did they lose the fucking film canister or something?"

He was very grumbly this morning which made my dick hard. "Pretty sure canisters haven't been involved much since the last millennium."

He made another growly noise which brought a smile to my face. "Thank you," I said sincerely.

"For what? Premeditated homicide?"

"For making me smile. You're the best. I gotta go."

"Be safe. Do you understand me? Tell those fuckers to—"

I cut him off before I came in my pants. "Enough dirty talk, Sheriff. You should get back to work, too."

"Text me when you're off the mountain."

"10-4."

When I ended the call, I felt grounded and ready to tackle the challenging scene again. An hour later, we were on the road toward Tempter's Chimney.

It took three hours to get all the shots Joel and Nolan wanted on the tyrol. Thankfully, the ropes were still in place, and Bo and Sara had both traversed them to check their integrity before I clipped in. The weather was gorgeous, and the wind wasn't high. The camera operator in the helicopter was able to get the angles she wanted. Both directors were chatting happily about the successful shoot. When I joined them in the craft services tent set up on the floor of the ravine, I thought I heard them mention making some changes to the final climbing scene on Slye Peak.

Crystobell came up to congratulate me on the shoot, so I didn't get to hear the rest of the directors' conversation about it. I hoped there'd still be time for Kramer to return before the Slye Peak shoot since it was a technical climb that involved a twenty-foot fall on the ropes. I'd feel better if he was there to triple-check all of the equipment before I put the stress of a fall onto the ropes. After being trained *not* to fall on the ropes and rely on your rigging, it was hard to do it on purpose.

Thankfully, that climb had a top rope I would be using as one of my redundancy anchors. We'd already gone over the choreography of the climb during some of the preproduction meetings, and Kramer had signed off on everything. My character had left his climbing gear bag in the back of his SUV before racing toward the mountain to rescue Crys's character, so we had an excuse to have high-end gear at hand for the stunt.

I blew out a breath and enjoyed the slightly shaky feeling of exertion in my muscles. It had felt good to be up high again in the gorgeous Colorado sunshine. What a difference a few days made.

I chatted with Crys for a little while before it was her turn to film. People came and went as I took a break at a portable picnic table with my plate full of grilled chicken salad and a couple of bottles of water. This really was a beautiful place to live. I couldn't imagine being so close to this many incredible climbs and being able to tackle them whenever I wanted.

Declan had mentioned mountain biking, and I wanted to try that, too. Colorado was like a playground for people who liked to be outdoors and active.

After another hour and a half, we were ferried over to another part of the mountain where the cave scenes were filmed. I'd already blocked and shot a hand-to-hand combat scene with Logan there and was very familiar with the layout of the area. The temporary set structure was in place, and I assumed that would be the structure they'd blow up for the explosion scene. It was made to look like an old hunter's shack near the mouth of the cave. Crystobell's character would be held in the shack until I rescued her, and we'd have to evade Logan's character in the cave.

Blocking the explosion scene ended up taking four hours, so when I returned to the set trailer, I was dead on my feet. All I wanted was a shower, a light dinner, and an early bedtime. Preferably with a certain bossy law enforcement officer plastered to my back in spoon fashion.

I picked up my phone to text him that I was finally off the mountain.

Me: *Am dead on my feet. Tell me you have sandwiches and a desire to stare at a sleeping actor for hours on end.*

Declan: *I definitely have a desire to stare at a naked actor for hours on end.*

I laughed.

Me: *I think you got part of that mixed up.*

Declan: *I don't think so.*

Me: *Can I stay at your place? My mom refuses to leave and the sofa isn't as comfy as your squishy body.*

Declan: *Is this how you woo a man? With dirty talk like "your squishy body"?*

I laughed and began to type a response, not realizing Kix had appeared at some point and was helping himself to a snack basket on the little kitchen counter in my trailer.

Me: *You didn't say you wanted dirty talk...*

"Who are you texting?" Kix asked.

I lifted my head up from the phone and grinned at him, feeling my face heat. "Hey. I didn't know you'd still be on set. How'd your day go? You were filming that scene at the baseball field, right?"

He nodded. "It was hot as hell, and all they had for us was bottled water. There was some mix-up with craft services. Anyway. Sorry about tonight. That sucks."

"What sucks about tonight?"

Kix looked surprised. "Your scene. The one on the rock face."

I got an uneasy feeling in my gut. "What are you talking about?"

A familiar head poked his head into the trailer. Bo looked apologetic and out of breath. "Sorry, I thought you'd gone back to your chalet. I didn't realize you were still here. Nolan and Joel want to shoot the Slye Peak scene tonight."

I let out a huff of laughter. "You're kidding."

He shook his head. "No. I wish I was. I'm beat. I can only imagine how you feel. But they changed their mind and want it filmed at sunset. Apparently they got a deal on the helicopter to keep them on a few more hours. Makeup and wardrobe are expecting you in an hour. Can I get you anything to eat before then?"

I stared at him. "You have to be joking. I've been on set since six this morning. It's almost seven already. If they're expecting me in an hour, when is the set call?"

"We'll depart for Slye Peak at eight thirty, and the actual set call is nine fifteen," he said, referring to a sheet he then remembered to hand me.

I looked at it in disbelief. They had plans to keep us on the mountain until eleven at night. The sun would be fully set by eight thirty. This couldn't be real.

My phone buzzed, and I glanced at it. Declan.

I answered the call. "Hey."

"Don't leave a man hanging like that, Finnegan," he said. The familiar sound of his voice washed over me with reassurance. I sat down hard on the sofa nearby.

"Sorry, I..." I took a breath. "I need a rain check on the staring thing."

The teasing tone was gone when he spoke next. "What's going on?"

"They added another call tonight. A climbing scene."

"Tonight? They're filming another climbing scene tonight?" He sounded as confused as I'd been. "Are they yanking your chain?"

"I don't know. But I need to eat something before reporting to makeup and wardrobe in an hour."

He sounded like he was trying to control his anger. I didn't blame him. "Did you know you'd be climbing in the dark and they just moved the shoot forward?"

"No. No mention of shooting a climbing scene in the dark. This is the first I'm hearing about it."

"Do you feel safe climbing in the dark?"

I opened my mouth to say no. I might feel safe climbing in the dark if I was fresh. But climbing at night after the day I'd already had? No way. But I didn't say it because the person I needed to say it to wasn't Declan Stone. It was the director who was playing fast and loose with my safety.

"Well, your hesitation answers that," he muttered. "This is ridiculous."

"I need to go," I said, knowing I'd lose my nerve if I didn't move quickly. I wanted to call my agent first and make sure I knew my rights before going to Nolan. "I'll call you later?"

"Finn, wait," he said.

"No, I need to do this. I promise I'll call you after, okay?" I hung up the phone and dialed Iris. When she didn't answer, I dialed her assistant, Dawson, who answered after the first ring.

"Finn! How's it going in Colorado? From all accounts, you're doing an amazing job. No surprise there, though."

I didn't have time for chitchat. "I need to talk to Iris, but she's not answering."

"She has a fundraiser at the Getty tonight. You might have caught her getting her hair done. What can I help you with?"

I explained my situation to him and the urgency of my request. "I need to know if I can refuse."

"Re... fuse?" he asked, like he was unfamiliar with the concept.

Kix's eyes lit up from across the small trailer, and he began nodding. "You should," he hissed. "You sooooo should. Give Nolan an ultimatum. What's he gonna do? Fire you? Pfft."

Something about Kix's words got under my skin. There was no way in hell he'd ever give the director of a feature film an ultimatum. But he wanted me to? Did he want me to stir up drama? Get fired?

I focused back in on what Dawson was saying. "I'll have to pull your contract and have an attorney—"

"Nope. I need it now. And I need you to get Iris on the phone for me. Make it happen, Dawson. I'll be waiting for your call." I took a page out of Declan's book and hung up after making my statement.

While I waited for a callback, there was something else I needed to do.

I turned to Kix. "Tell me about New Year's."

It took him a minute for my words to sink in, but then he gave me his cheesy grin. The one that made it seem like we were best bros. We'd never been best bros. Despite my efforts for over fifteen years, we'd never been more than slightly repellant magnets, the kind you keep pushing together just so you can feel that awkward rejecting force when they get too close.

"It was sick, man."

It *made* me sick, so he was close. "Why would you host a party at my house without telling me? When you know I would have hated having a bunch of strangers in my home?"

"Yeah, but it was New Year's. And I was avoiding that stalker chick, remember? I was crashing at your place. Where else would I have hosted it?"

Was he serious? "You violated my trust! You were fucking busted by the *cops*, and you never said a word."

He held his hands out as if to calm me down. "Wait just a minute. We weren't busted by the cops. We were joined by the cops. Not the same thing. Also? You're such a fucking Mary Sue. What do you care if I have friends over to celebrate a holiday? You're acting like your house is some kind of sacrosanct place when everyone knows it's like a fucking monastery. Just you and your nosy fucking mommy all up in your business."

I felt like I'd been slapped in the face. My "nosy fucking mommy" had been the woman he'd come to when he'd lost roles and faced heartbreaking rejections. His own parents were nice enough, but they didn't know the business. He'd come to my mother for help. Time after time he'd begged her for connections, advice, and help navigating the sometimes overwhelming machine of the film industry. She'd taken him under her wing as best she could. The only thing she hadn't done for him was ever, *ever* let him get close to getting a role she wanted for me. She'd protected my own career like a rabid grizzly with a single precious cub.

Instead of tears pricking my eyes as I would have expected, I felt anger, white-hot and all-encompassing. I wanted to punch the shit out of his smug face and tell him to stay the hell away from me and mine.

"Don't ever ask me for another goddamned favor as long as you live," I said instead, in a low voice shaking with irritation. Why hadn't I seen it more clearly before? I'd spent most of my teen years feeling guilt that I'd had success and Kix had been forced to settle for the leavings.

In reality, I'd had success because I'd worked my fucking ass off and had tried improving my skills while Kix had been off fucking around with friends or trying to make his way to the top with his ass instead of his head.

Why had I always felt like his own success or lack of it had anything to do with me?

"Don't worry," he said, sneering at me. "You don't have anything I'd ever want. You have no friends, no sex life to speak of, and no fucking idea what you want to be when you grow up. You're a washed-up child star whose mother has to sleep with directors to get you roles you're clearly not suited for. Hell, you can't even deal with getting a little roughed up on a shoot without calling Mommy to come take care of you and having to take the rest of the day off to snivel in your bed. Woe is poor fucking Finn Heller. Crying in his millions of dollars."

My stomach roiled with disgust and betrayal. I tried to ignore the nasty lie about my mother, but it was near impossible. I needed to know if there was any truth to it at all, and unfortunately, I wasn't thinking with a clear head at the moment.

I slammed my way out of the trailer, panning my gaze around to see if I could spot Nolan anywhere. My eyes landed on Joel sitting under the main craft services tent, eating a plate of some kind of pasta that was steaming in the cooling evening air.

"Great job today," he said when he saw me approach. "You hungry? Join me."

I stood across the table from him and clutched my hands together to keep from waving them around like a lunatic. "Where's Nolan?"

His chewing continued as he shrugged. "No idea. Why?"

I wasn't about to tell him the truth, that I needed to know if Nolan had ever had an inappropriate relationship with my mother. So I latched onto the other shitty situation at hand.

"I'm not okay with this evening's call sheet. First of all, climbing at night is dangerous. Climbing at night on a rock face you're unfamiliar with is downright idiotic. You can't be serious about this."

"You should talk to Nolan... oh look! There he is. He's on his way over here."

Sure enough, the director strode from his trailer to the tent while looking down at his phone. When he glanced up and saw the look on my face, he slowed.

"Don't throw a hissy fit, Finn. You're better than that," he said in a dry voice. "The scene needs to happen, and tonight's our best chance with the weather and the helicopter's availability."

I stayed a thousand times calmer than I felt. "When did you decide to add another scene to my already packed call sheet?"

"This isn't about you. It's about production. More goes into getting the shot than just one of the principals. Surely you know that by now."

His was one of those toxic personalities that relied on gaslighting. People like Nolan Trainor thrived in Hollywood, and they were treated like gods which only served to make them even more unbearable.

"I do know that. Know what else I know? You can't get the shot at all without the principals." I kept eye contact and willed the specter of Chip Clover away. I needed Nolan to see Finn Heller the adult actor staring back at him, asserting my rights as a man and an equal. Regardless of the reasons for casting me in this role, he *had* chosen me for it. And I wasn't going to be treated any less than any other principal in a big-budget film.

Before Nolan had a chance to open up his mouth and tell me where to shove my rights assertion, the whoop of a police car split the evening air around us. An Aster Valley sheriff's vehicle skidded to a stop in the gravel parking area nearby, throwing up a cloud of dust. All of the cast and crew who were still around at this time of night turned to watch as the sheriff of Aster Valley stepped out and approached us under the tent.

He did not look happy. And now, of course, was when my eyes began to sting.

Declan's voice was deep and commanding. Professional. "Finn Heller, you need to come with me."

My nostrils flared in irritation. As much as I wanted to see him, this was none of his fucking business. I was handling it myself. I needed another asshole fighting my battles for me like a damned hole in the head. I'd just been accused of not being in charge of my own shit, and now here he was trying to save the world for me.

While it was sweet as hell, it was piss-poor timing.

"What for?" I demanded. The people around us looked back and forth like they were at a tennis match.

His eyes hardened. "Do you really want me to share the particulars with everyone here?"

He seemed to be referring to... an actual police matter?

"What happened?" I asked, feeling my anger slowly replaced by concern.

"You were identified as the unauthorized driver of Mrs. Brainth-waite's vehicle on multiple occasions by multiple witnesses. I need you to come with me and answer some questions."

What the fuck was he talking about? I'd just been on the phone with the man not twenty minutes before, and now he suddenly thought I was a... car thief?

I threw up my hands in disbelief. "Why the hell would I steal the woman's car? I drive a—"

"I'm well aware of what kind of car you drive. And I'll allow you to come clear everything up at the station." His eyes were more intense than they'd ever been before. "Get in the vehicle."

"Don't be ridiculous. This is insane."

"Are you refusing to come with me voluntarily?" He moved his hands to the cuffs on his duty belt. Hypothetically, would it be weird if I admitted to popping a semi? I didn't. Obviously. But... but I kinda did. Just a little.

I glanced over at Nolan, who eyed both me and Declan suspi-ciously. He was between a rock and a hard place. Was he really going to call the sheriff's bluff and risk Aster Valley arresting one of his principal actors on set? Or was he going to admit defeat on his dangerous night climbing scene and let me go clear things up at the station?

Nolan pierced me with his gaze. "Don't say a fucking word until our lawyer arrives. Do you hear me?" He reached for his phone without waiting for my answer.

I glanced back at Declan and felt the familiar twist of excitement in my gut I got when he was near. How fucked-up was I when the man excited me even while quasi-arresting me?

I let out a breath and tried to shove the concerns about Nolan and my mother to the "later" box in my head and lock it down tight. The same went for the Kix situation.

"Slap the cuffs on me, Sheriff," I said, holding out my arms and meeting his eyes with a dirty challenge.

This was going to be good.

19

My back teeth were going to break off from the clenching.

As soon as we were alone in the car, Finn opened his mouth to speak. I could tell he was going to make an inappropriate comment, so I cut him off before he could say anything. "Cameras," I growled, reminding him we were being recorded for posterity.

I spent the drive back to town lecturing myself about being exactly where I'd known this would go all along.

Compromising my ethics on behalf of an actor, for god's sake. Just like all of my fellow officers in LA who'd gone down in the corruption scandal. And I'd been oh-so smug. As if I had the moral high ground.

Declan Stone would never cross that line for a celebrity.

Ha. The irony. Here I was making up bullshit just to get the man out of his job because I was worried about him.

Batshit terrified is more like it.

I bit back a sigh. I was a fucking idiot, but it was my own fault. I'd let this happen.

"You know I didn't steal some old lady's Buick, right?" Finn said softly from the passenger seat. I hadn't been able to bring myself to put him in the back of the vehicle like an actual suspect.

"I'm not talking about it," I ground out.

"Just tell me where you found false witnesses. At the diner? That's pretty rich."

I gripped the steering wheel tighter to keep from throttling him. "They aren't false witnesses." Even if they had been easily misled by the stupidly simple "disguise" of a *Hot as Heller* ball cap. A souvenir that was currently being sold at a hundred different locations in town, including the gas station next to the sheriff's department.

"Why would I even do something like that? Jesus."

"Celebrities get bored. They do stupid shit."

He turned to stare at me. "Ahh, there's that asshole chip on your shoulder. I almost missed it for a minute. Almost."

"Am I saying something that's not true?"

"Mpfh," he said before slumping down in his seat and crossing his arms. He looked tired. And dirty. Like he'd been on the mountain all day working hard.

I reached into the center console and pulled out a cold water bottle before passing it to him without a word.

"Thanks," he murmured. He cracked it open and took several large swallows. I almost wrecked the fucking vehicle watching his slender throat work.

"Are there beds in the jail? I could go for a catnap."

I loved that he wasn't scared. I selfishly hoped it meant he trusted me. He shouldn't have. But if he did, that was nice.

"Yes. It doesn't have a kitchen, though, so we'll have to pick you up some dinner on the way through town."

Finn's lips curved up in an absent smile as he watched the warm colors of the sunset paint the town outside the passenger window. "Does the Greek place have a drive-thru? I could go for some hummus."

I bit back my own smile. He was a damned delight, and I was a goner. This man had me wrapped around his little finger.

"I didn't want you on the mountain after dark," I admitted gruffly.

"I know." He turned and gave me an affectionate grin. "And I kind of want to smother you in ki..." He glanced at one of the cameras in the dash. "My gratitude right now."

206LUCY LENNOX

I cleared my throat. "That would be... inappropriate. But, ah... nice."

There'd most likely never be a reason for anyone to view the dash cam footage, but I still didn't want an official record of my goofy infatuation with Finn Heller. Later, when he was long gone, I would want to keep the memories to myself, held tightly in the deepest part of my heart where I already knew they would live on forever.

I swung into the Greek place and told him to wait in the car while I grabbed us some food. After placing a quick call to the overnight dispatcher to get her order, I went inside and waited for the food.

What the hell was I going to do with Finn when I got him to the office? It wasn't like he was a serious suspect for the Brainthwaite joyriding case. I was going to have to make it clear to him he was free to go. Would he feel obligated to return to the set and let them put him on that rock face?

Nerves twisted my stomach as I waited for our orders to be ready, but then damned if that cocky bastard didn't make the decision easy for me.

"Sheriff?" Castor said from behind the restaurant counter. He pointed past my shoulder to the scene outside the restaurant. There, framed by the large plate glass window of Kozani's was a scene I wouldn't have believed if I wasn't watching it with my own eyes. That blond-haired shitty sidekick of Finn's had pulled open the passenger door to my vehicle and was screaming in Finn's face about something I couldn't hear.

By the time I processed what was happening, Finn had punched the kid twice in the face and shoved him on the ground. I raced outside to intervene only to find Finn whaling on the kid on the hard asphalt. They both had rips in their shirts and bloody noses. I reached for the radio on my shoulder to call Janine for backup. I was sure I could break them up—both men were much smaller than I was—but I was definitely not transporting them both in the same vehicle afterward.

I grabbed Finn around the waist and hoisted him off the other man. "Hey, hey, cool it."

"Let me go," he growled. "You don't know what he did. What he said to me."

"Doesn't matter. Words aren't the same as punches. Stop. *Stop*."

Finn's voice had a tinge of hysteria in it. Something bad had obviously gone down between the two of them, but this wasn't the way to solve it. He wrestled to try and get out of my hold, but I pulled him back against my chest and stepped away from Kix. Several witnesses raced over to gawk.

Kix turned a vicious expression on Finn. "You're going to regret this. I'm pressing charges. See what that does to your perfect fucking pristine reputation."

Finn's hand on my forearm went from trying to shove me off to holding on tight. I wasn't even sure he realized it. He held my arm firmly against him like he was scared of letting go. "Dec..."

He was breathing heavy, and his rough voice broke on the word. Whatever this was about, it had cut him deep.

I moved him back toward the vehicle, only this time, I had to put him in the back. There were too many witnesses, and I needed to make sure Kix didn't run off.

"Get in there and catch your breath," I said, moving him as gently as possible into the back seat of the SUV.

He shot me a glare. "If you so much as mention a blank piece of fucking paper..."

I closed the door before he could finish the sentence.

Kix was already on his feet, making a scene. One hand swiped at the blood on his lip while the other pointed aggressively at me. "You'd better fucking arrest him. You were a witness. I didn't touch him! He came at me, and I was only defending myself."

I held out my hands in the universal "calm down" gesture and tried to keep my cool when my inner caveman wanted to pummel the kid just for daring to upset Finn.

I had it bad. It was clear I couldn't be the officer in charge of this case. I was way too personally involved to be objective. Where was my backup?

"Take a breath," I told him. "Let's let cooler heads prevail. Do you need medical attention?"

His eyes darted to Finn and back to me. I could see the calculations the kid was making in his mind. His injuries weren't serious enough for a hospital visit, but would it help an assault case? Would it help a media campaign?

Castor had run out of the restaurant with a first aid kit. "No need, no need. Looks like a simple case of a split lip and maybe a shiner. Bruises and scrapes. Boys being boys, eh?"

Now that his masculinity had been challenged by the older man, Kix gave up. "I'm fine. Whatever. But I am pressing charges."

My backup finally arrived in the form of Rolly Kepplow, who I'd had to keep on the force due to the simple issue of being short-handed with all of the fans in town for the *Gold Rats* shoot.

"What's going on, Sheriff?" he asked, stepping out of his vehicle and eyeing Kix with a combination of suspicion and awe. I already knew how much of a celebrity fan Rolly was, so this came as no surprise.

"Physical altercation between two males," I said, moving into work mode. "This man would like to press charges. The other is already detained in the back of my vehicle. I suggest taking them both in to take reports somewhere more private. Hopefully we can sort this out at the department."

Kix eyed Rolly wearily. "You're not taking me in. I'll come down there to file a report, but not in the back of your cop car."

Rolly looked at me, and I nodded. "Escort him in his own vehicle." I looked around to see where he was parked. It was only then I realized he'd shown up in the McLaren. Fucking Christ.

I returned to my vehicle and leaned in. I already knew Finn legally owned the car since I'd run the plates that first night.

"He's here in the McLaren. Do you—"

"Are you fucking kidding me? He stole my fucking car? Is he for real?"

Ooookay, so he wasn't cooled down yet. He'd obviously crumpled up the plain piece of white paper and set it on fire.

"Are you pressing charges, or are you letting him drive it to the department?"

Finn looked at me like I was two beats shy of a melody. "I am pressing charges. Big ones. All the charges."

I bit my tongue to keep from laughing. He was so goddamned cute, I couldn't stand it. Seeing him angry made me want to kiss his face off for some reason.

I didn't think he'd appreciate it at the moment, and I didn't really want to lose my job in a giant scandal either.

"Hang tight," I told him before returning to Kix. "Sir, it appears you are here in a stolen vehicle. Deputy Kepplow, please arrest this man on suspicion of auto theft. Once you've secured him in your vehicle, I'll need you to arrest the other suspect in my vehicle before we take them both in to get this sorted out."

Rolly looked at me funny but didn't ask questions. He simply began reading Kix his rights and escorted him to the back of the vehicle. Once Kix was secure, he returned to my vehicle and Mirandized Finn as well. Finn's eyes widened in surprise as they flicked over to me. I couldn't even give him a reassuring expression considering I didn't know how this was going to play out.

I turned back to the crowd of witnesses. "Can anyone here give me a witness statement about either the altercation or the arrival of the blue sports car?"

A few hands shot up, and I pulled out my little notebook to take down contact information and hand out my business card so the witnesses could come in at their leisure tomorrow to make statements. One of the witnesses was Gentry Kane's uncle Doran, who'd just pulled up to pick up dinner from Kozani's also. He wasn't known for keeping his mouth shut, and I knew he'd run right back to report what had happened to Gent and Winter, who'd probably tell Mikey and Tiller what was going on with the film crew who'd rented their property.

There were several witnesses for both crimes which made me both relieved and also angry as hell. Why had Finn thrown the first punch? If he'd just kept his cool and stayed in the vehicle, we'd be happily eating Greek food right now.

I looked over at the restaurant. Castor held up a finger for me to wait, so I re-entered the shop. "Sorry about all this," I said. "Is it okay if the sports car stays in the lot until tomorrow?"

He waved off the concern. "Yes, yes, of course. Your food is almost ready. Tell Janine I made extra so she has enough for a midnight snack."

I smiled my appreciation at him, taking a small moment to appreciate how much I loved living in a small town where everyone knew everyone and people looked out for each other. Even though I had strong feelings for Finn, I was going to be very happy when the film crew left town and Aster Valley returned to normal.

When the food was ready, I got back in the car and handed one of the bags of food to a stone-faced Finn.

"That motherfucker read me my rights and told me I was under arrest."

I glanced at him in the rearview as I settled into the driver's seat. "You are. You're under arrest for assault. Second-degree assault is a class four felony in Colorado with a potential jail term of two to six years."

The blood drained from his face. It was a familiar response to a law enforcement officer, but not one I'd ever wanted to see on his freckled face.

"But I was defending myself."

I chose my words carefully. "From what? Menacing? Menacing, or threatening bodily harm, is also illegal in Colorado. It's a class three misdemeanor. Up to six months in jail."

His eyes widened as he realized what I was saying. Not only could he hold the car theft over Kix, but he could also suggest the man had violated the law when he'd approached Finn with anger. The combination of potential crimes might make Kix rethink pressing assault charges against Finn.

This was all something a high-paid criminal attorney would know, but Finn wouldn't see an attorney for several hours at least. If he didn't want to spend the night in a jail cell, he might want to use some of this information before the fancy California lawyer arrived.

But it wasn't my place to suggest it.

Finn spent the rest of the drive shoving food in his mouth since he correctly assumed he wouldn't be able to keep eating once we began processing him in.

As soon as we walked into the department, Janine raised her head up and gestured to a man in the small seating area. "Mr. Heller's attorney."

I was stunned at how quickly they'd gotten someone here. Even a lawyer from Denver would have had to take a helicopter to get here this fast.

"I don't know you," Finn said carefully, looking at the well-dressed man. He was very good-looking with dark styled hair and a trendy bit of dark scruff on his cheeks and chin. A little niggle of jealousy wormed its way into my gut.

The man reached out a hand to shake Finn's. "I know. I'm friends with Tiller and Mikey, who own the property where you're staying. When they heard you'd been arrested, they sent me to help. I'm a corporate attorney out of Denver, but I was in town visiting Mikey to go over some business contracts. I figured I might be able to help clear this up before you go to the trouble of bringing in the big guns from LA. My name is Julian Thick."

Finn's signature smile appeared. "Julian, so nice to meet you. Thank you for coming to help out. I really appreciate it." He turned to me. "*Sheriff*, I'd like to meet with my attorney. Alone."

He was acting like any of this was my fault. I wanted to put him over my fucking knee.

"Right this way. I have an *interrogation room* you can use." Two could play at this game.

Once I got them settled in the room and closed the door, I let out a breath and returned to the front where Rolly was helping Janine enter Kix's information into the system.

"Kenneth Rowe, you say?" Janine asked with a raised eyebrow.

I wanted to laugh at how uncomfortable Kix looked.

"Yes, ma'am. Why did Finn get to see an attorney already? I want an attorney. And I want to make a phone call."

"His attorney was here waiting for him. I didn't arrange it for him," I informed him. "Would you like a public defender? It might take me a couple of hours to get one here, but I'm certainly happy to do that."

Kix lifted up his hands and stepped backward, away from the counter where Janine was preparing to take his fingerprints.

"Woah. Woah. Wait a minute. I'm the victim here, and I'm the only one being fingerprinted. That's not right."

Rolly met his eyes. "You're under arrest for stealing his car, remember?"

"He loaned me that car!"

Rolly shrugged. "He says he didn't. You can take it up with the attorneys and the judge. It's above my pay grade."

Kix looked between me and Rolly. "He's playing favorites. The sheriff is sleeping with him, and he's giving him the cushy attorney and the special meeting room. I'm going to sue your asses for preferential treatment of the man who assaulted me."

I held up my hands. "All I did was drive him here. Deputy Kepplow arrested him. Deputy, do you have any prior relationship with Finn Heller?"

"No, sir. I do not. And I placed him under arrest the exact same way I did Mr. Rowe here. The only difference as far as I see it was allowing Mr. Heller to meet with his attorney at his own request. We're not legally allowed to prohibit that at this juncture. The man has rights. You're welcome to do the same. *If* you have an attorney, that is."

I was going to have to reconsider Rolly's termination. He was impressing me with his cheek.

Kix's nostrils flared. "Get him out here. I want to talk to him."

I shook my head. "I don't think that's a good idea until we take your statements."

Before he could argue with me, Julian came out of the interrogation room and joined us at the counter. "I think we can clear this up easily without any charges being made. Is this Mr. Rowe?"

Kix narrowed his eyes at the hot attorney. "I am. Did the film send you? If so, that's not fair."

"No, a personal friend of Mr. Heller's sent me from Denver. I'd like to propose you both drop the charges against each other. You drop the assault charge, and in return, Mr. Heller will drop the first-degree aggravated motor vehicle theft charge, the class three menacing charge, the defamation charge, the perjury charge for bearing false witness, and the—"

Kix couldn't take it anymore. "Fine! Fucking fine! Jesus. I get it. Finn has more money than I do and can afford a fancy lawyer to pound me into the ground. Typical fucking Finn Heller maneuver. I'll bet his fucking mother sent you here, didn't she?"

Julian leveled him with a professional stare. "Do you agree to drop the charges?"

Kix looked suddenly deflated. "Yes. Fine. But that means there's nothing in the record about this for me either, right?" He looked at me, but Janine was the one who answered.

"No record, sweetie." She made a few loud clicks on her keyboard that probably did absolutely nothing to the data she'd entered.

Julian dropped his business face and replaced it with a kind smile. "Would you mind handing me the keys to the McLaren, please?" Then he held out his hand to the younger man. Kix looked like he wanted to shank the man, but he handed them over.

"Are you at least going to give me a ride back to the lodge?"

Julian's eyebrow raised. "You're staying at Rockley Lodge? That's where I'm headed. I'll give you a ride. No problem."

After they were gone, I thanked Janine and Rolly and made my way to the interrogation room which was still closed. When I opened the door, I saw Finn asleep with his head on his crossed arms on the table.

I closed the door quietly behind me and approached him, squatting down and running my hand through his hair.

"Hey, tough guy. You've been sprung from the clink," I said softly.

Finn blinked his eyes open. His makeup had worn off enough for me to see the dark scrape still healing on his cheek from the rock face incident the other day and a new bruise forming around one of his eyes from a punch Kix had obviously landed before I got there.

"Are you mad at me?" he asked in a whisper. His worried green eyes were a knife to my heart.

My heart flooded with affection. "No, sweetheart. I'm so fucking proud of you. When I showed up on set, it looked like you were standing up for yourself. And then with Kix... I don't know what he said to you, but I could tell it upset you. I don't agree with punching the guy, but again, it looks like you were defending yourself. I wouldn't have wanted you to sit there and take it. I only wish I'd come out quick enough to get him to back off before it turned physical."

"He said some bad stuff. About me. About my mom. And he thought I was being too sensitive about the house party thing. He's... it's a long story, and I just want to be done with him. We were friends for a long time. At least, I used to think we were friends. But I see it very differently now."

I got the impression the little punk had used Finn, but I didn't want to say anything when I truly didn't know the full story. Hopefully, Finn would tell it to me in time, but tonight he looked too worn-out for much more than sleep.

"Come on," I said, standing up and pulling him out of the chair. "You're coming back to my place tonight. I assume your mom is still at the chalet."

Instead of following me to the door of the interrogation room, Finn pulled my hand until I'd turned to face him, and then he walked right into my arms.

I held on tightly to this man I'd completely misjudged. The man who was trying so hard to figure out who he was and who he wanted to be in this big bad world.

The man who was damned near close to stealing my heart completely out of my chest and taking it back with him to California forever.

20

FINN

I fell asleep resembling an empty husk, but somehow, I woke up feeling whole again. Energized and empowered. Letting go of my unhealthy relationship with Kix was more freeing than I expected. And waking up with a hard cock riding through the cleft of my ass wasn't bad either.

"Fuck me," I said excitedly. "Sorry I fell asleep on you last night."

"Mpfh."

He wasn't awake yet, but his hands were all over me, I reached back and squeezed his ass. "Or I can fuck you. Either way. Someone needs to be fucked."

"Ngh."

The prickly scruff of his beard scraped against my shoulder as his lips nibbled a path up to my neck and behind my ear. Just his presence in the room made me hard, but this? The humping and growling? This made me short of breath and slutty.

"Okay, me. I'll be the one fucked. You'll be the one fucking. Where are the condoms?" I was talking to myself. Declan was way too busy getting handsy. His fingers were down the front of my underwear. I couldn't think with his hand on my dick.

"Con... condoms," I tried again. My brain very helpfully supplied the image of a clean sheet of white paper. "You're not helping," I told it, exasperated as hell.

"Stroking your dick isn't helping?" he grumbled into the hot skin of my neck.

"Oh Jesus Christ," I said on a gasp. My dick was leaking now. I needed him inside me before that voice brought me off prematurely. "You're not helping either."

I pressed back against his cock with my ass and tried reaching for the nightstand with my hand. The result was an unsuccessful Gumby maneuver. "Fuck."

Declan's rumble of laughter made me feel like I was flying. How was it possible to go from such a low yesterday to such a high this morning?

Declan. That was how.

"I can't... you have to let me get... oh god, more. More of that. Squeeze... just like that. Fuck." I'd forgotten all about the condom. His hand was magical.

"Nightstand. Go."

What that bossy voice did to me. I lurched toward the drawer and yanked it out, grabbing for whatever I could get my hands on. I came back with a handful of various items, including lube, cough drops, a phone charger, a small bottle of headache medicine, and—thank the blessed Virgin Mary—some condoms.

Declan suited up while I shimmied out of my boxer briefs. When I met his eyes, my heart did a little pirouette. "I want to ride you," I admitted. "Please."

His grin was sexy as fuck and all-knowing. Declan lay back on the bed and stretched that big, muscular body in invitation.

As if I needed an invitation to climb on that man.

I scrambled over him and straddled his hips, reaching for the lube bottle and pumping some into my hand. I reached back to make a quick pass at prep when all I really wanted to do was sit on his dick, prep be damned.

When I finally felt his thick cock head stretch me open, I groaned and threw my head back. Fuck, this felt good. I wanted it all the

fucking time. Day, night, midday, morning, twilight, bedtime. Whatever. Whenever. There was no such thing as enough sex with Declan
Stone.

I wanted all of it.

His hands spread out on my thighs, clasping firmly as I lifted
myself up and down and felt the incredible slide of his body in mine.
Our eyes met.

"Declan," I breathed.

He reached up a hand to clasp my cheek and brought my face
down for a kiss. It was sweet and gentle, tender. His hand moved
around to hold the back of my head, and his other one came around
my body to spread across my lower back in a possessive hold.

"You're perfect," Declan said. "Everything about you is... my
favorite."

It was awkward and sweet. I couldn't believe we were here, clearly
well past the hookup stage and obviously into each other for more
than just sex. But god, the sex was amazing. I wanted all of it. The sex,
the affection, the companionship. I wanted Declan Stone to be my
person.

My heart thumped merrily in my chest with the eager, naive
belief it would all work out. So what, we lived in different states? Pfft.
Logistics. So we had wildly incompatible careers. Whatever. Details.

After giving Declan another long kiss, I sat back up and used his
body to make myself feel good. I loved preening for him. His eyes
went dark and drank in every inch of my body like it was some kind
of life-saving elixir.

"Can't get enough of you," he said, spreading a hand along my abs
and up to my chest before tweaking a nipple and making me clench
around him in response. "Fuck, you're killing me."

He lurched up and grabbed me around the shoulders, twisting
me until I was the one on my back and he was above me, pounding
into me while my legs went every which way in the air. It didn't
matter. All that mattered was the sensation of his thick cock nudging
the spot that made me nearly swallow my tongue.

"That's it," he mumbled. "Feel good?"

That was a stupid question I didn't bother to answer. Presumably the sound of my breaths sawing in and out of my lungs was answer enough. Declan reached down to run a fingertip around my rim, to feel the way his cock was stretching me. The touch nearly shorted out my brain. I grappled for my dick and stroked it, crying out a warning that this was all coming to a crashing end whether he liked it or not.

"Fuck!" I shouted, forgetting all about the fact another person currently lived in this house. "Fuck, oh god. Fuck, *fuck*."

Declan let out his own release in a muffled roar against my neck. His taller body bent over me, and my hips were lifted up on his thighs as he thrust deep inside and shuddered through his orgasm.

I clutched his head and pressed kisses into his hair, biting back more curses of disbelief at how incredible sex with him felt.

"Not a bad way to wake up," he eventually said in a slow drawl that made me laugh. He grinned and kissed me again on the lips, lingering a few beats in a way that made me feel seen and appreciated. "Be right back. Don't move."

He wandered off to the bathroom, leaving me free to enjoy the view. His pale, muscular ass was topped by a tan line that made me curious what activity he did without a shirt on.

When he returned, Declan brought a hot wet cloth to clean me off, but I waved it away. "I need to take a shower and get going. I want to call my agent before I get to the set. There's no way I'm doing the climbing scene in the dark. At least without my climbing supervisor onsite."

He didn't say anything as he reached for my hand and led me to the shower. It wasn't until he was halfway through scrubbing me down that he finally spoke. But it wasn't to give me his opinions like I'd expected.

"Who does Solo hang out with?"

I turned to face him. "I don't really know. I can tell you the names of a few of the kids taking the summer school class with him. But I don't really know if he hangs out with them outside of it."

"I recognized Melanie Taggart and Joey Mixon. Who else was there?"

I tried to picture their faces. "Brandon Huber was the kid with the super-short blond hair. Marcus Bledsoe was the super-tall guy. Tay Hendrickson was the girl with the curly brown hair down her back, and let's see... the other girl's name was..." It took me a second to remember. "Kelsey, I think. But I don't remember her last name. Her mom is a pediatrician."

"Oh, Seibert, probably. Joann is her mom. Tessa and I met her last week when we were checking out the pediatrics office for the baby."

The casual mention of Tessa's baby brought up several questions, but I didn't have time to get into them now. I wanted to know what her plans were. Was she going to live here with Declan permanently? Was she covered financially, or did she need help? I wasn't sure what kind of living the sheriff of a small county in Colorado made, but it seemed like Declan probably had her covered if need be. But still. Was Declan going to help raise her baby? What was his role in all of this?

I kept reminding myself it wasn't really any of my business, but then again... I was beginning to think it might be. Rather, I *wanted* it to be my business. I wanted him to be my business.

But first, I needed to get my head in the game and finish out this film commitment.

It was obvious Declan wasn't very pleased with my rush to report to the set, but I was on a mission. My head was buzzing with plans. When Julian had pulled me aside in the interrogation room last night at the sheriff's department, he'd asked me what I wanted.

"I want to not be arrested," I'd said with a laugh.

"That's a given," he'd said, waving his elegant fingers through the air. "I can handle that. Your frenemy out there would be an idiot to press charges when you can pin him with motor vehicle theft and disorderly conduct."

That's when I'd mentioned the menacing. His eyes had danced. "Sounds like the sheriff likes you, Finn."

I'd huffed. *Not right now*, I'd thought to myself.

But then he'd doubled down. Julian had repeated his original question. "What do you want? In life, I mean."

I'd stared at him while my mind buzzed around with thoughts. "Why are you asking me this?"

He'd sighed and sat back. "My best friend just got engaged, and I just... I mean, what's it all about, you know? What's the fucking purpose of any of this?"

I'd blinked at him. "Con... grats?"

Then Julian had heaved an exhausted sigh. Suddenly, he hadn't looked like a put-together professional. He'd looked like a man who needed a nap. He'd looked like I'd felt. "Not really. I've been in love with him my whole life. But he's straight, so it's fine. I mean, it's not fine. Obviously. Anyway, forget I asked. I'm just feeling... melancholy. Ignore me. Let's get you out of here. Hang tight."

After he'd left, I'd thought about his question. What did I want in life?

Not this. Not this action film where the money was great but the conditions were dangerous because of a director's ego, because of the insane way Hollywood rewarded films and directors that "pushed boundaries."

I didn't want this life I had. The people in LA who claimed to be my friends but who most likely wouldn't show up if I suddenly lived in a place like Watts again. Hell, I'd had more fun here in Aster Valley than I'd had living in Santa Monica right on the ocean. Even the chalet felt more like home to me than my sterile, professionally decorated house in California.

But then I remembered Nolan's dangling carrot.

The Taming of the Shrew.

I could put my head down and get through *Gold Rats* if that was what was waiting for me at the end. My dream was to work on a Shakespeare project of some kind. To immerse myself in the language and nuance, the history and pageantry, of a quality Shakespeare production.

I wondered idly if Solo and his friends would have any interest in putting on an abridged version of *Hamlet* for their teacher. Would the teacher be impressed or pissed? There was no way to know unless I asked him, but I wasn't about to overstep. That would probably not go over well.

One thing at a time. I was here to film *Gold Rats*. Period. And I had high expectations of myself. I would act as well as I could and give this project all of me regardless of the director, the other actors, or any other detail unrelated to my own work ethic.

But that's not to say I wouldn't look out for myself.

I called Iris as soon as Declan dropped me off at my car in town.

"Finn, darling. I'm hearing wonderful things from your mother."

Way to set my teeth on edge from the first moment. I ignored the comment and got right into the reason for my call. I didn't have much time. The drive to the set's base of operations on the mountain wasn't that long.

"Yeah, well, hopefully Dawson filled you in on what they tried to pull last night. There was no mention of night climbing, and I'm not doing it without a stronger safety protocol, especially after what happened the other day."

"Where is Kramer?"

I wanted to scream. She already knew all of this. And if she didn't, she wasn't making me much of a priority. "Not here. So they either need to replace him with someone else certified at that level or wait until he gets back here to shoot a technical scene like that, someone AMGA-certified. I'm sure there are a ton of instructors out here in the Rockies."

"I consulted with our attorney late last night when I received your message. They don't see a place indicating that requirement in the contract. I'm sorry, Finn. It looks like you'll need to—"

I tried to focus on the road despite seeing red. "Go back and ask again, because I was sure there were safety protocol requirements mentioned."

"Well, yes, but the way it's written says the climbing instructor needs to *consult* on the shoot, not be present during shooting."

I felt wholly let down by this process. "Iris, I know we didn't discuss a lot about this contract and the stunts I was going to be required to do, and that's my bad because I trusted that you'd be looking out for my safety and my best interest. I won't make that mistake again. But I know for a fact that I told you I wanted a certified climbing safety inspector present at every shoot where I was in rigging. I told you so many times you rolled your eyes at me. You said of course that would be in there. You said it had been included in my terms since *Cast in Clover*. You said it was standard procedure."

Instead of sounding nervous, she sounded falsely patient, like she was attempting to *manage* me. "Finn, dear, you're an excellent climber. Hell, you have the same safety certifications Kramer does. Why in the world would we need—"

I cut her off before pulling down the road to the parking area. "Have the attorney call me directly in the next ten minutes, and make sure they have a copy of the contract in front of them. Do you understand?"

I hung up the phone and parked the car behind my trailer. Hopefully craft services had something hearty for breakfast because I was starving. Before heading over to the tent, I popped into my trailer to see if the call sheets were there yet. Instead of a call sheet, I found my mother.

"Mom. What are you doing here?"

She looked nervous. "Thank goodness. It's so good to see you. I was worried after I heard about the arrest."

Her hug covered me in a cloud of perfume. "It wasn't exactly an arrest," I muttered. "More like a mutual misunderstanding."

"Well, I saw how you *misunderstood* Kix's face. The poor kid is sporting a shiner today."

I glanced at her to see if she was joking. "I... I also have a black eye, Mom. In case you didn't notice. Also? I was sitting in a vehicle minding my own business when Kix came driving up in my car—taken without my permission—and began verbally attacking me out of the blue." I didn't mention the horrible things he'd said about her, but they were definitely on my mind again.

"You boys have always acted like brothers. It's just one of those things, I guess."

"No, Mom. Not one of those things. Not one of those things at all.

I felt guilty for years because I got the Chip Clover role and he didn't. But I'm done feeling guilty for that. I'd like to think I would have gotten it anyway. Despite what Kix has said for years, he wasn't a shoo-in for the role. Had they wanted him that badly, they would have waited for him. Also? How many times over the years did the casting agent preen about what an impeccable casting decision she'd made with me?"

Mom clasped my upper arms and smiled at me. "Don't for one minute think I don't believe you were the absolute best choice. You *are* Chip Clover. You defined that role, and history shows what a great casting decision it was. And look where it's led you. I hope you know how proud I am of you, Finn."

Her words were the typical roller-coaster ride of ups and downs. On the one hand, she was proud of me. Up. On the other, she saw me as Chip Clover. Down. She appreciated my acting chops. Up. But she thought it had led me to a place I really wanted to be. Down.

"Thank you. Did you need something? Otherwise, I'm going to grab breakfast and get to work."

She waved her hand in the air. "Oh, no. I just stopped by to... see how you were. I'm going to head back home this afternoon, but I was hoping you might let me watch whatever shoot you have today. I already ran it past Nolan, and he said it was fine."

My stomach dropped. "You... you already asked the director..." I didn't want to know. *I didn't want to know.* "How... how do you..." I bit my teeth together to fight sudden nausea. "Do you know Nolan Trainor?"

"Honey, everyone knows Nolan Trainor. Don't be ridiculous." She rummaged in her designer purse for something. "I happened to run into him this morning when I got to the set. He was very welcoming."

"How welcoming?" I asked, before I could stop myself.

My mother's blush and avoidance of eye contact told me all I needed to know about the truth of Kix's words.

I was gutted.

"Mom," I said, voice cracking. "Please tell me you didn't—"

Her eyes snapped to mine. "What I do in private is none of your business, understand me? None. And if you think for one minute someone with Nolan Trainor's reputation would ever cast someone who wasn't the right choice for the role, well, then you don't know Nolan Trainor."

I thought of all the smack talk I'd heard over the years about Nolan. How he was a player with a giant ego. He loved to be known for being edgy and pushing boundaries. How he treated people like commodities.

And suddenly, I was simply done.

I nodded and smiled at my mother the best I could. "Thank you for everything you've ever done for me. I know it wasn't easy being practically a child yourself when you were tasked with raising one. And I can't imagine what it would have been like growing up gay in Grandma and Grandpa's house. Because of you, I can live the life I want and make whatever choice I want for my future. Please don't ever think I'm ungrateful for that, because I'm not. Because of you and this work, I'm able to follow my dreams."

And my words were true. She just didn't know what dreams I was referring to.

21

DECLAN

When I got to the office after dropping Finn off in town, I was whisked right into one situation after another. Mrs. Brainthwaite's car had been stolen again, only this time she had the video doorbell. After figuring out how to retrieve the footage, we saw it was Mrs. Brainthwaite herself who'd driven off in the vehicle before being dropped back home an hour later by her sister.

We contacted Alicia to ask how she'd come to bring her sister home and discovered Mrs. Brainthwaite had been turning up at Alicia's house mysteriously from time to time with no recollection of how she'd gotten there. Alicia lived within easy walking distance of all the locations the car had been abandoned in.

Unfortunately, Alicia was now tasked with making sure Mrs. Brainthwaite got the proper medical assessments, and I was tasked with recommending she voluntarily give up her driving license until and unless a doctor could approve her mental clarity.

It was a sad situation all around, but I was glad to at least not have to interrogate Solo's friends. I hadn't wanted to believe any of them would have used possible information from Solo's job running errands to take advantage of the older woman, but I'd been at my wit's end on finding the answer to the abandoned car mystery.

With that solved, I moved on to scheduling some additional training for Rolly and putting in a request for an additional part-time deputy now that tourism was picking back up in Aster Valley. Crime hadn't increased at all, but other needs were. Patrol requests, motor vehicle incidents, noise and disorderly complaints, and trespass violations were up. We needed a part-timer now, and we'd need to add a couple more full-timers as soon as the ski resort opened. I made a note to contact Tiller and Mikey to discuss their plans.

The day went by in a blink the way it usually did. This job kept me on my toes, and I loved that part of it. Shawn came in for a late shift with a goofy grin on his face and confessed to having real feelings for Tessa. He poked his head in my office to say hello and told me he'd had lunch with her.

"I'm going on that annual fishing trip I told you about with my dad and my brother tomorrow, and I think I'm going to tell them about her. I know it's quick, though. I don't want to freak her out or anything, but she's like... god, Declan. She's everything. You know?"

"She's pretty great," I admitted, spotting the woman herself over his shoulder. He must not have realized she was coming to take me to dinner. "And I think she'd appreciate hearing you say so. She's going through a scary time right now and can use all the support she can get." I shot her a wink, but Shawn must not have noticed.

His grin dropped, and his face became serious. "I'm here for all of it. If she'll let me. The baby and everything. I'm serious, Declan. This isn't just a fling for me. I've had girlfriends before, and I never felt a fraction for them the way I feel for Tessa. I want to make her happy. Whatever it takes. And... I'm not in a hurry. I don't want to rush her or pressure her right now. I just want to be there for her. I... I really care about her."

Oh shit.

The tears came right on cue. It was the first big sniffle that clued Shawn in to his inadvertent eavesdropper.

His face dropped. "Baby, hell. Oh hell, I didn't mean... Come here." He held her in a tight hug and ran his hand over her hair, making sweet shushing noises and rocking her gently.

"I should have said those things to you." He chastised himself quietly into her hair. I stood up and walked over to the pair of them before nudging them both into my office and closing the door to give them privacy. Then I caught Penny's eye across the office. Her hand was on her heart, and she had a Kleenex under her eye.

I laughed. "There you go. An office romance and you didn't even have to work for it."

Finn had texted around lunchtime that he'd agreed to do the night climbing scene after all. He'd arranged for an experienced climbing instructor from over in Steamboat Springs to be on set for it to help oversee the safety issues, and I got the feeling he was paying for it out of his own pocket.

I tried not to spend too much time thinking about it or I'd need to get back in my office for the bottle of antacids in my desk.

Instead, I'd decided to reach out to Mikey, who reached out to Sam and Truman, who reached out to Winter and Gent, to see if they wanted to grab a beer somewhere. Julian was still in town, so he joined us at Pie Hole.

The first thing Truman said when I sat down was, "Tell me everything. Oh my god he's so stinking cute. Don't you think? Those freckles." He clasped his hands in front of his chest and sighed. Truman's blond, bearded boyfriend blinked at him.

"Do we need to give you a private moment?"

Truman laughed and leaned over to kiss the edge of Sam's jaw. It wasn't until his lips were on his big boyfriend that Truman's ears turned pink.

"There's only one man for me, big guy. Especially if that man knows how to hang closet shelving."

Sam broke out in a laugh, trying not to spit out his beer. "Fine. Alright. Enough. I'll do it tomorrow, I swear."

Truman looked over at me with a grin. "The cobbler's family has no shoes, or in our case the contractor's partner has no handyman around the house."

Mikey broke in. "Sorry, that's our fault. We're keeping him too busy with resort business."

Julian nodded like Mikey was doing the same to him.

Truman agreed. "That's true. But I know he's loving every minute of it. Aren't you, babe?" He turned an expectant expression on Sam, who gave a satisfied nod and stretched his arm around Truman's smaller form.

"I never knew I could work outside all day in the height of summer and not think I was on the verge of heatstroke. Aster Valley summers beat Houston ones, hands down."

I pictured Sam sweaty and shirtless on a Houston summer jobsite. That wasn't a bad image, but my brain quickly replaced Sam on urban scaffolding with Finn on a rock face, shirtless and sweaty. His muscles stretched and bunched as he reached for the next hand-hold or toe hold. The rope harness cupped his junk, and his ass and veins were visible on his forearms.

"... homicide. I just can't decide if I want to kill him slowly with a boning knife or quick-like with a semi-automatic."

My attention snapped to Mikey, who was looking at me with mischief in his eyes. "What the fuck?" I asked. "Who are we killing?"

The table of guys all broke into laughter at my expense. Mikey pointed to me and called me out for zoning out during the conversation. "Dude, it's nice to know when the convo around you turned to premeditated murder, your ears at least did you a solid."

Truman stopped giggling long enough to add, "And I love the use of the word 'we.' No matter what nefarious plans were afoot, our intrepid sheriff was all in."

Even Sam, who normally kept his emotions fairly close to the vest, was laughing his head off. I took a deep breath and let myself join them. It felt good to be out with friends. It felt good to be off duty and drinking beer with men I enjoyed and admired. I took a moment to appreciate what I'd gained when I'd made the decision to leave LA.

These men were my community. They cared about me, and the feeling was mutual.

"You didn't answer my question," I said to Mikey when the laughter died down. "Who are we killing?"

"Whoever it is that has stolen our precious friend's attention," he said, watching me carefully for a reaction. "You going to tell us what's going on? I left town for like a week, and I came back to Sheriff MoonyEyes."

"Sheriff I' Some," Julian mumbled into his copper mule mug. If I wasn't mistaken, this was his third. He'd already sucked down a couple of them in the time it took us to order our food. I hadn't even known the pizza place offered more than beer and wine.

I felt my face ignite and tried to hide it behind a sip of cold beer. "I'm, ah... seeing someone."

Truman looked positively bubbly with excitement. "Someone *famous*?"

Winter shot a wink at his celebrity husband. "Famous people are the best."

"Someone you swore off as a prima donna the last time we were together?" Mikey teased, ignoring Winter and Gent's quick kiss. "I believe you were going to steer clear of anyone even associated with *Gold Rats*."

"Not all Gold Rats are bad," I admitted with a smile. "Some of them are very, very good."

Julian muttered, "At least you have a rat. I don't have anything. The love of my life is marrying someone else, and fucking Christ, I need another drink."

Mikey reached out to rub Julian's shoulder. "We're going to hatch a plan. I told you. Sam has helped me strategize my way through many a love challenge. He even helped me land a pro football player. He can help you land a measly ski instructor."

"I don't want to *land* Parker. It's too late. Besides. Straight. Remember?"

Sam squinted at him. "Isn't Parker the one Tiller kissed in high school? Or am I remembering that wrong?"

From the look on Mikey's face, Sam had just spilled beans that had been locked up tight. Julian stared at him. "What?"

Mikey kicked Sam under the table, and Sam put on the fakest smile ever. "Ha! Just kidding! I think... I think that guy's name was... Clark-er."

Truman facepalmed and muttered something under his breath. Mikey's nostrils flared. "Are you trying to break his fucking heart? Samson Rigby, you're a monster."

Julian looked drunkenly between Mikey and Sam. "Tell me everything."

Mikey shook his head. "No can do. Tonight is about Sheriff Happycock and the actor who begged him to manhandle his stick shif... hey! Hey, ha, Finn! Wow. You have... impeccable timing, don't you?"

I felt arms come around my neck from behind, and Finn's unique scent hit my nose. I closed my eyes for a beat to drink it in. "My ears were burning," he said before leaning in to press a kiss against my cheek, then temple, then neck. I shivered and reached for his wrist to pull him around so I could see him.

He was drop-dead beautiful, this sexy leading man I wanted so desperately to be a fixture in my life. "I thought you were filming the night scene?" I asked, pulling him onto my lap. The guys around us scrambled to get a chair for him, and after giving him a quick squeeze, I let him settle into it.

"They moved it to tomorrow night because of a maintenance issue with the helicopter. It means I have to bring the climbing supervisor back tomorrow, but that's fine. I was hoping to find you here. Janine said to try the Roadhouse or Pie Hole. I was hoping you were here because I could go for some pizza. I'm starving."

It was so good to see him, I couldn't stop staring.

The guys around the table welcomed him and introduced themselves if they hadn't already met him. I strode up to the bar to grab a cup and another pitcher of beer as well as put in an order for a greek salad I knew he'd probably want in addition to the pizza. When I got back to the table, I saw him laughing with my friends. I froze for a minute and thought back to the last time I'd been here and how I'd felt looking around the group of men, wishing I could feel a part of them and realizing I did.

Now it was even better. Not only did I truly feel like I had a group of friends, but there was Finn Heller, sitting and laughing with them as if he was simply... one of us.

Mine.

He glanced over at me with a frown, obviously wondering why I'd stopped before reaching the table. I continued over to him and set down the glass and pitcher before taking his face in both hands.

"Please tell me I can kiss you in public," I said softly.

"Please tell me you will," he replied. Before I had a chance to lean in, he added, "But know there are consequences. Like..."

Suddenly, I saw the fear in his eyes. I knew he meant media interference, attention I may not want. But if that was part of being with Finn, then that was inevitable anyway. I didn't want to hide my feelings about him from anyone.

I leaned in slowly so he had plenty of time to stop me.

He didn't.

We kissed for a full minute before the guys at the table began throwing up score numbers with their fingers. When I pulled away from Finn, he looked a little pink-lipped and dazed.

"So fucking gorgeous," I murmured before sliding into my seat again.

"You're dangerous, Sheriff Happycock," he said, revealing he'd heard plenty of the teasing that had gone on before I'd noticed his arrival. Mikey snorted out a mouthful of beer, and everyone else started laughing.

"Not sure happy is the word to describe it at the moment," I grumbled to Finn.

"Take me home later. I'll make sure to fix it."

The rest of the evening was some of the most fun I'd had since coming to Aster Valley. My friends were used to spending time with celebrities, and it didn't faze them. Gent and Finn talked about some mutual acquaintances they knew in the entertainment industry, and Mikey updated us on Tiller's upcoming season.

We left the restaurant on a high. Good food, decent beer, great company. When Finn mentioned his mother returning to LA, it was even better. "My place?" he suggested with bouncing eyebrows. "I had housekeeping come through after Mom left. Should be fresh and clean for us."

"Did they smudge it with sage? If not, Truman might have—"

Finn elbowed me in the side. "She's not an evil spirit. Just a misguided one. I've decided to forgive her for being young and ignorant and for making bad choices. She made a lot of good ones, too."

I pulled him closer before we reached his car. "Hey, I'm sorry. I was just joking about—"

"No, I know. I just... I've learned some not great things about my mom this week, and I'm coming to terms with it."

When we returned to the chalet, we sat curled up together on the sofa while he told me more about his mom, how she'd gotten him into acting and become "that" stage mom. He talked about his conflicting feelings, knowing she was desperate but also wishing he'd been able to have a "normal" childhood out of the media spotlight.

I loved hearing so much about his experience and his feelings. It made me feel closer to him. We hadn't talked about our relationship yet, but we shared the kind of vulnerabilities with each other that created that kind of intimacy. We'd blown well past casual sex territory into "I want this to become something real" territory.

But tonight wasn't the night to press. He was tired and a little sad, mourning the last vestiges of thinking his mother was anything more than a regular person with regular faults.

After brushing our teeth and stripping off our clothes, we slid between clean sheets and made love slowly and silently, using our hands and lips to tell each other how we felt. It was both intense and familiar, something I'd both already had with him and desperately wanted from him again and again.

I fell asleep wondering for the first time in six months if I would even consider moving back to LA in order to pursue a real relationship with Finn when *Gold Rats* filming wrapped.

I had it bad. And it was time for me to tell him.

The next day, Finn went to work, and I did the same, but just when I was ready to clock out for the day and check in with Finn before his night climb, Penny came racing into my office.

"It's Tessa! She couldn't get a hold of your cell. She's having pains and bleeding. Should I send a bus?"

I scrambled for my cell phone and noticed three missed calls and two missed texts. My phone's ringer had been acting up ever since the night I'd gone to Slye Peak in the rain and gotten it wet. It was supposed to be water-resistant, but at this rate, that appeared to be bullshit.

I quickly got her on the line. "Where are you?"

"The house. I'm scared. I think we should go to Denver. To the specialist. Remember what they said about—"

I snapped to get Penny's attention and nodded at her, mouthing, "Get a bus." An ambulance would be the best way to make sure she was in good hands as soon as possible. Penny ran off to arrange it.

"Tess, I'm sending an ambulance to the house," I said, keeping my voice calm. "I'm sure it's overkill, but let's not take any chances. I'll call the specialist and ask what they want us to do, but at least at Aster Valley Med you'll be in good hands in case it's something that can't wait." Or in case it needed transport by helicopter, but I didn't want to scare her.

I raced out to my SUV and went straight to the hospital. When they arrived, one of the EMTs I knew from the job gave me a look that said we'd probably be going to Denver in the air ambulance. Sure enough, within twenty minutes of being seen by the resident OBGYN, we were off to the city. I wasn't allowed to ride in the helicopter, but I got on the road in the SUV as quickly as I could, calling Penny to give her an update and then leaving a voicemail for Finn to tell him I wouldn't be back that night.

After trying Shawn with no success, I remembered he was deep in the middle of the backcountry somewhere fishing with his dad and brothers. "Fuck," I muttered, calling Penny back. "Hey, do you have an emergency contact for Shawn? I need to get a message to him about Tess."

She patched me through to Shawn's mother, and I explained politely who I was and that there was an item I needed to speak to him about as soon as possible when he came out of the woods. It wasn't a long trip, I didn't think. He'd only asked for one full day off work. If I wasn't mistaken, it was a one- or two-night thing.

When I finally arrived at the hospital in Denver, Tessa had already been examined, and the doctors had decided to do a C-section in order to alleviate the preeclampsia and avoid abruption. None of that sounded good. I knew preeclampsia had been the fear that had sent us to the specialist in the first place. She'd had some childhood cardiac issues that had caused the need for additional monitoring, but I hadn't expected it to culminate in an emergency C-section like this.

The doctor asked if I wanted to suit up and come into the operating room with them.

I glanced at Tess. "Mother's prerogative."

She got teary at the word "mother" and shot me the bird. "Of course I want you in there."

She didn't mention Shawn, but I knew she was thinking of him.

"I left a message with Shawn's mom to have him call me as soon as he gets back in range."

The next few hours were a whirlwind that resulted in the most perfect baby boy who'd ever lived. He was fat and purple, squinch-faced and loud as a siren. But he was healthy, and so was she.

And I was so incredibly grateful.

It was five in the morning when I finally had a chance to check my phone. I didn't want to wake Finn yet, but I was happy to see a missed call from Shawn. I called him back right away.

"Is she okay?" he asked without even saying hello.

"She's perfect. And so is her baby boy. We're at the hospital in Denver, and I'm sure she'd love to have you here."

I could tell he'd started crying. "It's a boy? Really? And they're both healthy? She's okay? He's okay? Are they—"

I cut him off with a laugh because I knew exactly how he felt. "Hang on, let me turn on FaceTime." I stepped back into Tessa's room and showed Shawn the new mother and my little siren of a faux nephew. "Aren't they incredible?"

"Yeah, they are! I'm heading to Denver now! Be there by midmorning."

Tess heard Shawn's voice and immediately reached for my phone, I handed it over and left the room again in search of much-needed coffee after my sleepless night. I took a few minutes to sit by myself in the hospital cafeteria and think of what an incredible experience it had been holding Tessa's hand during the delivery and what a fool Nick was for giving all of it up so easily.

"You fucking idiot," I murmured under my breath. "You had everything anyone could have wanted, and you fucked it all up."

It made me double down in my decision to lay my feelings on the line for Finn. As soon as Shawn arrived, I was going to head back to Aster Valley and tell that man I had strong feelings for him.

When I returned to the room and Tess handed me back my phone, I noticed a missed call and a text from Finn. I glanced at Tess. "You could have answered the call from Finn. He probably wants to congratulate you. I sent him some pictures."

She crinkled her brows. "The phone didn't ring."

The damned ringer. I toggled the mute switch back and forth and made sure the volume was all the way up. Then I checked the text.

Finn: *Congrats Uncle Sheriff! I'm so glad you were there for the delivery. That's pretty amazing, and you're right about him looking like a fat raisin lol. I'm at work. Night climb went well last night, but Nolan's trying to rework some things. Don't worry, though. Nothing I can't handle. I'll tell you about it when I see you. Go enjoy the baby, okay? I miss you. I can't wait to see you. I have some things I want to talk to you about. All good stuff, I promise.*

I tried calling him back, but it went straight to voicemail. I texted him back.

Me: *I miss you too. Have a good day at work, and good luck with whatever is going on. I know you can handle it, baby. I'm going to head back to Aster Valley as soon as Shawn gets here to hang out with Tessa. I don't know what time, but if you want to meet me at the house after* *work, the keypad code is the way Penny would relay confidential information ;-)*

"You're so gooey over that guy," Tessa gloated as she cuddled the baby. "You're texting with a big grin on your face, and you don't even realize it."

"Am I?"

"Mmhmm. And it's hella satisfying to see. I'm just glad to know there's someone else in the world who recognizes how special you are. You deserve that, Dec."

"He's the special one." I shook my head. "He came in like a shot out of the blue and shook my whole life up. I'm not sure I could go back to the way it was before."

And I knew for sure I didn't want to.

Finn Heller was a dream come to life.

But when Shawn arrived a couple of hours later, wide-eyed and white as a ghost, that dream quickly turned into a nightmare.

"Sheriff!" Shawn panted like he'd run the whole distance from the campground to the hospital, and I instantly jumped out of my chair. "Penny's been trying to get in touch with you for half an hour. There's been an explosion. Up on the mountain. By the film set."

I blinked, and my blood instantly ran cold. On the film set? The film set where Finn had an early call?

I had to work to keep my hands steady as I called Penny back, vowing to replace my broken phone as soon as possible. "What's going on?" I demanded. "Shawn said there was an accident on the set?"

I couldn't bring myself to say the word explosion. I couldn't bring myself to ask about Finn.

"Sheriff, thank god. It's a 10-80. There's a report of an explosion on the mountain that triggered a rockslide." She sounded harried, and I heard several phones ringing in the background. "Multiple 911 calls for medical and fire response. I called in Janine for backup and all hands on deck."

My brain couldn't even process what she was saying. I met Shawn's eyes. "The film crew wasn't supposed to set off their pyrotechnics until late next week, and the structure they were demo-ing shouldn't have been close enough to the side of the mountain to trigger a slide. How the hell did this happen?"

"Initial reports are saying it's not the temporary structure that exploded. It was the cave." Penny's no-nonsense voice quavered. "And it caused... hold on..."

I could hear her talking quickly, and I recognized the voices of Deputies Farmer and Kenton in the background. When she came back, she said, "Witnesses are reporting a rockslide and a cave-in. Missing persons from the cast and crew. Not sure who or how many. The director was hit with flying debris, and no one's able to tell us if there are any other charges set. We might need a bomb squad."

"I'll get back there as soon as possible. In the meantime, do the best you can. Tell Farmer to take the lead until I get there. I'll call the bomb squad here in Denver County, then I'll call Cort and get Routt County to give us a hand. Tell Kenton to call in mountain rescue if needed. Give me updates as often as you can."

I felt my training kick in—observe, assess, delegate, execute—and I was grateful for it. It held me together despite the fear gripping my chest.

I called the state folks and arranged for a bomb crew. They had access to a helicopter and told me to be ready on the hospital's helipad in ten minutes for departure.

I declined Shawn's offer to come with me and said a quick goodbye before making my way to the helipad and dealing with hospital security. While I waited, I made all the necessary calls to arrange extra support from the neighboring county and continued to touch base with Penny and the deputies onsite. When I finally had a minute on the helicopter to try and get Finn on the phone, the call went straight to voicemail. I tried again and again with no success.

I told myself it didn't mean anything. In an emergency like this, cell signals were jammed. For all I knew, a tower had come down in the explosion.

As much as I tried to focus on helping organize the emergency response, my thoughts kept spinning with thoughts of Finn missing, maybe trapped in that cave-in. I knew he was on set today, but I didn't know where he was supposed to be filming. Was it at the cave?

When we finally touched down on a meadow near the scene, I saw right away the response was still in chaos. Cast and crew wandered around in a daze, some with injuries and debris on their hair and clothes. I was desperate to find Finn, but I had to keep my focus on the job. Doing my job was the best way to get to Finn as fast as possible.

I found Deputy Farmer. "Do we know how many people are trapped?"

He was the most experienced deputy in the department. As a father of four and grandfather of fifteen, the man had no interest in the responsibility of being sheriff, but he certainly had the personality and know-how for the job. I'd felt confident putting him in charge, but I hated seeing any small-town deputy have to handle something of this magnitude. We simply didn't have the resources.

"No. The closest we can guess is at least six people. We've sent two buses to the hospital with fairly minor injuries so far and have one waiting here in case of a more serious injury. The rest are scrapes and bruises from what we can tell. One of the EMT crews is setting up a station to treat those over there." He indicated a nearby tent that had probably been used for some of the film crew during the shoot. "The good news is it wasn't a bomb. One of the crew members mentioned pyrotechnics for a scene they were filming. It was supposed to happen late next week, I guess, but they moved it up."

Rage churned in my gut, and I tried to hold it down.

That was the scene Finn was supposed to be in with Crystobell and Logan. Where Finn's character comes to save Crystobell's character from Logan's clutches and Logan dies in the explosion. But all of it was supposed to happen in the structure, not the cave. The shack structure that was still standing nearby, completely untouched, when everything around it seemed covered in rock dust.

I finally got close enough to see the mouth of the cave behind the temporary shack. Only it was no longer the mouth of a cave; it was a pile of boulders. My stomach dropped. Clearing an opening in that was going to take hours, and meanwhile, the people inside would be...

Do not imagine Finn trapped under those rocks.

A man I vaguely recognized shouted commands to a work crew nearby. I blinked and asked Deputy Farmer who it was.

"Coleman Harrow. He runs an excavation company used by the mining companies mostly. He lives over on Thistledown, so he was one of the first on the scene. The man's an expert at earth moving and managing big rocks. We're lucky to have him and his crews."

The street name reminded me how I knew Coleman. He'd been attacked by the squirrel while trying to feed the raccoon. Finn's life was in the hands of someone who thought it was brilliant to try stealing food out of a squirrel's mouth.

If I hadn't trusted Deputy Farmer's assessment, I would have thought we were screwed.

"Sheriff, we found Mr. Trainor," Deputy Kenton said, pulling the director along by the elbow. He was covered in just as much debris, but he also looked very confused.

"Sir, who was in the cave when the explosion happened?" I asked.

"What explosion?"

I wanted to throttle him. Right now I had to keep reminding myself to stay professional. Do what it took to get answers.

"The explosion that collapsed the cave. Which of your cast and crew were inside when it happened? How many people are missing?"

Trainor glanced around as if seeing the scene for the first time. "Oh my. Something happened." Once he turned completely around, I saw his head sported a big bloody gash. "Creation sometimes means destruction! You have to keep innovating, Pushing the envelope. Pushing, pushing, pushing the... what was I saying?"

I gritted my teeth. "Deputy, where did you find Mr. Trainor?"

"He was just wandering around."

"Get him medical attention, please." Even though he deserved it less than anyone else on set. "It looks like maybe he hit his head."

I wanted to beat the man to a bloody pulp, but that wouldn't help me get Finn back any faster. Instead, I looked around to see who else

I could find who might know who was in the cave when the explosion happened.

Deputy Blackrock was having trouble keeping the media away, the show runner was busy trying to wrangle concerned cast and crew away from the critical area, and Aster Valley's two big ladder trucks were parked on the nearest logging road that cut across the slope to the cave. They seemed to have already finished their portion of the job, but I could tell from other scattered emergency vehicles there were alpine rescuers, K-9 units, and medical personnel already hard at work.

I rushed over to the show runner and pulled her aside. "I need to know who's missing."

She looked shell-shocked. "I... I don't know. I wasn't paying attention. I just remember Nolan talking to the pyro techs right before it happened. It looked like... like god. It shook the whole mountain. It scared us to death. And then the sounds of the rocks tumbling."

Tears filled her eyes. "I hope everyone's okay," she said in a small voice. "I don't think he meant for it to happen."

I didn't care what the fuck he'd meant to happen; I wasn't going to rest until Nolan was arrested for this. "Who was supposed to be in the cave scene when it happened? We need to know how many people might be trapped inside."

"I don't know!"

I took a breath and tried not to shake her. "Call sheet. Isn't there some kind of record like a call sheet that would say who was involved in that scene or who was in what location at a certain time?"

She looked down at the tablet in her hands. "Oh god. Yes. Yes! I have that all on here."

Shelly pulled it up and began tapping at it until she turned the tablet around for me to see.

My eyes went straight to the name as if there was nothing else on the page.

Finn Heller.

My person was trapped inside that mountain. He'd even told me in the text message earlier that there was some shit going down on set today. He'd said he was going to handle it, but I knew from how he'd acted earlier in the week that handling it meant putting his nose down and getting through it. Yes, he'd arranged for additional climbing safety, but this hadn't been a climbing scene. And no one had realized what Trainor was up to.

Fuck. Finn was in the damned mountain, and there was nothing I could do about it but my job. According to this call sheet, there were probably at least six people trapped behind the rocks. Finn, Crysto-bell, a camera operator, a boom operator, a key grip, and the DP.

I would have to work to get everyone out just as hard whether Finn was in that group or not.

When I looked back at the pile of boulders we were dealing with, my heart clenched in my chest. Machines had already begun care-fully removing them, piece by piece, but it was a slow process due to safety protocols.

In the meantime, I left the excavating to the experts and helped disburse unnecessary personnel from the area. We found Mikey and had him move all media personnel off his private property which included most of the entire mountain, we helped the film crew find transportation back to their lodging or the main set area depending on where they wanted to congregate, and we finally finished processing all of the minor injuries.

At one point I tried Finn's phone again, even though I knew he wouldn't have had it on him during filming. It went straight to voice-mail again.

I gave Shawn an update and told him not to worry Tess with the news Finn was missing. There was no reason to upset her when I was bound and determined to believe he was fine and simply bored and restless waiting for us to get to him.

There'd been no word from anyone inside the cave, but Deputy Blackrock assured me the cave was too thick for cell reception, even if someone inside had their phone.

"We don't have any evidence they were crushed. I've been up here hiking and skiing many times, Sheriff, and I can tell you this cave is plenty deep for them to have gotten to safety when the rocks started falling. I'm confident they're mostly hungry and scared in there. Shouldn't be anything but minor injuries once we get to them."

His words helped keep me from completely flipping out, but at dinnertime, when the light started slipping behind the nearest peak, we got confirmation he was right.

The excavation crew finally breached the mouth of the cave and found five fairly intact individuals.

But no Finn Heller.

22

I'd just arrived to the set first thing in the morning when a flood of baby pictures came streaming in over text.

"Oh my god, who's that?" the lady at craft services squealed.

I stood shoulder to shoulder with her to flip through the shots and tried explaining that this was my boyfriend's... friend's baby. "So this little nugget is kind of like my nephew. Kind of. I mean, not really at all, but maybe one day."

I felt so happy for Declan and Tess. The pregnancy had brought some health scares, so knowing the baby had safely arrived was cause for celebration. After celebrating my way through an omelette, a cup of fruit, and a giant vat of coffee, and trying unsuccessfully to call Declan with my congratulations, I finally arrived at my trailer to find the day's call sheet.

And it was complete bullshit.

Location: Hideout shack

Exterior shot of Ladd sneaking around shack and approaching mouth of cave.

Location: Mountainside cave

Interior shot of Ladd confronting Mona near stack of gold bars.

Location: Mountainside cave

Interior shot of Ladd, Mona, and Murdoch arguing.

Location: Mountainside cave

Exterior shot of Ladd pulling Mona out of cave as cave explodes behind them.

I reread it several times. The explosion was supposed to be the shack only, not the cave, and it wasn't scheduled to happen until late next week when we wrapped filming on location in Aster Valley.

Never in my entire career had I come across such an unprofessional and unorganized shoot. This was completely unbelievable.

I shot off a quick text to Declan, congratulating him and telling him I had some stuff to talk to him about that night. Part of me wanted to call him and cry on his shoulder about it all, but he was dealing with Tessa and the baby. And I didn't want to start what I hoped would be a long and happy life together by giving Declan the impression I was a child. I wasn't.

I was going to handle this like an adult.

When I knocked on Nolan's trailer, one of the PAs answered. "He's already up at the site for this morning's shoot," she said. "He sent me back to grab him a jacket because it's windy up there."

Instead of going straight to the site, I went ahead and reported to makeup and wardrobe, hoping like hell I could talk some sense into Nolan once I got to the set location. I was happy to film everything except the explosion scene. That shit wasn't happening until and unless he could convince me it was all legal and set up according to official safety protocol.

I'd reached out to my union rep the day before and asked several hypothetical questions. Now I was armed with some language about safety protocol and my rights. And I was interested to find out how the hell the stunt coordinator had signed on to such a shoddy production. He had a good reputation in the industry, but his complicity with Nolan's corner-cutting was mind-boggling.

Once I'd been to makeup and wardrobe, I got a shuttle to the site higher up the mountain. I found Nolan right away.

"Nolan, I'd like a word, please," I said when I noticed him finishing up a conversation with a crew member.

"You look great, you look great!" he said, bouncing on his feet. "Look at this gorgeous day. Could it be any more perfect? I don't think so. No, I do not. What do you have for me, Finn?"

He patted my shoulder like we were best buds. "I'd like to talk to the stunt coordinator about the explosion scene. It's my understanding we're only permitted to blow up the shack, so I think I have misunderstood the blocking we went over the other day."

"Heh, no. That's... we're going to change the blocking this morning. See, it's all changed. I had some great ideas, absolutely fabulous ones. It's going to be amazing. Trust me. You've never seen anything like this."

I stepped away from him so I could meet his eyes. "That's what I'm afraid of. I've never seen anything like this. So far this production isn't adhering to union safety protocols, so I just want to make sure—"

"Don't be such a fucking square. Jesus, Finn. There's annoying principals, and there's you. Stop whining like a baby. Follow the damned script, and let Joel get the shots we need. Don't use your head. Let us be the brains of the operation, m'kay? Okay. Great chat, great chat."

He began to wander off, calling for Joel's attention.

"I'm walking off the set, Nolan," I said in a calm, professional voice. "If you can't respect my contractual rights to safety protocols during filming, I am within my right to walk away from the production. It's breach of contract, and you're in it."

He turned back to me with a narrow-eyed glare. "Remember our deal, kid? You do this for me, and I'll give you Merchant of Fucking Venice. Got it? But if you insist on giving me hell over every single fucking aspect of this—"

"You mean *The Taming of the Shrew*," I said, knowing with absolute certainty he didn't mean either one. How had I been so gullible? I'd believed his ridiculous promise even though the man was known for filming action movies.

Kix had been right. And I'd been a fool.

"You were never doing a Shakespeare project, were you?" I asked quietly. I didn't want people to overhear the disappointment in my voice. Sixteen years in the film industry and I was still that naive eight-year-old walking onto my first set with stars in my eyes and an idealistic vision of the way it all worked.

Nolan's face settled into an ugly sneer. "Don't be ridiculous. Me? Putting out some Kenneth Branagh bullshit? Pfft. I'm in this for money, Finn. Just like everyone else, including you. Don't kid yourself. This movie is going to put you on the map as an action star. It's going to make you millions, and it's going to lead to more multimillion-dollar roles for you. And you can thank me when that happens. But you know what's not going to happen? You walking off the set of this fucking film. Now get over there and prep for the first call."

His PA came running up with his jacket. I ignored him even though I was glad he was there to bear witness. "Are you blowing up the cave during a scene I'm in?"

"You're damned right I am. I'm the director of this film. You are not."

I nodded. "Then I'm sorry. I'm leaving. Let me know when you change your plans or can prove this shoot meets legal requirements. I will return to fulfill my legal obligations at that time."

After making eye contact with the PA to make sure they'd heard every word, I walked calmly back to where the shuttle had just arrived with Crystobell and her makeup coordinator. I nodded to her and asked the shuttle driver to return me to my trailer lower on the mountain.

As soon as I got there, I changed back into my clothes, washed off all my makeup, and hopped in my car.

There was a text from Declan on my phone.

Declan: *I miss you too. Have a good day at work, and good luck with whatever is going on. I know you can handle it, baby. I'm going to head back to Aster Valley as soon as Shawn gets here to hang out with Tessa. I don't know what time, but if you want to meet me at the house after work, the keypad code is the way Penny would relay confidential information ;-)*

After referring to my trusty police code cheat sheet, I learned confidential information was a 10-36. Declan was a total geek.

I knew if I told Declan what had happened, he'd want to leave Tessa and race back here right away. So I decided not to call him. Instead, I'd tell him about it over dinner, a nice quiet dinner at home just the two of us.

Before I got the top down on the McLaren, my phone was already buzzing with calls from Iris, my mother, Kix, and one of the PAs. I powered it down completely and stashed it in the glove box.

Once the top was down, I realized Nolan had been right. It was a perfect day.

I shifted into Drive and sped away from the *Gold Rats* set. With no destination in mind, I drove and drove. Music blasted from the speakers, and the sun bore down on my head and shoulders. This part of Colorado was stunning, and since I wanted to move here permanently, I decided to check it out.

I drove for hours, simply enjoying the weather, the views, the music, and the blessed silence from my glove box. When I pulled into the town of Steamboat Springs, I saw a bicycle shop.

On a whim, I parked the car and went in.

"Help you?" a guy said from down by the floor where he was unpacking some water bottles from a box.

"Yeah, I think... I want to buy a mountain bike?" It was the silliest thing I'd thought or said in a long time, but it felt incredibly right.

He glanced out the open door to where I'd parked the car. "You got some kind of bike rack for that thing?" he asked with a laugh.

"Oh, uh... I was thinking maybe you could have it delivered? Except I live... I live..." I swallowed and took the leap. "I live in Aster Valley."

He stood up and reached out to shake my hand. "Name's JT. Nice to meet you. This your first bike, or are you replacing one?"

He clearly recognized me because later in the conversation he teased me that I'd forget all about rock climbing as soon as I got out on the trails, but he treated me like a normal person, and I appreciated that more than I could say.

Once I'd picked out a high-end Trek with full suspension, JT convinced me to try a SeaSucker bike rack which used big suction cups to hold the bike onto the car. I had to drive back with the top up, but it was worth it. As soon as I got to Declan's house, I took the bike off the rack and rode it to the nearby grocery store to pick up food for dinner.

When I got back, my thigh and calf muscles reminded me rock climbing and running weren't the same kind of exercise as biking in a mountain town. I was exhausted. After unpacking the groceries, fixing the marinade for the steaks, and soaking in a relaxing bath, I crawled into Declan's bed and inhaled his pillow.

I fell asleep hugging it and sniffing it in a way that might have come off as creepy in a teen slasher flick but was totally normal in real life.

I slept for hours. When I finally woke up, I realized the sun was getting low in the sky. I made my way down to the kitchen and pulled out the green beans to wash them when I realized I didn't know if Declan was even going to make it home at a decent hour.

I went out to the car to get my phone from the glove box. When I powered it on, the damned thing took on a life of its own in my hand.

Stress and guilt tried to flood back in my gut, but I forced it away. Even if I'd been in the wrong, I still wasn't even close to the worst case of actors behaving badly on set.

But the messages weren't about the film. Not exactly.

"What the fuck," I said, feeling the blood rush out of my head so quickly, it left me dizzy. I read text after text about an explosion on the set. People trapped, injuries, emergency response.

Fuck. *Fuck.* I quickly dialed Declan's number, but there was no answer. Did he know about it? Had they reached him in Denver to tell him about it?

I raced back to the house for my shoes before jumping in the car and screaming my way up the mountain in the McLaren. When I came to a stop at the barricade, I jumped out and began running.

I couldn't believe my eyes. There were emergency vehicles everywhere. Rescue crews in safety harnesses and helmets. Floodlights set up and K-9 units wandering around. The media were clamoring to get access to the property, but they were held back on the road. The only way I managed to get past was one of the deputies recognizing me and giving the attendee at the barrier permission to let me through.

"The sheriff was looking for you," Deputy Kepplow called to me. "He's over by the cave-in."

My heart jumped in relief. Declan was here. He was here, and I was going to be able to see him in person.

I still couldn't believe this had happened. Who was hurt? Were people still missing? Had there been fatalities? I couldn't even wrap my head around it. What if I'd been here? What if I'd been in the cave when the explosion had happened?

I jogged past some cast and crew who still looked dazed, when my eyes finally landed on the sweaty sheriff in the crumpled uniform. He looked like hell.

"Dec?" I called, slowing down in case he was busy. I didn't want to distract him from his job.

His head whipped around until his eyes landed on me. I could see the disbelief on his face. "Finn?"

I nodded and began walking closer.

"Finn?" he asked again, incredulous. His voice broke a little, and he lunged for me. "Oh god, baby, shit. Oh, Finn."

He grabbed me and held on so tightly I nearly lost my breath. "I'm okay," I said over and over.

"I thought you were in the cave. And then... and then they opened it up and you weren't there. *You weren't there.* No one knew where you were. I wondered if you'd gone climbing. If the concussion from the explosion had knocked you off the mountain. I wondered if—*fuck.*"

He clutched my hair in a fist and kept his other arm wrapped all the way around my waist so I was pressed against him from hip to head. Declan's entire body shook against me.

"I'm sorry," I said against his collarbones. He smelled like sweat and dust, maybe even smoke. "I didn't know. I turned off my phone. I refused to stay here when I learned he was going to blow up the mountain. But I didn't think... I didn't think he would actually do it!"

Declan pulled back just enough to grab my face in his big hands.

"I thought you were in there. I thought you were hurt. I can't lose you. Finn... I can't..."

I grabbed the front of his uniform in two fists. "I love you. You're not losing me."

As soon as I said the word, his eyes closed in a kind of prayer before opening back up. "Are you just—"

"No," I said, shaking my head. "No I'm not just saying it. I bought a bike."

Declan's eyebrows furrowed in confusion. "I don't understand."

Of course he didn't. My brain was leaping all over the place. "I bought a mountain bike. And I told the guy at the bike store I lived in Aster Valley. With you. Because I want it to be true, and I... I..." It was too soon and too inappropriate of a situation to talk about this, so I simply repeated what I'd said already. "I want it to be true."

He kissed me hard and fast, lingering for several long beats before pulling back. "I want it to be true, too. I love you, too. So much. I'm so glad you're okay."

I began apologizing again for worrying him, but he simply pulled me into another hug and grunted for me to stop apologizing. "None of this is your fault. I'm so fucking glad you weren't in there. I was so scared."

"Is everyone okay? Are they still trapped?"

He released me but took my hand in a firm grip as if unwilling to let us be separated. I liked knowing he needed to be sure of me.

"Everyone's out. The five cast and crew stuck in the cave are all okay. Just pissed as hell. I have a feeling this production will be bankrupt before the movie even gets out the door."

I blew out a breath, feeling the final weights drop from my shoulder. A breeze lifted my hair and cooled my hot face. It was the sensation of one door closing and another... well, I was looking right at the other one opening.

EPILOGUE
DECLAN - SEVERAL MONTHS LATER

"I feel like I'm going to puke."

I rubbed Finn's lower back in the soothing way he liked. "You're not going to puke." I wished there weren't so many layers between my palm and his skin, but I had to deal with it. Not only was it cold in Aster Valley in December, but as the director of the play, he was expected to wear a coat and tie.

Finn Heller in a coat and tie was a borderline violation of public decency laws. I was staying extra vigilant by keeping my eyes laser focused on him just in case I needed to make an arrest.

"This is worse than the time I had to sing at the Emmys with Dolly Parton," he said, shocking me out of my inappropriate—and honestly way too frequent—sheriff/perp sex fantasy.

"The Emmy people put *you* in a duet with Dolly Parton?" I asked incredulously. I'd never heard that story, even though we'd been living together four months now. And Finn was a talker. I loved his stories, but I'd have remembered a Dolly story.

He shot me a glare. "I can sing. I can sing just fine."

"No, of course you can." He couldn't. "Of course. It's just..."

"Fine. It was a gag sketch between award presentations. Whatever. Anyway, this is way worse."

I bit back a laugh. "They're going to be fine. You've been practicing every night for weeks."

Finn and I looked out onto the Aster Valley High stage while the curtain was still closed. Solo was trying to laugh silently at something Abbie Vollmer had said. Every time she shot him her "moody Kate" look, as Finn called it, Solo cracked up again.

"It's going to be good, isn't it?" Finn asked me in a soft voice only I could hear. The crowd made enough noise on the other side of the curtain to cover up his words. They were still busy finding their seats and chatting with friends.

"Babe, it's going to be amazing. Last night's dress rehearsal had me in tears I was laughing so hard. Plus, they're clearly having so much fun with it. I love that you let the kids put their own spin on the story."

Finn's smile was shy but proud. "That's the whole point of what I wanted to teach them in class. This stuff is timeless. The themes and issues can be put into modern..." His cheeks darkened as his voice trailed off. "And you've heard me talk about this a million times already. Sorry."

"I never get tired of seeing how happy you are in your new job. You have to know that by now. Even if I have to send a patrol vehicle over here to lure you out of work sometimes."

Tessa came rushing up and handed Finn something tiny along with a bottle of water. "Headache medicine. Trust me, it's a preventive for afterward when all the parents come to meet you under the guise of 'thanking you' for putting on the play for little Timmy and Tonya. Remember the night of the parent-teacher conferences?"

Hell. That night had been sheer hell. Finn had come home looking like he'd been jumped and stripped for parts. "They're uh... really excited I'm their kids' new teacher..." he'd said in a daze.

Finn took the pills and threw them back in his mouth before gulping water. He muttered something about the poorest service being repaid with thanks. I was fairly sure it was a quote from the play.

After swallowing the meds, he winked at Tess. "Thanks. Where's Hoss?"

She laughed. She didn't think it was funny when *I* called Conley the same nickname, but Finn could get away with murder when it came to that baby, and anything else for that matter.

"Shawn's parents came to town to watch him so we could come see the show. We're going out to dinner after this. By ourselves. *Without the baby.*" She looked almost reverent. "Like a real date that real people get to go on. By themselves."

I narrowed my eyes at her. Finn and I had offered to watch Conley plenty. It wasn't our fault she didn't trust us to be alone with him.

Finn leaned over to me and spoke under his breath. "10-32."

I sighed. Fine. So there'd been one teeny time when we came a little bit too close to letting the kid drown in his bathtub. But it had been fine. And who had better access to EMTs than the sheriff? No one.

Finn straightened back up and gave Tess his red-carpet smile, the one I couldn't wait to see in person on the actual red carpet when *Gold Rats* was released next spring and I accompanied Finn to the premiere.

Nolan Trainor's shocking diagnosis of a degenerative brain disease had rocked the film industry and shocked the cast and crew of *Gold Rats*, including Finn. Ironically, it had been the medical testing after he hit his head that had led to his diagnosis. It had explained his rapid mood shifts and inability to retain critical information such as safety and legal regulations.

That hadn't explained the DP and stunt coordinator who'd been complicit, though. The three men would be wound up in red tape for a long time to come. Meanwhile, the film was able to finish under the directorial guidance of a woman named Lan Iradia, who'd been about the quirkiest human being I'd ever met.

But she'd been a rule follower which was good enough for me.

As soon as filming wrapped, Finn had packed up his house, shipped everything to a storage unit in Aster Valley, and driven straight through until pulling into my driveway and flinging himself bodily at me.

I'd been on cloud nine ever since, but I hadn't actually fully relaxed until he'd gotten the job as the head of the drama department at Aster Valley High. The look on his face had been enough to convince me this was it. He was here for good.

"We'd better get this show on the road," Finn said. "Go find your seats."

Tess grabbed my hand. "Come on, we saved you one with us."

I squeezed her hand and asked for a minute before looking back at Finn and taking his hands in mine. "You're going to be amazing. You *are* amazing. Your kindness and passion overwhelm me. Your love for others and for fun and growth and giving back..." I took a breath. "I am in awe of you, Finnegan Heller. And tonight is proof you can do anything you put your mind to. You have so much talent to share with the world, and this is just one of many, many examples."

He scraped his lip with his teeth. "Damn you," he breathed. "I hate you so much right now."

I leaned in and pressed a long kiss against his cheek. We'd agreed a long time ago not to be too "ooey-gooey" in front of the kids while he was at work, but this was a moment that deserved coming close.

"I love you so much," I whispered against his skin, the skin that felt warm and familiar against mine. That smelled like coffee, woodsmoke, and the floral shampoo he special-ordered from his stylist in LA. He smelled like comfort and home.

He smelled like mine.

And I was never letting him go.

"I love you, too, now go!" he said before turning and hustling away.

I took a minute to make sure his ass was to code before turning and allowing Tessa to lead me to our seats.

"Did you decide on a Christmas gift for him?" she asked softly without looking over at me.

"Yes. And it's a good thing you reminded me to shop early. Mikey and Sam called to ask for security help with some big family reunion group that's staying at the lodge this weekend."

"What did you decide on?"

"A ring."

Tessa had learned the art of the slow-pan from the master.

"Tell. Me. Everything." She yanked me down in my seat and ignored Shawn on her other side.

My heart thumped excitedly in my chest. I couldn't wait to see his face on Christmas morning when I asked him to be mine forever. "It's black zirconium on the outside and rose gold on the inside."

"Oooh! He's going to flip."

I nodded. He really was. "And I had it engraved with a Shakespeare quote from *Taming of the Shrew*."

Tessa fluttered her hand over her heart where her own engagement ring sparkled under the bright auditorium house lights. We'd come a long way from our lonely single days in LA.

The lights suddenly dimmed, and Tess and I had to stop talking. I tried to focus on the show, but when scene two began, I couldn't help but listen out for the line I'd selected for Finn's ring.

"Sit by my side and let the world slip..."

I blew out a slow breath and sat back. Neither of us was in purgatory anymore.

And our piece of paper would never be blank again.

Up next: Will the giant family reunion at Rockley Lodge turn out to be any families we know? Find out in *Forever Wilde in Aster Valley*!

LETTER FROM LUCY

Dear Reader,

Thank you for reading *Hot as Heller*.

I hope you are enjoying Aster Valley as much as I am! The next book set in Aster Valley is a Wilde/Marian holiday story featuring a brand new romance, but after that, we will get Julian's story in *Thick as Thieves*. Here is a list of all the stories coming soon:

Hijacked, the next Licking Thicket collaboration with May Archer comes out on September, 2, 2021.

Hostile Takeover, my steamy, enemies-to-lovers standalone comes out October 26, 2021.

Forever Wilde in Aster Valley comes out November 16, 2021.

Thick as Thieves (Julian's story) comes out February 2, 2022.

I am writing as fast as I can to bring you all of my favorite new stories :-) You can pre-order them now for the earliest delivery by clicking the highlighted titles above or visiting my website.

All Lucy Lennox novels can be read on their own so find a story that appeals to you and dive right in.

Please take a moment to write a review of this book on Amazon and Goodreads. Reviews can make all of the difference in helping a book show up in book searches.

Feel free to stop by www.LucyLennox.com and drop me a line or visit me on social media. To see inspiration photographs for all of my novels, visit my Pinterest boards.

Finally, I have a fantastic reader group on Facebook. Come join us for exclusive content, early cover reveals, hot pics, and a whole lotta fun. Lucy's Lair can be found here.

Happy reading!

Lucy

ABOUT THE AUTHOR

Lucy Lennox is a mother of three sarcastic kids. Born and raised in the southeast, she now resides outside of Atlanta finally putting good use to that English Lit degree.

Lucy enjoys naps, pizza, and procrastinating. She is married to someone who is better at math than romance but who makes her laugh every single day and is the best dancer in the history of ever.

She stays up way too late each night reading gay romance because it's simply the best thing ever.

For more information and to stay updated about future releases, please sign up for Lucy's author newsletter here.

Connect with Lucy on social media:
www.LucyLennox.com
Lucy@LucyLennox.com

WANT MORE?

Join Lucy's Lair

Get Lucy's New Release Alerts

Like Lucy on Facebook

Follow Lucy on BookBub

Follow Lucy on Amazon

Follow Lucy on Instagram

Follow Lucy on Pinterest

Other books by Lucy:

Hostile Takeover

Made Marian Series

Forever Wilde Series

Aster Valley Series

Twist of Fate Series with Sloane Kennedy

After Oscar Series with Molly Maddox

Licking Thicket Series with May Archer

Virgin Flyer

Say You'll Be Nine

Visit Lucy's website at www.LucyLennox.com for a comprehensive list of titles, audio samples, freebies, suggested reading order, and more!

Made in the USA
Monee, IL
13 September 2021